The Lost Brother

The Gareth and Gwen Medieval Mysteries:
The Bard's Daughter (novella)
The Good Knight
The Uninvited Guest
The Fourth Horseman
The Fallen Princess
The Unlikely Spy
The Lost Brother
The Renegade Merchant
The Unexpected Ally
The Worthy Soldier
The Favored Son

The After Cilmeri Series:
Daughter of Time (prequel)
Footsteps in Time (Book One)
Winds of Time
Prince of Time (Book Two)
Crossroads in Time (Book Three)
Children of Time (Book Four)
Exiles in Time
Castaways in Time
Ashes of Time
Warden of Time
Guardians of Time
Masters of Time
Outpost in Time
Shades of Time

The Lion of Wales Series:
Cold My Heart
The Oaken Door
Of Men and Dragons
A Long Cloud
Frost Against the Hilt

A Gareth and Gwen Medieval Mystery

THE LOST BROTHER

by

SARAH WOODBURY

The Lost Brother

This is a work of fiction.

www.sarahwoodbury.com

To brothers everywhere
but especially to
Carew, Gareth, and Taran

Pronouncing Welsh Names and Places

Cadwaladr – Cad-wall-ah-der
Cadwallon – Cad-WA/sh/-on
Ceredigion – Care-eh-dig-EE-on
Cynon — KIN-on
Dafydd – DAH-vith (the 'th' is hard as in 'they')
Deheubarth – deh-HAY-barth
Dai – Die
Dolwyddelan – dole-with-EH-lan (the 'th' is hard as in 'they')
Gruffydd – GRIFF-ith (the 'th' is hard as in 'they')
Gwalchmai – GWALCH-my ('ai' makes a long i sound like in 'kite; the 'ch' like in the Scottish 'loch')
Gwenllian – Gwen-/sh/EE-an
Gwladys – Goo-LAD-iss
Gwynedd – GWIN-eth (the 'th' is hard as in 'the')
Hywel – H'wel
Ieuan – ieu sounds like the cheer, 'yay' so, YAY-an
Llelo – /sh/EH-law
Llywelyn – /sh/ew-ELL-in
Meilyr – MY-lir
Owain – OH-wine
Rhuddlan – RITH-lan (the 'th' is hard as in 'the')
Rhun – Rin
Rhys – Reese
Sion – Shawn (Sean)
Tudur – TIH-deer

Cast of Characters

Owain Gwynedd – King of Gwynedd (North Wales)
Cadwaladr – Owain's younger brother, former Lord of Ceredigion

Rhun – Prince of Gwynedd (illegitimate)
Hywel – Prince of Gwynedd (illegitimate)
Cynan – Prince of Gwynedd (illegitimate)
Madoc – Prince of Gwynedd (illegitimate)

Gwen – spy for Hywel, Gareth's wife
Gareth – Gwen's husband, Captain of Hywel's guard
Tangwen – daughter of Gareth and Gwen
Llelo – adopted son of Gareth and Gwen
Dai –adopted son of Gareth and Gwen

Evan – Gareth's friend
Gruffydd – Rhun's captain
Meilyr – Gwen's father
Gwalchmai – Gwen's brother
Taran – King Owain's steward
Tudur – King Owain's manservant
Father Alun – priest of Cilcain church

Godfrid – Prince of Dublin

Ranulf – Earl of Chester

1

November 1146

Gwen

"Gwen! Dear God, Gwen, what are you doing here?" Gareth's oldest friend, Evan, loped towards her, coming from the lines of picketed horses. His blonde hair was mussed, stuck to his head with sweat from the recent wearing of a helmet, and his blue eyes were full of concern.

Gwen gestured to the bag she'd slung over her shoulder. "I brought supplies for Gareth and Prince Rhun, and letters for the king."

Shortly after she'd last seen Gareth, the cart carrying his belongings had overturned while crossing a swollen river. All its contents had been lost downstream. According to the letter Gareth had sent her, he'd lived these last weeks in what he'd stood up in that day, plus whatever he could borrow from his companions. Prince Rhun, apparently, had been forced to do the same, since his possessions had been swept down the river too, and not even a prince had time to visit a seamstress in the middle of a war.

Even glared at her. "Yes, but Gwen—"

She cut him off, lowering her voice so it barely carried. "Evan, I need to see him."

Gwen hadn't intended to admit that much, even to Evan, but behind the admission was the daily ache Gareth's absence had become. Every night, Gwen lay awake missing him, her mind roiling with visions of his death in battle. They were vain imaginings, and she knew it, but it took an incredible effort of will to get them out of her head. It seemed impossible that she loved him as much as she did.

On the worst nights, she wished she could simply cut out her heart and put it in a box, because it was so painful to have its continued presence inside her body. Women had felt this way about their husbands and sons going to war from the first day men had gone to war. Gwen herself had felt it before. But except for a brief furlough in early October, during a lull in the fighting, Gareth had been gone for the whole of the last three months. It was getting into winter, and this war needed to end.

The look on Evan's face told Gwen he understood without her saying more. Evan had avoided female entanglements—or perhaps it was simply that he hadn't found the right woman yet—but that didn't mean he didn't understand love. He didn't embarrass her by further comment and instead looked past her to the activity going on behind her.

His eyes widened. "I was going to ask if you came alone, but I see that you didn't!"

"No, I didn't." Gwen grinned. "I brought Hywel some friends from Aber. Do you think he'll be pleased to see them?"

She turned to look with Evan at the group of twenty riders who'd arrived in the camp with her. Six feet tall to a man, the soldiers who conferred fifty feet away spoke in Danish, brandished long swords and axes, and were of a lineage that had struck fear into the hearts of Welshmen for five hundred years. None of the newcomers were bigger, taller, and more dangerous than the man at their center: Prince Godfrid of Dublin. An old friend.

Evan shook his head. "You are a wonder! And you know full well that not only will Prince Hywel be pleased, but we need every last ally we can find." His expression turned serious again. "I won't pretend that we haven't been hard pressed the last few weeks. The English always have more men than we do, and when one of them falls, he is replaced by two more."

But then he laughed to see Prince Hywel, who'd come out of his tent in order to see what the commotion was about, lifted into a bear hug by Godfrid. The two princes contrasted sharply in coloring and size. While Hywel had dark hair, Godfrid's hair was so blond it was almost white. And though Hywel wasn't exactly a small man, Godfrid was twice as wide and four inches taller. They both had blue eyes, though, which sparkled with amused intelligence—and at the moment, mutual pleasure and respect.

Turning away from the scene, Evan took Gwen's elbow. "Let me bring you to Gareth. He's just returned from scouting our northern perimeter. You'll have to pardon the muck on him. We've had nothing but rain for the last week."

"At least winter has held off," Gwen said.

Evan made a *maybe* motion with his head. "Those who know more than I about it say we're due for colder weather within a day or two. I'd like to see the ground harder myself, since it's better for riding and for moving across the countryside with fighting men, but I'm not looking forward to snow or freezing rain."

They squelched through the mud towards a cluster of tents on the north side of Hywel's encampment. Located roughly twenty miles due west of Chester, in a sheltered valley to the west of the Clwyd mountains, the camp was close enough to England to be within striking distance of Mold Castle, but far enough away that any raid into Wales on the part of the Earl of Chester's forces would be seen before his soldiers could get this far.

Even coming from the west, Godfrid's company had been stopped by three separate pickets keeping watch, ready to blow a horn at a moment's notice if the enemy had managed to breach the mountains and come at the camp from an unexpected direction.

The princes' tents overlooked the main camp, which had grown up in a farmer's field and held nearly five hundred spearman and archers. The presence of the army wasn't affecting the farmer's livelihood, however, since the field had been harvested at the end of the summer. Now in late November, grass grew in what had once been straight furrows, churned and rechurned by the hooves of horses and the feet of men.

Since it was winter, trees denuded of foliage descended down the mountain sides towards the camp. Only during the night would an enemy company be able to approach from that direction without the watchers being aware. From where Gwen stood, she could see anything that moved on the hills above her and the fields around. She let out a sigh and allowed a true sense of relief to comfort her. Gareth wouldn't be safe until he returned home again, but now that she had seen where he was sleeping, maybe she could sleep better herself.

Near the outdoor kitchen, Gwen recognized the blacksmith's apprentice from Aber's village. She made Evan stop for a moment to give the boy the best wishes and greetings his mother had charged her with bringing to him before she left. Every woman at the castle and village had burdened Gwen with the same task. Looking around the camp, which was much larger than Gwen had anticipated, she saw that it was going to take her a bit longer than she'd thought to fulfill those requests. First, however, she had to complete her own mission.

Men of Prince Hywel's *teulu* raised their hands to Evan as he passed, and several nodded to Gwen, recognizing her. Evan didn't stop to greet them, however, continuing to hustle Gwen along.

It was cold—colder than it had been so far this year—and she was glad she hadn't spent the last three months living outside as these men had. Several nearby soldiers sported bandages on their heads, and one man limped along in the opposite direction from the one Gwen and Evan were taking. He saluted them as they passed, and gave Gwen a wide grin, making her feel better about his injury. For all that the men were clearly tired and dirty, bursts of laughter came from around the campfires, and the overall mood she was sensing wasn't of gloom or despair.

"You've never been in a war before, have you Gwen?"

"No."

"It's no place for a lady."

"I wasn't always a knight's wife," she said.

Evan glanced at her. "I forget that sometimes, but you've never been a camp follower either, and I would have you avert your eyes from some of what goes on here."

Gwen scoffed. "I know what goes on—" She came to an abrupt halt, unable to speak, only to stare.

They'd arrived at the edge of the camp. A washing trough had been set up a few paces from the entrance to the nearest tent. Gareth, who hadn't noticed Gwen's approach, pulled off his shirt and tossed it towards a pile of clothes, heaped by one of the tent lines, awaiting laundering. Then he plunged his head into the trough. While still submerged, he scrubbed at his hair and neck with a cloth, and then he came up, shaking his head and spraying water everywhere.

It had been a month and a half since Gwen had seen him, which even then had been for only a single night. Hywel had tasked Gareth with bringing news of the war to Taran, the steward at Aber. It had been a kindness on Hywel's part, knowing Gwen's need to see her husband. As soon as she had a moment, Gwen meant to thank him for sending Gareth when he had.

Evan had been right to warn her about Gareth's scruffiness. While six weeks ago he'd sported a full beard and his brown hair had been long, he'd kept them trimmed and neat, pulling his hair back and tying it at the base of his neck. Today, his hair was newly shorn—badly done too, with uneven ends, making it likely that one of Gareth's companions had been tasked with it. And he sported a three-days' growth of beard that was bound to scratch Gwen when he kissed her. Far worse, however, was the newly healed scar across his right breast.

Gwen drank in the sight of him. She didn't care what he looked like. He was alive, and that was all that mattered. He still hadn't seen her, and even with him standing in front of her, she wasn't completely convinced that he was real.

Then she shook off her hesitation, picked up her skirts, and ran forward. Gareth became aware of her a heartbeat before she reached him and turned in time to catch her in his arms as she barreled into him. She clutched him tightly around the neck, and he embraced her fully, both of them heedless of the water dripping from his hair, down his back and neck, and onto her.

Gareth's arms circled her waist, he lifted her off her feet, and she finally got to kiss him like she'd wanted to for so long (she was right that his beard was scratchy).

When they broke apart, he said, "*Cariad.* My love. What are you doing here?"

It was the same question Evan had asked, but this time she ignored it. "You were hurt!"

"I'm fine." Gareth threaded a hand through the back of her hair as he held her. "You shouldn't be here."

Gwen squeezed her eyes shut, finding tears pricking at their corners. "I've missed you so much." Her voice broke.

"I've missed you too." Gareth didn't let go, but he turned his head a little, trying to see into her face. "Are you going to answer my question?"

Gwen still didn't have the voice to reply.

Gareth eased her back down to the ground. When her toes touched the earth, he kissed her once more and then gripped an upper arm in each hand so he could look fully into her face. "Is something wrong?"

It was only then that Gwen became aware of the fear in her husband's eyes and hastened to dispel it. "No! No! Nothing like that. Tangwen is well. Everything is fine at home. I just needed to see you."

Gwen had left their daughter, Tangwen, who was nearly two, back at Aber Castle, fifty miles to the west. Gwen hated being separated from her young daughter, but Tangwen couldn't visit the front, even to see her father. Tangwen's new nanny, Abi, whose own daughter had been born within a few months of Tangwen, was capable and caring. Tangwen had a surrogate sister to play with until Gwen came home, which she had promised to do just as soon as she could.

Relief swept across Gareth's face, a match to what Gwen herself had felt when she'd finally seen the camp with her own eyes.

"If that is the sole reason you are here, you should not have come. It isn't safe."

That was exactly the reaction Gwen had been expecting. She brushed a stray lock of brown hair out of her eyes. No matter how she'd tried to preserve her attire for the ultimate meeting with Gareth today, she still looked a sight: dusty, the hem of her dress permanently stained with mud from the road, and her hair falling out of its pinnings—as it always did no matter how tightly she braided it or how carefully she wound it up at the back of her head. Hywel's wife, Mari, had perfect hair that could remain unmussed even in a windstorm.

Gwen had known there was an even chance her husband would take one look at her and send her away immediately—and it would have had nothing to do with what she looked like. She'd entered a war zone, and he didn't like it. Gwen didn't want to upset him, and she would leave if he ordered her to, but at the very least, she was touching him for the first time in a month and a half.

"I was safe enough on the journey." Gwen's tears had subsided, though traces of them remained on her cheeks. "I brought a packet of letters and messages for King Owain that Taran received at Aber, and—" she had to gesture with one shoulder to the men behind her since Gareth still held both of her arms, "—I brought some friends."

Gareth's eyes had been only for Gwen. He hadn't even acknowledged Evan, so Gwen was delighted to see his jaw drop when he finally looked past her to the activity that was ongoing nearer the camp's entrance where she'd come in.

At that moment, Prince Godfrid spied Gareth too. His face split by a wide smile, he strode through the camp towards him.

Gareth moved forward too, and since his arm was still around Gwen's waist, she came with him. Thus, when Godfrid reached them, his choice was to take Gareth's outstretched arm or to hug them both.

Unusually, Godfrid settled for decorum. "How is my favorite sleuth?"

"I am well," Gareth said.

Gwen knew the word from previous visits with the Dane. *Sleuth* was from the Norse and meant 'tracker of men'. Godfrid meant it entirely as a compliment.

Smiling too, Hywel had followed Godfrid. "You got off easy. I should see the healer because I think he cracked my ribs."

"It is good to see you, my friend," Godfrid said.

Gareth and Godfrid grinned at each other, their more subdued greeting no indication of how happy they were to see one another.

Then a wary look came into Gareth's eyes. "I'm delighted as I always am when you have the opportunity to visit Gwynedd, but if you're here, it can't be for a reason that will please me."

"I don't know about that." Godfrid laughed. "My men were getting rusty. Every now and then, they need a good fight to keep their wits sharp."

Gareth snorted. "And—"

"And—" Godfrid's friendly face became completely transformed by a sudden sadness. "My father is dying. I need to discuss with your king what will happen to Dublin when he does."

2

Gareth

"I am very sorry to hear that, Godfrid," Gareth said.

Godfrid looked down at his feet for a moment, and then back up to Gareth's face. "You remember my elder brother, Brodar?" At Gareth's nod, Godfrid continued, "He and I have abided by my father's wish not to challenge Ottar's rule. My father fears we will lose. I intend to see to it that we win."

This conversation wasn't one that should be held out in the open with Gareth half-undressed, but Godfrid's intensity was such that Gareth didn't want to suggest they move before at least giving him some assurances. Unfortunately, he had none to give.

Nor did Hywel. "This war with Ranulf has become far more widespread than my father hoped it would when we first came east. We have lost many men in the fighting."

"I know," Godfrid said. "I am not suggesting—nor would I ever suggest—a direct exchange. We will join your side no matter what King Owain promises. In truth, with only twenty men, I offer him far fewer men than I hope he will offer me when the time comes."

"Still, for the immediate future, King Owain will owe you," Gareth said.

A mischievous look came into Godfrid's eyes. "Far better than the other way around."

Gwen patted the big Dane's upper arm. "I, for one, am very happy to know that you will be fighting alongside my husband."

Gareth gave his wife's waist a squeeze and tipped his head to Godfrid. "I'm disturbed you allowed her to come with you."

"Allowed?" Godfrid said in mock surprise. "I am quite certain that my permission was neither asked for nor given."

"I told Taran I was going, whether he wanted me to or not," Gwen said. "And I was safe on the road, as it turned out."

Gareth felt a growl forming in his throat at Gwen's willfulness. "Gwen—"

She threaded her fingers through his. "I was as safe as I could be in Godfrid's company, and Taran did have several letters that needed to be delivered to King Owain. Taran decided that he wouldn't test my obedience by denying my request, and I promised not to challenge his authority, or yours for that matter, by doing anything foolish. Now that I have seen you, I can turn for home again—tonight if you wish."

"Perhaps not tonight, but I cannot promise you more than a day or two with Gareth." Hywel lowered his voice. "The siege of Mold will begin soon. I would not have you here when we move the men forward."

"One day is more than I've had in over a month," Gwen said. "I will take what I can get."

"Besides, I'm sure my father would like to speak to you about the goings-on at Aber, beyond the letters Taran sent," Hywel said. "Who wrote them, specifically?"

"King Cadell of Deheubarth has written to King Owain several times," Gwen said, "though typically he has promised no aid. The king has also received a formal letter from King Stephen of England, the seal to which Taran did not feel he could break, but he assumes it is in regard to Chester's action against us. That is the real reason he needed someone to ride east as soon as possible."

Without further ado, Gwen reached into the bag on her shoulder, removed the packet of letters destined for the king, and handed them to Hywel.

Hywel glanced at them as he took them from her and then slipped them into the long interior pocket of his coat. These were hardly the first messages he'd carried to his father, but the letter from King Stephen might be the most important.

Gareth raised his eyebrows. A letter from Stephen could be very good news for the Welsh cause if the English king was in any way willing to give them aid against the Earl of Chester.

Ranulf had a long and complicated history with both King Stephen, the current occupant of the English throne, and Empress Maud, his cousin and the challenger to it. While Stephen was nephew to the former King Henry, Maud was his only surviving legitimate child. But she was a woman. Upon the death of King Henry, instead of supporting Maud's claim, which had been

Henry's wish, many barons had thrown their support behind Stephen's claim.

The dispute was—if it was anything—a family one. Not only were Maud and Stephen cousins, but Ranulf was son-in-law to King Henry's bastard son, Robert, who was in turn Maud's half-brother, her chief supporter, and a very capable general. That connection hadn't tied Ranulf permanently to Maud, however, and he'd switched sides at least three times in the ongoing war between these royal cousins.

At the moment, having been imprisoned by King Stephen for treason as late as August of this year, Ranulf wasn't supporting either side. He had retreated to Chester to lick his wounds, to plan whatever new intrigue against King Stephen appealed to him next, and to wage war on his closest Welsh neighbor, King Owain Gwynedd.

If King Stephen assented to come into King Owain's dispute, the war could be over before Christmas. It all depended upon what the letter said, and what King Owain would have to promise King Stephen in return for his support.

"Why did Llywelyn not bring the letter to the king himself?" Hywel said.

At the start of the war, King Owain had sent Llywelyn to London to act as his emissary to the court of King Stephen.

"He sent his servant on to Aber alone," Gwen said.

His expression a match to Hywel's, Gareth frowned down at Gwen. "That's odd. Why would he do that?"

"The servant could only say that Llywelyn appeared nervous and unsettled," Gwen said. "The man hadn't wanted to leave his master, but Llywelyn ordered him to, and the servant obeyed because he knew how important the letter was. When Llywelyn put him on his horse and sent him away, he went. If you haven't seen Llywelyn, then nobody has heard from him since."

Gareth looked over at Hywel. "This news about Llywelyn is disturbing, my lord. It makes me wonder if someone shouldn't be sent to England to seek word of him."

"Would that someone be you, Gareth? Tired of my company already?" Hywel said.

Gareth made a sour face. "Of course not, my lord. I may have words with Taran later about using Gwen as his errand boy, but I can see why he thought Godfrid's arrival seemed the perfect opportunity, not only to see his letters delivered but to get Gwen out of his hair."

"Are you sorry I came?" Gwen said.

Gareth barked a laugh, not willing to dignify that question with a response. He looked again at Hywel. "May I accompany Gwen to see your father?" At Hywel's nod, he added to Gwen, "Let's find something for me to put on that isn't coated with mud. If we are going to see the king, I should look my best."

"I brought you some clothes in my saddlebag, perhaps better than what you have." Gwen gestured to where her horse had been picketed. One of the stable boys, who'd been brought to the encampment from Aber, had watered him, and he was munching happily from his feed bag. "I also have supplies for Prince Rhun—and a letter to him from Angharad."

Gareth pressed his lips together, trying to hide his smile. Prince Rhun's marriage prospects had been the subject of much speculation over the years, but he had finally settled upon Angharad as his choice. She was niece to the King of Deheubarth, a fickle ally if ever there was one and the ruler of a kingdom to which King Owain had been seeking closer ties for years. King Owain had approved the match—partly out of relief that his son had finally chosen a wife, but also because it was good politics.

King Cadell himself had no daughters, so marriage to his niece was the best that could be hoped for. The wedding would take place in the spring. Everybody was trying to avoid thinking about the last time a marriage had been arranged between Deheubarth and Gwynedd. In that instance, the wedding had ended before it had begun: with a dead bridegroom and Cadell on the throne of Deheubarth. They could only hope that the outcome of this match would be better. Gareth didn't see how it could be worse.

"Where is King Owain?" Gwen said as she and Gareth detoured to her horse to pick up Gareth's fresh clothes, and then walked back towards his tent, leaving Hywel and Godfrid to ready themselves in their own way for the short journey to King Owain's headquarters.

"He has taken over a nearby monastery, recently abandoned, and refitted the buildings for his own use," Gareth said.

"This isn't the convent where you learned to read, is it?" Gwen said.

"No," Gareth said. "That was located farther to the south. Many holy sites have been destroyed or abandoned since the war between Stephen and Maud began."

"I didn't realize the fighting between them had affected monasteries all the way up here," Gwen said.

"In itself, it hasn't," Gareth said, "but lawlessness has taken hold in remote corners of Wales such as this. Monks prefer to build as far away from lay settlements as they can, but isolated lands are precisely the places where masterless men can operate with near impunity. Gwynedd's reach has rarely stretched this far. King Owain's father was on the verge of conquering here when King Owain's elder brother, Cadwallon, was killed and, since that day, control over these roads and lands has shifted back and forth between Ranulf and King Owain a dozen times. Mostly, the people look to their local lords for guidance."

"As they do most places," Gwen said.

"True," Gareth said, "but usually a shift from one overlord to another doesn't involve changing countries."

"And Ranulf hasn't exactly been a good steward." Gwen nodded her understanding. "I feel sorry for the monks, but sleeping safe in a monastery sounds like a much more comfortable situation for King Owain than I expected. Cristina has driven us all mad with her endless grousing about how he hasn't come home for three months. He might not wish to subject himself to her nagging, but I wondered how he could stand sleeping on the ground all this time."

Gareth laughed. It felt good—genuine and familiar—as it bubbled up in his chest. That Gwen walked beside him, that she was *here*, even if she shouldn't be, covered the whole world in a rosy glow. "Though he would deny any suggestion that he is slowing down, the king nears fifty years of age. I, too, have been surprised that he hasn't left more of this war to his sons."

"I do think it's Cristina," Gwen said flatly. "Motherhood has made her shrewish."

Gareth eyed his wife. "Has she directed her bile at you?"

"Not often," Gwen said.

Gwen's words came out short, bitten off even, and Gareth decided not to harp again on Gwen's decision to make this trip. It had been nearly a year since he'd spent more than a few days at Aber Castle, so he couldn't judge the state of the queen's mind. She had her two sons now, Dafydd and Rhodri, and her devotion to them was fierce and uncompromising—perhaps to the boys' detriment.

Certainly, her protectiveness and her constant defense of their birthright had kept most of the king's many other sons away from Aber, Hywel and Rhun among them. Even with the loss of his possessions in the river, Rhun hadn't made any effort to leave the front in favor of a few days at home.

"Mari—" Gareth began.

"—never left Ceredigion. She chose to remain in Aberystwyth until the birth of her child," Gwen said.

It took two days of hard riding for a message to travel from eastern Gwynedd, where the war was being waged, to Aber Castle, west of the Conwy River. It would take many more to reach Ceredigion. The atmosphere at Aber must be truly foul if Mari would prefer to live so far away from where Hywel fought. "Provided the passes remain open, after you leave here you should collect Tangwen and ride to visit Mari," Gareth said. "Since Hywel cannot, you should be with her for the birth of the child."

Gwen gave a small cry and threw her arms around Gareth's neck. "I don't want to be so far from you, but if my husband commands it, what can I do but obey?"

Gareth laughed again, pulling her tightly to him, and then kissed her hard, forgetting for a moment their surroundings and the many watching eyes.

"Time is a 'wasting," Hywel said, coming up behind them on his way to his own tent. His words were a rebuke, but his tone was mild.

"Yes, my lord," Gareth and Gwen said at the same time, not without a giggle on Gwen's part, and they hurried into Gareth's tent.

Hastily, Gareth stripped off his clothes. Although he would have much preferred to wrap Gwen up with him in the new thick black cloak she'd brought and lie down on his pallet with her, they couldn't keep Prince Hywel waiting. Instead, he dressed in the clean items from Gwen's pack. It was probably just as well they'd hadn't taken any time for themselves. As Gareth was pulling on his shirt, Dai tossed back the tent flap and entered.

"Mum!" The boy flung himself at Gwen, and she hugged him back. His brother, Llelo, appeared in the doorway a moment later. Taking in the scene, he approached more slowly, but with as much joy, and hugged his mother too.

"My boys," Gwen said.

Gareth could hear the tears that had formed in Gwen's throat at the presence of her two adopted sons. Gareth and Gwen had rescued them from England after the loss of their parents two and half years ago when the boys were ten and twelve. Now old enough to wear the mantle of a knight's sons, Llelo and Dai were being fostered and taught by one of King Owain's illegitimate sons, Cynan.

The next oldest son after Rhun and Hywel, Cynan was Hywel's half-brother, a year younger than he. King Owain had given Denbigh Castle to him and to his younger brothers, Madoc and Cadell, as a base from which to protect eastern Gwynedd. On his way back from Aber last month, Gareth had spent an evening with Cadell, since he remained at Denbigh as its guardian while his older brothers were fighting. Cadell chafed at his charge, viewing it as a form of exile, but when he'd spoken to Gareth of the king's trust in him, Gareth had heard pride too, both for himself and for his brothers.

In recent weeks, Cynan had been promoted to captain of the king's *teulu*. King Owain's former captain had been wounded and lay recovering at Denbigh. Gareth had inspected the injury in his right leg, and while he would live, the wound had cut deeply into the muscle. He might ride again one day, but it wouldn't be into battle.

Llelo and Dai had spent the summer at Denbigh Castle, starting their apprenticeship to become knights, before the outbreak of fighting on the far eastern border between Gwynedd and Chester had brought them here in Cynan's wake. Early on, the fighting had been farther to the south, but in recent weeks it had moved closer to Chester and become focused around Mold Castle, to which King Owain was preparing to lay siege.

Having reached manhood, Llelo was a few inches taller than Gwen and wore a sword on his hip. Dai was tall enough to look her in the eye. She hugged them again and said, "You boys have been staying out of trouble, haven't you?"

Llelo rolled his eyes. "Of course, Mum."

"We haven't seen any real fighting," Dai said.

Gareth nodded. "We've been using them as scouts mostly."

And then, with accomplished movements, Llelo moved to help Gareth arm himself. He'd done it before, of course, though Gwen had never witnessed it. Gwen stood with her arm around Dai's shoulder, watching, and then while Llelo belted on his father's sword, Dai left her to help Gareth adjust the bracers on his forearms.

Gareth kept his eyes on his wife's face, proud beyond measure of their sons, but trying not to show it. "How is our daughter?" he said softly.

Gwen smiled. "She is well. Bright and loving. I found her a new nanny, since Elspeth is married and expecting a child of her own. The woman's name is Abi. She lost her husband in the early summer while we were in Ceredigion. Sickness."

It was an all too common story. Gareth had lost his own parents to measles when he was five years old.

"She is some relation to our Dai and Llelo." Gwen said.

Llelo stopped in the act of tightening Gareth's belt and looked up. "I heard you say her name, and I thought I might know of her." He tugged on the end of the belt so it would stay and not flap annoyingly. "She's my father's sister's husband's cousin."

Gareth smiled. Welsh genealogy being what it was, every man could name his ancestors to seven generations, but it became complicated trying to remember the family trees of those who had married in. It didn't surprise Gareth, however, that Llelo could do it. He probably had Gareth's and Gwen's families memorized too.

"And what have you been doing, Gareth?" Gwen said.

"I've hardly drawn my sword, Gwen. You needn't worry so."

Gwen didn't believe him—and said so. "What about your new scar?"

"Oh. That," Gareth said.

She gave a mocking laugh. "Yes, *that*. You allowed an enemy to come far too close to you when you weren't wearing your armor."

Gareth put his hand on his eldest son's shoulder. "I was scouting with Llelo. He already knows how to read the landscape and listen to a forest, so studying the terrain comes naturally to him. Unfortunately, it did to Ranulf's scout too, and neither of us saw each other before we were face to face, each coming around the opposite side of a large bush. He was quicker with his knife than I—"

"Gareth!"

Gareth put out a hand to Gwen, "—let me finish. I was going to say that my aim was more accurate."

Gwen bit her lip as she looked at the calm faces of Gareth and Llelo. "I understand why you didn't want to tell me, but I need to know the bad as well as the good." She looked at Llelo. "And what about you?"

"I learned a valuable lesson," Llelo said, sounding far more like a man than the boy she'd last seen at Aber.

"We have both been more careful since then," Gareth said.

"I am so scared for all of you, every day," Gwen said. "After this, if I ride to see Mari in Aberystwyth, it might be months before I see you again."

"I know you're scared for me," Gareth said, "but please know that I am not. Trust me that I know what I'm doing."

"It isn't your skills that I question," Gwen said. "It's those of the men you face I'm worried about."

Gareth actually laughed. "The real difficulty ahead is wresting control of Mold Castle from Ranulf. King Owain is determined to take it before Christmas. We weren't fully committed to the effort before last week, and until yesterday some of the lords remained reluctant to agree to a siege. From what Hywel has told me, King Owain hopes to move the men forward by the end of the week, and then the whole army will converge on Mold."

"The boys too?" Gwen said.

Llelo stepped back from Gareth, eyeing his attire and nodding, satisfied with his work. Gareth was satisfied too, which was why he had no qualms about stealing his son from Cynan every now and then when he needed him.

"I will keep my eye on them," Gareth said.

Dai grinned. "That's what he says, but it's really that we'll be keeping an eye on Da for you, Mum."

"For which I am very grateful," Gwen said, reaching for Dai again and bringing him into the circle of her arm.

Then Dai said, "But you shouldn't be here, Mum."

"I'm only here for a day, and then I'll return to Aber. I needed to see you all, and Lord Taran had a letter for the king." Gwen looked at Gareth. "I suppose we should see about speaking to him."

Leaving Dai and Llelo to their duties—both were due to stand watch on the perimeter of the camp—Gareth and Gwen left the tent and found Godfrid and Hywel waiting for them by one of the fire pits. Hywel stood with his hands outstretched to the warm flames. He'd taken off his leather gloves, and his fingers were white. Gareth eyed them, watching the color gradually return to them. It appeared that the prince's sensitivity to cold was growing worse.

From Gwen's report, Hywel's hands and feet had reacted strongly to cold since his early teens. It wasn't something a soldier—or a prince—was allowed to complain about, but Gareth remembered the first time Hywel had shown him the forefinger of his right hand after it had turned white and lifeless. Warm water was best for heating it up, but Hywel had been known to plunge his fingers into a bowl of cooking porridge when he was desperate to feel his fingers.

Hywel saw Gareth looking at his hands. He grimaced and hastily pulled his gloves back on. He never went anywhere without them in winter, and his boots had an interior layer of wool to better keep out the cold. Living outdoors all the time might be more difficult for him than for King Owain.

"Do we walk to the monastery?" Gwen asked.

"It's a half-mile through the woods," Hywel said. "Better to ride in this weather."

Even if he suspected the prince wanted to ride because of the condition of his fingers, Gareth didn't protest. The air had turned colder over the last hour, and given its size and the exposed nature of the field, the camp was open to the weather. Warm winds and rain, both of which they'd had plenty of this autumn, came from the southwest. But it was a cold north wind that was blowing this afternoon. They could have snow by morning.

Gwen shivered beside him. Concerned, Gareth pulled up her hood and retied the scarf around her neck so that it held her cloak closed and prevented the wind from getting into the core of her body. Beneath the cloak, she was already wearing wool breeches, a shift, an underdress, and an overdress. Any more layers and she'd barely be able to move. As it was, the only bits of her that were showing were her nose and mouth.

It took only a few moments to mount, and then the companions rode down the track to the monastery. They arrived in the clearing in front of what had once been the main gatehouse but was now something of a ruin. The base of the wall had been originally built in stone, but it had crumbled on either side of the gate to a height of less than three feet and no longer provided any serious barrier to the courtyard behind it.

The wooden gate stood open, and a half-dozen horses cropped the grass that had grown up between the slate stones that paved the courtyard in places. Dismounting, the companions led their horses through the gate. At that moment, Prince Rhun, Owain's eldest son and Hywel's blood brother, appeared out of the entrance to the cloister with a man dressed in priest's robes. The pair had been talking intently and looked up at the sudden arrival of the visitors.

Rhun broke into a smile and, sounding very much like his father, said, "Well, well. Look what the cat dragged in." He walked towards Godfrid, who tossed his reins to Gareth.

The two princes reached each other in three strides. Godfrid didn't give Rhun as exuberant a greeting as he'd given Hywel, but they shook arms with genuine affection. They were near to each other in height and weight, attributable to their mutual Viking ancestry.

"Cousin." Godfrid stepped back from Rhun. "I bring you greetings from my father, as well as twenty good fighting men."

Rhun dipped his chin. "I am very glad to hear it—and to see you. I am looking forward to hearing your news from Dublin, but—" His eyes strayed first to Gareth, and then to Gwen, who'd pushed back the hood of her cloak so Rhun could see her face.

Gwen smiled. "My lord."

Rhun was in his late twenties, a few years younger than Gareth. He'd been his father's right hand since he'd become a man and knew his father's mind better than anyone except Taran, King Owain's longtime friend and the steward of Aber Castle.

"I do not know how it is that you are here, Gwen, but somehow I can't be surprised. It is just as well. The good father has need of your services."

Gwen put a hand to her breast. "My services?"

"Yours and your husband's." Rhun tipped his head towards his brother. "It appears, once again, that your captain is needed for other duties for a few days."

"Why is that?" Hywel looked nonplussed. "The siege of Mold is imminent, Rhun."

"Our preparations will have to continue without Gareth, at least for now," Rhun said. "Father Alun, of the parish of Cilcain to the east of here, has found a body in his graveyard."

3

Gwen

Prince Rhun gestured Father Alun closer. The priest, a rounded, somewhat squat man somewhere in advanced middle age, obeyed, stepping out from under the eave that sheltered the doorway into the monastery proper. He'd waited there while Rhun had greeted Godfrid.

Arrayed in the undyed robes of a country priest, simple and plain down to the sandals and a belt made of rope, he couldn't have been comfortable in this weather. Gwen felt colder just looking at him. He had a kind face and eyes, though, which were currently riveted on her face with an intensity that was disconcerting.

Gwen didn't know the reason for it, so she tried to ignore it, saying instead, "Aren't bodies supposed to be found in graveyards?"

Gareth squeezed her hand briefly, probably glad that she'd been the one to ask the obvious question rather than leaving it for him.

"Indeed," Father Alun said, his eyes still fixed on Gwen. "One would expect it. But this is something of a different situation. I was wandering among the stones at the back of the churchyard, looking for a burial spot for a parishioner who died, when I came upon a body in a freshly dug grave."

Gareth's eyes narrowed. "One, I gather, that shouldn't have been freshly dug?"

"And a body that shouldn't have been in it, freshly dug or not," Rhun said.

Father Alun's gaze skated to the prince, who tipped his head in a possible apology for interrupting, or merely to indicate that the priest should continue his tale.

Father Alun sighed. "Earlier in the day, one of the village pigs was found inside the churchyard wall. We rousted him and thought we'd undone the damage from his rooting, but we hadn't investigated very far behind the church. I wish I had, because he'd been digging at the grave with his hooves and uncovered a woman's hand."

Gwen wrinkled her nose in distaste. "That must have been unpleasant."

Father Alun nodded. "It was. I'm sorry to say that I did not keep my dignity as well as I would have liked."

He admitted his failing with complete serenity, and Gwen felt a sudden warmth towards this humble priest, who seemed to have no agenda but to discover the name of the poor victim who'd been left in his charge.

Prince Rhun waved a hand, dismissing Father Alun's admission. "Go on."

Father Alun certainly knew how to tell a story. While he didn't relish the telling of it, he laid out the salient facts with a clear voice: the grave lay in the far corner of the graveyard under a spreading oak. The initial grave had been dug long ago, and the man in it buried while the tree was still young and its root system less extensive. The wide boughs had prevented the robust growth of grass beneath the tree, which may have deluded the man who'd buried the woman there into thinking the digging would be easy. Instead, he'd encountered roots two feet down, gave up, and buried the woman in a far too shallow grave.

"Even without the pig," Father Alun continued, "I might have noticed how the earth was more mounded under the tree than it should have been. At the very least, even a cursory inspection would have shown that someone had tried to get rid of extra dirt by mixing it with fallen leaves and strewing it over the spot where the digging had occurred."

"Is the body of the man whose grave it is still in place?" Gwen said.

"Yes, it is." Father Alun said. "We confirmed it without uncovering him entirely, and then laid the dirt over him again. We tried to be respectful." For the first time he showed real discomfort, wringing his hands at the sacrilege done to the dead man's remains.

"Could someone have buried the body because they didn't think—" Gwen broke off, trying to find a better way to articulate the ugly thought. She started again, "Could it simply be a matter of burying a loved one whose interment in holy ground you might not have approved of?"

"That was, frankly, my first thought." Father Alun spread his hands wide. "I am not one to deny burial unless the circumstances are extreme, and I hadn't heard of a woman dying in the region other than the old woman for whom I was looking for a burial site. We are a small parish, and any death would have been known throughout Cilcain."

"Anyway," Rhun said, obviously having heard the whole story already, "the man's grave was old and had a stone to mark it."

"What about grave robbers?" Godfrid said, speaking for the first time. He'd been listening to Father Alun with an amused expression on his face, which was typical for him.

Father Alun shook his head. "We are a poor parish—poorer in recent years with all the fighting. My people aren't buried with expensive rings and trinkets."

"Perhaps it's time you tell us why you came all this way," Hywel said. "A dead woman is one thing. Are we to understand that you believe she was murdered?"

"Her throat was cut." Father Alun gave an involuntary shiver.

Gwen had been waiting for him to admit something along those lines and spoke gently, "You don't recognize her as someone from your parish?" It was one thing for Gwen herself to become far too familiar with murder, but this might be the first time the good father had encountered it.

"No, but—" Father Alun shook his head, his attention back on Gwen's face. Then, strangely, he came forward and took one of

Gwen's hands in both of his. "I am accustomed to being the bearer of bad news, but I have never had to bring news to a relation in a situation such as this. My dear, I apologize for staring at you, but even in death the woman we found bears some resemblance to you. Do you—do you have a sister? Or-or-or a cousin, one who could have come to grief near Cilcain?"

Gareth leaned in between Gwen and Father Alun. "Wait. Are you saying that the murdered woman looks like Gwen?"

"Yes." Father Alun said. "I came here hoping for help in putting a name to the woman's face, but I had no idea that discovering her identity was as simple as speaking to you, my dear." Father Alun looked helplessly at Gwen. "Please tell me her name so that I may give her a proper burial."

"But I don't have a sister." The words came blurting out before Gwen could think about them or stop them. "I don't even have a female cousin that I know of. My mother died birthing my brother."

She looked down at the ground, not wanting to see the sympathetic expressions on the men's faces. It was perfectly possible that her father had loved another woman besides her mother. Gwen knew virtually nothing about her father's life before her own birth and might not know everything about his conduct afterwards. He might never even have known that he'd sired a daughter other than Gwen.

It would have been unusual for the mother of the child not to tell him. In Wales, illegitimate children were counted as legitimate as long as the father acknowledged them. King Owain had many illegitimate sons and daughters, and he'd acknowledged them all. Rhun was his father's favorite and the *edling,* the chief heir to the throne, even though King Owain hadn't married his mother, an Irishwoman who'd died at Hywel's birth. It was one of the many ways that Welsh law differed from English law, and why the Welsh were fighting so hard to maintain their sovereignty.

Gwen was still shaking her head. "My mother was an only child, and my father's sisters have no daughters. I don't know who this woman is."

Father Alun pressed his lips together for a moment, and then said, "That may be, but would you consider coming to see her for yourself?"

"I think you should," Hywel said, before Gwen could answer, "except that Cilcain is very close to the territory controlled by Earl Ranulf's forces. Cilcain itself was ruled by him until we drove his men back towards Mold a month ago."

Gareth slipped his arm around Gwen's shoulder and directed his words at Prince Hywel. "My lord, this isn't just about the girl's connection to Gwen. It's murder too."

"As I was saying to the prince before your arrival, my lords, Earl Ranulf's men have moved south and east," the priest said. "A few of us alone won't invite notice or comment, even if he has men scouting the region."

"Looking for us, you mean," Hywel said. "He knows that we are preparing to move on Mold."

"All of Wales knows that," Father Alun said, "but Chester doesn't have the men to stop you."

Prince Rhun stepped closer. "How's that?"

Father Alun's head twitched as he looked at the intent faces of those surrounding him. "Didn't-didn't you know that? He is facing pressure from King Stephen on his eastern border. Small skirmishes only, but Ranulf has pulled back many of his men all along the border with Gwynedd."

Rhun's face took on a rare intensity. "Is that so? We hadn't heard."

Godfrid touched Gwen's elbow, and he jerked his head to indicate that he would like to speak to her and Gareth a bit away from Father Alun, who was now being pressed harder by Rhun and Hywel to explain exactly where his information had come from.

"Father Alun could be a spy for Chester and his story a ruse, as a way to deliver this piece of information to King Owain," Godfrid said. "What if his intent is to draw the king into a trap?"

Gwen looked up at the Dane. His size and enthusiasm sometimes made her forget the sharp mind behind his twinkling blue eyes.

But even with Godfrid speaking low—and in accented Welsh—Father Alun overheard him. He cleared his throat and said loudly, "What I have told you isn't news today to any man living east of the mountains. Chester has refortified Mold as best he can, it is true, but we haven't seen any of his soldiers pass through Cilcain in days. I swear it."

"My lord," Gareth said, speaking to Hywel, "I am the captain of your *teulu*. If I were to go, I can uncover the truth of Father

Alun's words. Cilcain is a small village, and the people will all know about the woman's death and be concerned about a murderer running free among them. They will need reassurance that their king—in the absence of Ranulf—has taken an interest in their wellbeing. I can show them that he has."

Hywel rubbed his chin, studying Gareth and Gwen, and then turned to his brother. "I agree with Gareth. I think we should help the good father, and Gareth can also discover if what Father Alun says about Ranulf's forces is true."

Rhun looked east, though all he could see from where he stood were the trees that surrounded the monastery. "You know as well as I that determining the course of events that led to this woman's death is unlikely to be quick or simple."

"Which is why I should go, my lords," Gareth said. "If it's only Gwen and me, we will have access to homes and crofts beyond those which a company might find open to them, and we can ask questions of everyone."

Hywel looked at his brother, who was behaving very much the *edling* today. "You know how good at this they are."

In adulthood, the brothers had become closer than they'd been as children, providing each other with real support and without a shred of jealousy or acrimony. Though Gwen had never had a sister herself, Hywel had been like a brother to her at times, and she recognized real camaraderie when she saw it.

"I do." Rhun contemplated Gwen and Gareth for another few heartbeats, and then he nodded his consent.

Gwen gave a small sigh of relief. Father Alun had been right to come to King Owain's headquarters, since he was the new ruler of the region, but control of that lordship remained precarious. If King Owain was going to rule in fact as well as name, he needed to be seen doing so. And that meant solving a murder in his lands.

Gareth held out a hand to Godfrid. "It was good to see you. Hopefully Gwen and I can clear this matter up quickly and return before the assault on Mold begins."

"But—" said Godfrid.

Gwen almost laughed at the look of consternation on his face, which was mirrored in Hywel's and Rhun's expressions as well. The part about Gareth and Gwen going alone hadn't sunk in until this moment. All three had been involved in Gareth's and Gwen's murder investigations at one time or another, and each man wanted to come on this journey. She could appreciate the tug of intrigue and discovery, though she herself wasn't looking forward to examining the dead body of a possible sister.

But then Rhun gave way to the necessities of his station and said, "Be careful."

Hywel sighed and punched Godfrid's upper arm. "This time we'll have to leave them to it, old friend."

Though his eyes remained on Gareth and Gwen, assessing them, Godfrid grunted his assent. "At a minimum, a conference with the king shouldn't wait."

"I agree, Godfrid," Rhun said. "While my father hasn't been receiving visitors today, perhaps he will make an exception for you."

"He is unwell?" Hywel stepped closer to Rhun.

"So much so that he admitted it." Rhun tipped his head to Godfrid, indicating that the Dane should come with him.

His brow furrowed in concern, Godfrid patted Gareth's shoulder, nodded at Gwen, and followed Rhun into the monastery, leaving Hywel with Gareth and Gwen.

"I don't like hearing that your father is ill," Gwen said.

"Neither do I, but you'll have to leave him to Rhun and me for now." Like Godfrid's, Hywel's face showed worry. "I suspect you understand what is happening here as well as I, but I'm going to spell it out for you anyway, just to be clear: you are to solve this murder in the name of the king while at the same time keeping your ear low to the ground. Our scouts have not reported a withdrawal from the region around Mold, which they should have if it were true."

"Maybe this just happened," Gwen said.

"Prince Cadwaladr's men have had the duty these past few days," Gareth said, though he looked down at the ground as he said it, not meeting Hywel's eyes.

Prince Cadwaladr, King Owain's younger brother, had arrived on the border with Chester before King Owain's forces last summer, having hastily departed Ceredigion in advance of the king. Gwen and Gareth had met during a time when Gwen's father sang in Cadwaladr's hall, and Gareth had served him as a man-at-arms. Both had left Cadwaladr's court years ago—in Gwen's case because she went where her father went, and in Gareth's for refusing what he believed to be a dishonorable order. Gwen and

Gareth had caught the wayward prince out in wrongdoing several times since then.

"I know," Hywel said.

"I don't like leaving you under these circumstances," Gareth said.

"I trust no one more than you two to get to the bottom of this," Hywel said, "but it would be good if you could hurry."

4

Gwen

"I will send a query to Lord Goronwy's men on the chance they know more about Ranulf's movements than Cadwaladr's men have reported," Hywel said.

"Where is Lord Goronwy camped?" Gwen said.

"Farther south," Hywel said, "beyond Cadwaladr's forces and alongside some of the other lords from eastern Gwynedd."

Gareth nodded. "Meanwhile, Gwen and I will question the people we meet." He paused. "Some may not like it."

"My father rules these lands," Hywel said, "and if Earl Ranulf wants to take them back, my father is prepared to meet him. Father would prefer to avoid the necessity, however. Our focus is on Mold Castle, not on the little villages and hamlets between here and there. We aren't interested in fighting hand-to-hand and house-to-house."

"We understand," Gwen said. "You want us to go to Cilcain to solve this murder and spread goodwill, while at the same time spying out the lay of the land. You'd prefer, also, that we don't call attention to ourselves such that one of Earl Ranulf's informers hears of it and tells him where we are."

Hywel studied her a moment. "This is an old tune for you, Gwen. You should know it by heart by now."

Gwen just managed to refrain from making a face at him like she might have done had they still been ten and twelve. Or even nineteen and twenty-one. He was right, of course. She'd spied for him before she'd investigated murders for him, though this wouldn't be the first time one task had blended with another.

Gareth was chewing on his lower lip. "Now that you agree, I'm having second thoughts. I hate to leave the men and you so close to the time for real battle."

"Evan is here, and while he is not you, he will do for now. You need to go," Hywel said. "I would send only you, Gareth, if this dead girl wasn't possibly Gwen's sister or relation."

"I need to go with Gareth," Gwen said.

"I know," Hywel said. "I won't bar you from seeing her into the ground with a proper burial."

"Besides, as a couple, we will cause less comment," Gwen said. "Now that I think about it, it wouldn't be a bad idea for Gareth to travel as a common man."

Gareth put a hand on the hilt of his sword, which stuck out from underneath his cloak. "I will not sneak around like a thief. Either I'm representing King Owain and the rule of law, or I'm not."

"You are," Hywel said. "Wear your sword."

"We'll try not to get caught between opposing forces," Gwen said, a smile on her lips. "Or get you caught between them."

Hywel pointed a finger at her. "That isn't amusing. If you come upon Earl Ranulf's forces, you turn and run."

"What if we can't run?" Gareth said.

"You are a knight and my father's representative. You speak for me."

Gareth bowed, acknowledging the burden Hywel had placed on him, though truthfully, he carried that burden every day.

Hywel touched Gwen's shoulder briefly. He didn't speak, but she saw concern and love there, and then the prince grasped Gareth's forearm. "Good luck."

Gwen and Gareth mounted their horses to follow the priest, who'd watched their conversation from his perch on his mule.

"How far is it to Cilcain?" Gwen said as she began to follow the priest down a different pathway from the one on which Gwen and Gareth had ridden to the monastery. Instead of heading north, back towards the camp, they rode south. The trail here was slightly narrower than the one from the camp—understandable since that road had experienced an upswing in traffic in recent weeks—but still well-trodden.

The ground had been churned up during the spell of rainy weather they'd had, but the ruts had dried today in the colder air, becoming more rigid and easier to stumble over. Tree branches overhung the road as well, and Gwen kept having either to swerve to avoid them or to duck under them.

"A little more than three miles as the crow flies, but we need to take the pass that runs south of Arthur's mountain, so it will take a little longer. Thanks to King Owain, Gwynedd now runs to within a mile of Mold. We breathe easier under Welsh rule."

"Which puts the border of Wales how far from Cilcain?" Gwen said.

"Another three miles east," Father Alun said. "I know your prince is concerned for your safety, but even when Earl Ranulf's forces controlled the area, they never bothered us. You will be perfectly safe."

Father Alun might be only trying to comfort her because she was a woman, but it never paid to be complacent, especially when one lived on the border between two warring lords. And while on first acquaintance Gwen had liked Father Alun, all of a sudden he seemed more self-satisfied than he ought to for someone who'd found a murdered woman in his graveyard. Godfrid could be right about the misinformation and the trap.

Still, Father Alun had said his parish was poor, and Gwen consoled herself with the reminder that Ranulf of Chester wanted to rule these people too. Sacking a village that tithed to you, whether or not the inhabitants were Welsh, wasn't a good way to ensure that the people continued to obey.

The journey required nearly two hours of riding, in large part due to the slow pace set by Father Alun's mule. A horse couldn't run at a gallop for long, but if they'd at least been able to ride more quickly than at a walk, they could have reached the chapel in half the time. On another day, the delay between learning of the existence of a dead girl who looked like her and seeing her body might have set Gwen's teeth on edge. But she was perfectly willing to put off what lay ahead of her as long as possible.

During the first part of the journey, the hills which rose up on either side of them and the thick woods that surrounded the road sheltered the riders from the cold wind. But once they reached the open fields that characterized the land east of the Clwyd Mountains, the road widened, which Gwen preferred, but the wind picked up too, screaming down the valley towards them from the north.

Gwen cinched her hood closed under her chin, such that the only part of her body that showed was her face. She was sure her nose was red, though with the light starting to fade as the end of the day neared, soon nobody would be able to tell. The close of autumn in Gwynedd meant that they had less daylight every day, until by the time of the winter solstice, the days were hardly more than seven hours long.

Here in late November, that date was rapidly approaching. It wasn't any wonder that King Owain wanted to move on Mold in the next week rather than continue to fight through the long winter months in the dark and the cold. Victory by Christmas sounded wonderful to Gwen too.

As the road continued to descend into the lush valley, green even at this time of year, they approached the village of Cilcain from the west. Villages were few and far between in most of Wales, but in eastern Gwynedd, they were more common because the most prevalent livelihood for the people was farming rather than herding. When people were able to live in one place year round, communities were more likely to spring up. The village of Cilcain consisted of three dozen houses clustered around a central green.

A small tavern, which was hardly more than a few wooden benches and tables set outside someone's home, occupied pride of place at the entrance to the village. Its benches were full tonight, and as Gwen and the others passed by, every single head in the place turned towards them to watch their progress down the road.

Father Alun raised his hand to the crowd and gave an extra nod to the tavern keeper, who came to stand in the doorway to the hut, the light from the fire behind him making him little more than a silhouette in front of it.

Cilcain didn't have an inn, which weren't common in Wales anyway. They hadn't passed one on the road either. With no castle nearby, she and Gareth would have to beg for a bed tonight from Father Alun or one of his parishioners.

From the tavern, the road led Gwen, Gareth, and Father Alun past the southern side of the green to a crossroads, at which point they turned north, effectively passing through the bulk of the village in order to reach the chapel, which was located on the north side of Cilcain. Along the way, women and children came out to inspect them.

Gareth had fallen back a length or two, his intent expression one he wore when he was carefully studying his surroundings. In particular, he would be committing the faces of the villagers to memory and taking note of any who looked quickly away as he passed or disappeared from among the onlookers before he could make them out.

Gwen settled back into her saddle and lifted a hand shyly to several women as she passed by. Father Alun gestured to a little chapel fifty yards ahead of them, and his mule, sensing home, picked up speed such that he outpaced her horse's walk.

"So much for being discreet," Gareth said from his new position on her left side, having caught up to her again. "Any spy of Ranulf's can see for himself that a Welsh knight from Gwynedd has come to Cilcain."

"At least their glances aren't resentful," Gwen said.

"The people here are Welsh," Gareth said. "Let's hope they know it, and nobody is running right now to the Earl of Chester to tell him we're here."

Far too knowledgeable about intrigue and treachery to wonder why someone might report their presence, Gwen looked down at her hands as they once more clenched the reins. The answer would be for the usual reasons: because the spy was paid to do so, or because he believed in his cause. And she had to admit that if she lived in Cilcain, and Ranulf had sent his knights to the village, she would have been the first to tell Hywel of it if she could. Loyalty and treason were two sides of the same coin.

"It might not be just for the money," Gareth said, reading her thoughts. "People here have lived under Norman rule more often than Welsh for the last hundred years. Some will have done better for themselves because of it. Some might truly believe the Normans bring order, or even that they are the future and to fight them is only to put off the inevitable while making things worse for themselves in the process."

"I don't want to live in a world where Norman rule is inevitable," Gwen said.

"God and King Owain willing, Gwen, you never will."

They left the main road to follow a northerly track, just wide enough for one cart, and halted in a grassy clearing in front of the main gate that led to the west side of the church. Like every chapel in Wales—and maybe all of Christendom—the nave was oriented on an east-west axis, with the door on the western end of the church and the altar on the east. This was so the morning sun, if and when it broke through the cloud cover and shone through the eastern window, could fill the church with light from behind the altar.

Graves were dotted here and there in the grass on the north side of the church, and were even more numerous farther back, under the trees, which, as Father Alun had said, appeared to have grown up since the people in those graves had been buried. There were so many tombstones within her line of sight that Gwen quickly recalculated the age of the church. It was newly white-washed, which had given her the mistaken impression that it had been built recently.

Gareth dismounted and surveyed the little church. "When they come, our men will march right through Cilcain."

Gwen dropped to the ground too. "I saw that gleam in Rhun's eyes too when Father Alun mentioned the pulling back of Ranulf's forces."

Gareth nodded. "I don't know when it will happen, but it could be as soon as tomorrow or the next day. King Owain will move our camp forward, past Cilcain, but not close enough to Mold to be seen. And then he will attempt to circle the town and castle completely."

"Can you take the castle?" Gwen said.

"Honestly?" Gareth said. "Yes. It's an earth and bailey castle, built in wood, not stone. We can take it."

"You could simply burn it down," Gwen said.

"We could," Gareth said, "but King Owain wants it for its strategic importance. He'll burn it if he has to, rather than leaving it for Ranulf to refortify, but he'd prefer to take it intact. If we hold Mold, we have a good chance of controlling the eastern lands all the way from the Conwy River to the Dee. Even right up to the gates of Chester. Gwynedd hasn't had that kind of reach since King Gruffydd's time."

"I heard you mention Prince Cadwaladr's forces," Gwen said in a tentative voice. It went without saying that Gwen neither respected Prince Cadwaladr nor trusted him. She didn't want to know what he'd been doing since she'd last seen him because she cared about his wellbeing, but because she cared about Gareth's. As far as she was concerned, even when he was on King Owain's side, he was a danger to her, Gareth, and everyone she loved.

"You knew he was here, Gwen." Gareth was speaking so low his words barely reached her. "He's made Ruthin Castle his base, in the same way that King Owain has fortified Denbigh."

"But the king is staying at the monastery, not at his castle," Gwen said.

"Denbigh isn't in a forward enough position for King Owain's tastes. Riding back and forth from the encampment to the castle takes too much time, and he doesn't have any other castles closer to Mold. That's one of the reasons he *wants* Mold." Gareth canted his head. "By contrast, Cadwaladr prefers to lead from behind. I actually haven't seen him in weeks."

Father Alun, who had dismounted and approached without Gwen noticing, cleared his throat in what Gwen interpreted to be a subtle protest against the aspersions cast on Cadwaladr's character. Gwen thought—hoped—he'd only heard the last few sentences Gareth had spoken, because any discussion of King Owain's strategy had been intended for her ears, not his.

Gareth faced the priest. "I apologize, Father, if I offended you by speaking of the king's brother in that way."

Father Alun raised his hand. "It is good counsel never to speak ill of anyone, especially a prince, but do not fear that I am judging you. Your reputation has preceded you. Prior Rhys of St. Kentigern's monastery in St. Asaph is a friend of mine."

Gwen let out a breath. Father Alun didn't have to say more. If he and Prior Rhys had discussed the politics of Gwynedd, Rhys would have told him of some of the more heinous crimes Cadwaladr had committed over the years, many of which hadn't been made common knowledge among the populace, but which Prior Rhys knew about from Gareth.

And if he knew of Gareth, than he knew of her too. Some priests were uncomfortable around a woman who investigated death, but Father Alun had taken her presence at a murder investigation far more in stride than he had her resemblance to the dead woman. In fact, now that Gwen thought about it, he hadn't balked at all when Prince Rhun had instructed both her and Gareth to return to Cilcain with him to look at the dead body. It was refreshing, really, not to have to justify her presence.

"I should show you the grave site before it grows any darker. We've already moved the body into the chapel," Father Alun said.

That answered the question Gwen hadn't asked, regarding whether or not he and his helpers had disturbed the burial scene. He had, but she couldn't blame him for doing so. It would have been unseemly to leave the body outside all day, awaiting Father Alun's return.

"We understand," Gareth said.

"She may not have been killed here anyway," Gwen said.

Gareth glanced at the sky. "It smells like snow. We need to work fast if we're going to beat both it and the night."

"Snow will cover the murderer's tracks nicely," Gwen said, as she followed Father Alun towards the northeast corner of the churchyard, where the graves were set off slightly from the rest and had bigger grave markers.

"This area of the graveyard has been set aside for the family of the local lord." Father Alun halted at a hole in the ground, approximately a foot and a half deep, which was marked by a large stone, too weathered for Gwen to make out the name of the deceased unless she put her nose right up to it. But from the size of his stone, he had to have been an important man.

Gwen wrinkled her nose as she looked down into the hole. As Father Alun had said, the diggers had taken great care to protect the body of the man whose grave it had been for so many years. The one who'd buried the body of the girl had made her grave just deep enough to hide the body but hardly the depth required to keep a stray pig from uncovering it.

Father Alun gestured helplessly with one hand. "You see what has been done? Why could he not have simply buried the poor woman in the woods? Why defile a grave?"

"Father, even with the rain we've had, it isn't so easy to bury a body six feet in the ground," Gareth said.

Nearly two years ago, Gwen and Gareth had investigated the death of Hywel's cousin, Tegwen, who also hadn't been given a proper burial. One of the men involved had said the exact same thing as Gareth had just told the priest, though he'd thrown up his hands in despair when he'd said it.

"Far easier to dig up soil that's already been dug once. And since this spot is farthest from the church and any spying eyes, you can see why the killer chose it," Gwen added.

"Whoever did this may have thought burying her here wouldn't attract attention," Gareth said. "Graveyards are supposed to have bodies in them. What's one more?"

"It is of great importance to me, I can assure you," Father Alun said, sounding offended. "He must think me simple—or a fool—if he thought I wouldn't eventually notice."

"More likely he was in a hurry, panicked even," Gwen said. "Most murders aren't planned, and that means most murderers are unprepared to face the consequences of what they've done. Nobody thinks about how to get rid of the body of a person he's just killed until he's actually done it." She gestured to the grave. "As you can see."

Father Alun peered into Gwen's face. "You are so young. I wish you couldn't speak of murder with such familiarity, my dear, but I suppose I'm not sorry for it either if your knowledge will help us find the one who did this."

"Gareth and I have investigated untimely deaths many times in the past few years," Gwen said. "I don't mean to imply that I'm used to it, however."

"What I hear most in your voice is weariness with the evil ways of men, and that is a sentiment I can understand," Father Alun said kindly.

"You should hear determination too," Gwen said. "Truthfully, it isn't murders we investigate, but *murderers*. The dead are with God, and their souls are your purview. It's the living who concern Gareth and me."

5

Gareth

Gareth directed Gwen and Father Alun to search around the graveyard in an ever-widening circle from the grave, in order to look for anything the murderer might have left behind. He was anxious to examine the body, but with darkness coming on, a thorough search of the area took precedence. He was already regretting the lack of manpower resulting from being here with only Gwen.

If it didn't snow in the night, they could try to get a more complete picture of the grave and its surroundings in the morning, but it was important to do what they could before any more time passed. Another loose pig in the graveyard, and the scene would be completely destroyed.

For his part, Gareth crouched by the pile of dirt, which the gravedigger had left at the gravesite when he'd removed the body of the woman, and began to sift through it. He'd borrowed a lantern from Father Alun, accepting the loss of his night vision in favor of being able to see well enough to distinguish pebbles and leaves from artifacts left by a man. Gareth was hoping for a piece of cloth or a memento—a ring, a necklace, a broach—but he wasn't exactly surprised not to find anything more significant than a few stones and sticks.

"Whose grave is this?" Gareth gestured towards the stone marker, the carving on which he was having trouble making out. "Did you know him?"

"Huw ap Morgan." Father Alun turned his head to look at Gareth. "And yes, I did know him. I was new to the parish when he became Lord of Cilcain." Then he approached, peering closely at the carved letters. "My eyes aren't what they once were, but perhaps you can read what I can't. Does it say he began his rule in the year of our lord 1118?"

Gareth crouched beside Father Alun, feeling at the numbers beneath the illegible name. "I'd say so."

Father Alun rested his hands on his knees, still bent over. "That was the year King Gruffydd, King Owain's father, annexed Rhos and Rhufoniog. Here, we were still ruled by the lords of Dyffryn Clwyd and Tegeingel, Queen Cristina's family, in tithe to the Earl of Chester. But we knew without seeing King Gruffydd's army approaching that we would soon fall to Gwynedd."

"Caught between two powerful lords is never a comfortable place to be," Gareth said.

Father Alun lifted one shoulder. "We are simple folk and have few needs. We farm, as the Saxons do, and we care for our flocks, as our ancestors did. Our lands have not been ravaged." For the first time, his face took on a fierce look. "Woe betide the lord who cares so little for his people that he strips them bare a month before winter."

Gareth chose not to reply to that, rather than assure Father Alun that King Owain would never do such a thing, and instead indicated the stone again. "Could there be a reason other than convenience that the murderer chose to bury the woman in this grave?"

Father Alun straightened, looking south, beyond the wall of the graveyard towards the village. "I can't tell you. I know the family, of course. Morgan, Huw's grandson, rules these lands from his fort on the bluff above the ford on the road to Mold. I would say he is of an age with you."

"And whom does he serve?" Gareth said.

Father Alun barked a laugh, revealing a bit of acid beneath the kindly exterior. "Not King Owain, not yet. But not Ranulf of Chester either, except when forced to bend a knee. Things aren't what you're used to here, Sir Gareth. Allegiance is a tenuous thing, and a man has to look to his own people and flocks first and foremost."

"Would you say Morgan is good at that?" Gareth said.

"Better than some," Father Alun said. "He hasn't filled the seat as well as his father or grandfather did, but he is young yet and inexperienced."

"Will he speak to me, do you think?" Gareth said.

"Are you asking if he will answer your questions truthfully?" Father Alun gave a cant to his head. "He won't blame you for what's happened, if that's what you're wondering, as much as he won't like hearing that a murdered woman was buried over his grandfather's body. That he won't like at all."

"Such was not my concern," Gareth said. "I was wondering, rather, if he would view speaking to the captain of the guard of a prince of Gwynedd as taking sides in the war. While King Owain has moved into this region, his soldiers haven't yet occupied the village, and with Mold Castle so close, Ranulf could send in his men at any time. Will he not want to risk meeting with me in case it rouses Ranulf's ire were he to hear of it?"

"I am not a former soldier like Prior Rhys," Father Alun said. "I have never involved myself in politics, but I can tell you that Earl Ranulf has proven himself to be a reasonable man, even if he doesn't appear so to you."

Reasonable had never been a word Gareth would have applied to Earl Ranulf of Chester, but he'd met him only that one time at Newcastle, and the circumstances had certainly been tension-filled. Stuck in England, they'd been faced with traitors, spies, and dead bodies—though come to think on it, Earl Ranulf had been one of the few people who turned out to be exactly as he seemed: arrogant, ruling his lands as an almost-king, and resentful of any encroachments on his own power.

Father Alun continued, "The earl would understand if your inquiries took you to Morgan's doorstep, but if you wish, I will come with you in the morning to introduce you to Morgan and explain your task."

"I would appreciate that. Thank you—"

"Gareth." Gwen's voice carried to him from within the woods.

"Coming." It was dark enough now that Gareth couldn't see more than a few paces into the trees. He picked up the lantern and carried it with him, keeping it low to the ground so it would illumine the dirt, grass, and fallen leaves. It was impossible to make out much beyond the small circle of light, but Gareth wasn't worried about an attacker hiding in the darkness. He wanted to catch a glimpse of a piece of cloth, torn from the corner of a cloak, or the glint of light off metal.

He saw nothing useful, however, and found Gwen crouched on the far side of the patch of trees, next to a stone wall that demarcated a farmer's pasture. She pointed to the ground.

Father Alun had come with Gareth, and he peered at the place Gwen was pointing. "I see churned earth. What are you seeing that I don't?"

"At least three sets of boot prints," Gareth said, instantly recognizing why Gwen had called him over, "and the hoof prints of three horses."

Gwen gestured to one set. "Those belong to a big man, not just one with big feet."

"I would say so too." Gareth moved at a half-squat among the tracks to look for another that he could distinguish clearly from those around it.

"How is it you can determine something like that?" Father Alun peered at the tracks with an intent look on his face. "Just because a man has large feet doesn't mean he's big. One of the tallest men I know has smaller feet than I do."

Gwen straightened to answer him. "A heavier man sinks more deeply into the ground than one who is lighter, regardless of the size of his feet."

Father Alun's expression blanked for an instant, but then cleared, and he smiled. "Of course. I should have known that. I have been unobservant."

"He would also sink if he was carrying something heavy, Gareth," Gwen said.

"Something like a body." Gareth held the lantern close to another one of the prints and measured his boot against it. Gareth's feet were of average length and width, and so was this print. He shot a quick grin at Gwen, pleased to have acquired a piece of solid information already. "They never learn, do they?"

Gwen smiled. "Don't play your harp before it's tuned, my love."

"Who never learns?" Father Alun said. "And what is it they don't learn?"

Gwen gestured to the prints. "Murderers always think they're more intelligent than anyone else. They believe they can hide their tracks, or that the body they buried won't be found. But here we are."

Gareth nodded. "As a priest, you probably see the worst of people too, like Gwen and I do, but honestly, I don't believe most men are suited to great evil. It weighs on them. They feel shame or guilt. Even a man who doesn't, who has become so accustomed to the loss of his soul that he doesn't notice its absence anymore, still can't think of everything. He slips up. He can't help it."

"He betrays himself, you mean?" Father Alun said.

"Exactly," Gareth said.

Father Alun lifted one shoulder. "I don't know if I can agree, Sir Gareth. I have seen great evil in my time."

"Surely great good too." Gwen tipped her head to Gareth. "We have."

"I'm not saying that in the heat of the moment a man can't do the most heinous deed imaginable. I'm just saying that it eats at him afterwards. What's left of his soul prevents him from thinking his actions through to the end—and as a result, you end up with this." Gareth gestured to the ground around him, a little embarrassed about discussing theology with a priest. Something about Father Alun's manner invited confidences. "You end up with a woman buried inexpertly in another man's grave and clear marks of boot and hoof prints, which might lead us ultimately back to the one who killed her."

Gwen tipped her head, calling Gareth's attention to the fence. "See here? Many of the stalks are shorter than the surrounding vegetation. It looks to me like the horses were tied here and cropped the grass while they waited."

Father Alun looked from Gwen to where she indicated. "Prior Rhys was right."

"What was he right about?" Gwen picked up the lantern and began to walk along the fence line, her eyes on the ground.

"That men should beware of committing murder in your vicinity," Father Alun said. "I see now that you know your business, and I understand why Prior Rhys speaks so highly of your skills. King Owain was right to place his trust in you."

Gareth pressed his lips together, feeling satisfaction himself. The more men who thought as Prior Rhys and Father Alun did, the fewer murders Gwen and he would have to solve. That their reputation preceded them could only be a good thing.

Even if Prior Rhys had exaggerated his skills to Father Alun, he and Gwen had a history of success. That wasn't to say that dozens of men hadn't succeeded in getting away with murders nobody knew anything about.

"Is there more to find here, or would you like to see the body now?" Father Alun said.

Gareth looked at Gwen, who put her hand to the small of her back and stretched, before straightening and sighing. "I suppose we should see the body." She returned to his side, the lantern swinging from her hand.

Gareth put an arm around her shoulders and squeezed. "You don't have to see her if you don't want to."

"Yes, I do," Gwen said.

Gareth didn't question her decision again. She had more courage than most men, of a kind that had less to do with the strength of her arms than with her mind and character.

They walked back through the woods, past the open grave, which the grave diggers would now be able to fill in, to the churchyard, and then into the vestibule of the little chapel. One foot inside the door, Gareth caught the first whiff of the smell left by a dead body. Gwen, whose nose was more sensitive than his, recoiled on the threshold. Putting the back of her hand to her nose, she took a step outside, drew in a deep breath, and then started forward again.

"You'll need to bury her in the morning," Gareth said. "It really shouldn't wait another hour, but it's too late in the day now."

"I can sense that," Father Alun said, dryly. "The body didn't smell at all when I left this morning."

"It's only a guess, but I'd say we're still in the first full day since her death, putting her murder yesterday before midnight." Gareth said. "The earliest part of the decaying process occurred while she was in the ground, so the smell was something you might not have noticed at first."

"Why is that?" Father Alun said.

Gareth glanced quickly at Gwen, who wore a tense look on her face and didn't seem to be listening. "The body releases its fluids—" Gareth broke off at the way Father Alun flinched.

The priest held up a hand. "Say no more."

"It isn't something most people spend any time thinking about," Gareth said. "We usher our people into the ground within a day, usually, and I imagine it is the women of the parish who clean and dress the body, not you."

"It is as you say," Father Alun said. "I will pay more attention in the future."

"As it is, it's a blessing the weather has turned cold," Gwen said, proving that she'd been listening to their conversation after all. "If it were a summer's day instead of almost winter ..." her voice trailed off, and Gareth was glad she'd decided not to regale the priest with any more of what she knew either. She could have said that a body decayed much faster in hot weather. Likely Father Alun knew that instinctively already.

Fortunately, the priest was already moving across the flagstones that made up the floor of the church and didn't comment on what Gwen had said.

The body was being kept to one side of the nave in a little alcove. The chapel was really only one large room, smaller than many great halls, with a central area in which people could worship and an altar that lay at the eastern end on a raised platform. It was a far cry from some of the more ornate churches in which Gareth had examined bodies over the years.

Gareth and Gwen followed Father Alun to where the woman lay on a table, covered from head to foot by a sheet. One candle guttered in its sconce on the wall above her, but as Gareth and Gwen gazed down at the body, Father Alun busied himself with lighting whole banks of them, arranged in four candelabras, until the area around the body was lit up nearly like day.

Despite his earlier revulsion, Father Alun had turned matter-of-fact, which Gareth appreciated. If he was going to have to examine the body in the presence of someone other than Gwen or Hywel, he would prefer the onlooker wasn't losing his dinner on the floor beside the table.

"May I ask why you rode all the way to King Owain to tell him of this murder instead of going to Lord Morgan in the first place?" Gareth said, still not pulling back the cloth that covered the woman's face. Gwen remained a few paces away, her eyes unfocused. "He is the local lord."

Father Alun's expression turned somewhat sheepish. "I took this matter to King Owain because I was looking for you specifically, with the hope that the king would consent to relieve you of your other duties and send you home with me."

Gareth looked up at him. "This is because of your conversations with Prior Rhys?"

"Yes. I realized that the king couldn't involve himself in every incident, but as this was murder ..." Father Alun's voice trailed off as Gareth continued to study him. He'd known intellectually that word of their investigations may have traveled far and wide across Wales, but he hadn't given Father Alun's interest in him much thought beyond that simple notion.

"How did you know I was with the king's company?" Gareth said.

"It is well known that you lead Prince Hywel's men," Father Alun said. "At the very least, if you had been otherwise occupied, I hoped that King Owain could find someone else he could task with the investigation. I didn't know that I would be fortunate enough to acquire the services of both you and your lady wife."

Gareth didn't mind at all that Father Alun wanted them to investigate the murder—he just didn't understand why he hadn't said so up front, back at the monastery. Then again, maybe he had mentioned it to Rhun and the prince hadn't seen the need to talk to Gareth or Gwen about it.

"Despite what you said in the graveyard, am I to understand, then, that you don't trust Morgan?" Gareth said.

Father Alun raised both hands, palms outward, in a gesture of defense and denial. "I felt the girl deserved the best, and we have no experience with murder here, neither in the village nor the castle."

Father Alun hadn't actually answered Gareth's question, suggesting to Gareth what he'd already concluded: this Lord Morgan had Norman leanings. It wouldn't be an uncommon position to take, not along the border. Welsh and Norman had mingled for a hundred years. In good times, intermarriages created valuable alliances. In bad, it split families in two. By now, most of the nobility in the March—what everyone called the border region between Wales and England—had mixed ancestry.

"I wish we didn't have that experience, Father Alun," Gwen said, "but since we do, and we're here, we'll do our best for you and for her."

Gareth glanced at his wife. "Are you ready?"

Gwen took in a shallow breath and nodded.

Father Alun took the last three paces to the table where the body lay and folded back the cloth that had been covering the woman's face.

Gwen and Gareth reacted at the same instant—Gwen with a gasp and Gareth with a muttered curse, which he immediately swallowed back and apologized for to the priest.

"I did warn you," Father Alun said, sadness in his voice, "though now that I have seen the two of you together, your resemblance to her, Gwen, is more a sense of similarity in size and shape, rather than your specific features."

Gareth circled around the body, peeling back the rest of the sheet as he went. The body had already been washed and dressed in a white shift for burial. The woman had been dumped unceremoniously in a shallow grave, unshrouded. Had someone not cared for her since she was found, her clothes would have been reeking and her tissues crawling with tiny insects and creatures that lived in the ground. The act of cleaning her might have erased evidence that could have led to her killer, but Gareth couldn't be sorry that Gwen didn't have to see her in such an extreme state.

Besides, any damage to her body beyond her throat would be easier to spot and wouldn't require them to strip her, an act that would surely make the priest—and Gareth himself—uncomfortable.

Gareth focused on the body, aware even as he did so that Gwen was still standing a few feet back from the table. He was worried about her, but he also knew that if he didn't make a thorough examination of the body now, he would never get another chance. He told himself to take his time, that he was growing used to her resemblance to Gwen, and that this strange reluctance to touch the woman's body could be worked through.

"Now that I look closely, I can see why you thought she was my sister, Father Alun," Gwen said, finally coming out of her reverie. "But it's more that her hair is the exact color of mine, and her skin has the same tone to it. Her features actually remind me more of Gwalchmai than me."

"They remind me of you," Gareth said. "Still, though she might well be a relation, she isn't your twin." The woman had been several inches taller than Gwen, too, though perhaps that impression derived from the fact that she was lying full length on the table.

"Her feet are bigger," Gwen said.

Gareth allowed himself a quick smile. Gwen had dainty feet, dwarfed by his large hands when he kneaded them after a long day. He was glad to see that she seemed to be recovering from her initial shock and dismay.

"You say you never had a sister?" Father Alun said.

"No," Gwen said. "Nor cousins, nor anyone that I have ever met who looked so much like me. That's not to say what you were all thinking back at the monastery couldn't be true—that my mother gave birth to a child before she married my father, or my father loved another woman besides my mother."

"The latter more likely, surely," Gareth said. "Children stay with their mothers."

"I would have thought so," Gwen said.

Gareth longed to be alone with Gwen so he could delve into what was going on behind his wife's calm features, but with Father Alun here, any questions along that line would have to wait.

He turned to the priest. "Was she put into the grave fully dressed?"

"Yes." Father Alun pointed to boots and clothing that had been carefully folded and placed on the lone chair in the chapel.

"Those are hers. My housekeeper washed them and must have returned them while I was gone."

Gareth shot a look at Gwen, who nodded and moved towards the pile, taking on their examination as her task. "May I speak to the housekeeper?" she said over her shoulder to the priest.

"Of course," he said, but he didn't move to find her, mesmerized, it seemed, by what Gareth and Gwen were doing.

Gareth bent forward to examine the wound at the dead woman's throat. Her neck had been slashed, probably from behind and by a right-handed person, from the way the wound had been cut deeper into her flesh on one side of her neck than the other. The shift she now wore showed no blood, of course, since it had been placed on her recently and her body had stopped bleeding at death.

Gwen unfolded the clothing and held up the woman's dress to show Gareth what he expected to see: a pattern of blood across the chest and shoulders, which even an enthusiastic scrubbing couldn't entirely get out. It indicated that once the murderer had slashed the woman's throat, she'd dropped to the ground on her back, bled out, and died.

"Somewhere there should be a pool of blood and no body. It would be nice to find it," Gwen said.

"It could be anywhere," Gareth said. "I didn't see any blood in the graveyard or where the horses were tied." He turned to Father Alun. "You didn't notice anything unusual during the last few days—either in the village or near the chapel? Or perhaps someone behaving strangely, as if he knew a secret he couldn't tell?"

Father Alun shook his head. "Nothing like that. I certainly didn't notice anyone digging in the graveyard. I was tending to the needs of my flock, I'm afraid, not looking for a murderer."

"They could have brought her body in from anywhere," Gwen said. "She could have been killed a mile away and been brought to the church flung over the back of a horse."

"But only in the dark," Gareth said. "She couldn't have been carried anywhere—or buried in the churchyard for that matter—in broad daylight."

Gwen folded the woman's dress, laying it back on top of the pile of clothing, and then she picked up the woman's boots. Even from here, Gareth could see the dirt and scuff marks on the backs of the heels, indicating that she'd been dragged. But they could have guessed that.

Gareth gave a rueful laugh. "At least I won't have to sketch her face to show to the people we question."

"No, you won't." Gwen gave a little sigh as she set the boots on the floor. "You'll only have to show them me."

6

Gwen

Gwen had been taken aback at the initial sight of the body, but she was getting used to the similarities between herself and the dead woman. It helped that the woman's face appeared less like her own the more she looked at it. She could see why Father Alun had been stunned to find her at King Owain's headquarters, however, and why Gareth had taken the name of the Lord in vain.

"Now that you've seen her, do you still think she was murdered yesterday evening?" Father Alun showed no signs of leaving them alone to do their work, even after Gwen had tried to get him to leave by asking to speak to his housekeeper. After a quick glance at Gareth, whose face indicated resignation, she resolved to ignore the priest's wide eyes while she worked.

"It has to be that recently," Gareth said.

"How do you know?" Father Alun said.

"The body is cold and a little stiff," Gwen said.

Father Alun's face went suddenly blank, like it had out in the graveyard. It was a look Gwen recognized as an instinctive balking at her bald statement. *So much for ignoring his wide eyes.*

She'd spoken without thinking and now put out a hand to the priest. "Do you think I'm uncaring? I assure you I am not."

Father Alun shook himself, as if trying to clear his head. "Your straightforwardness is refreshing. You are thinking of this poor girl as a problem to be solved rather than a lost soul whose life ended all too soon."

"I am thinking of both," Gwen said, "but her soul is in heaven and was always your concern. Giving her justice here is ours."

Gareth grunted his agreement. "It's as Gwen said earlier. We did not choose this path, but now that we are on it, our charge is to uncover the truth, especially when someone has gone to such great lengths to hide it from us—and to hide from it."

"And in so doing, we have to remain detached," Gwen said, "or we can't function."

Over the years, she and Gareth had (quite naturally) talked at length with each other about the murders they'd investigated. At one time, Gareth had tried to protect her from them, but he had mostly come around to seeing that they were better off working together.

Gwen didn't know that either of them had ever before articulated to anyone, to quite this extent, the *why* of what they did. Gwen was surprised at herself for revealing so much about what was going on in her head on such short acquaintance with Father Alun. His easy manner must have come in very useful when it came to confession.

Father Alun uncrossed his arms and gave them both a little bow. "Perhaps it would be best if I leave you to your work." He turned on his heel and strode purposefully for the door, his steps quickening the closer he came to it.

Gwen watched him go and then turned back to her husband with a rueful smile. "He seems like a good man, a good priest."

"I wish we had more like him." Gareth held up one of the woman's hands. "Look at this."

Gwen peered closer. While the body had been cleaned from head to foot, eliminating whatever dirt, blood, or skin might have been left under the nails, the condition of the nails themselves was permanent. And in this case, the nails on the woman's right hand were ragged and torn.

"She marked her killer," Gwen said.

"She marked someone. We can't say yet whether or not he was her killer. The cut to her throat was clean and very likely came from behind," Gareth said. "I wouldn't have thought she'd have had the chance to hurt him."

"She could have fought him earlier," Gwen said. "He might have had to subdue her before he killed her. He could have tied her to a chair, for example."

Gareth grimaced. "I'm torn, *cariad.* I don't want you to have these thoughts in your head, even as I need you to think them. Worse, I keep seeing you in her. I don't like it—but I think you could be right. Her wrists are bruised as well."

"So she was held or tied," Gwen said.

"Maybe both," Gareth said. "Maybe she was tied when she was brought to the woods and killed there, close to the grave. We merely haven't found the spot yet."

Gwen shivered. The sense of violence that hovered above the body was palpable to her, like a miasma in the air, mixing with the scent of death. When Gwen had first seen the woman's throat, she'd viewed this murder as somewhat straightforward—or as straightforward as murder ever got. But thinking about the woman struggling against her captors and fighting for her life before she was murdered had Gwen's stomach churning.

"Go get some air, Gwen," Gareth said. "I'll finish up here."

"But—"

Gareth canted his head towards the door. "Go."

Gratefully, Gwen went. Gareth still had to see what other damage the killer had done to the woman, even to the point of undressing her completely. Gwen knew she should stay with him, but she hurried away anyway, mimicking the quick steps Father Alun had taken in his last rush to the door. Even so, she resolved to remain outside only briefly before returning to help.

Once she crossed the threshold of the chapel, however, she found Father Alun sitting on a bench outside the door. The air was even colder than before, and their breath formed a fog in front of them. Gwen pulled her cloak close around her body and approached the priest, her boots crunching on the small stones that made up the pathway.

"You're done already?" Father Alun started to rise to his feet.

"No. No, we're not." Gwen put out a hand in a request for him to stay seated. "I just needed some air."

"I can understand that." Father Alun subsided, shaking his head. "I don't know how you do it."

"Sometimes I don't know how either." Gwen took in several heaving breaths, trying to expel the smell that lingered in her nostrils. She knew from experience that it would remain in her clothes until she scrubbed it out of them. She was thankful she had a spare dress in her saddlebag. "But it has to be done, and if not by me, then by whom? And who better?"

"Some would say investigating murder is no job for a woman," Father Alun said.

"Women deal in life and death every day," Gwen said. "Occasionally, the killer is even a woman. Again, who better than me to discover her?"

"That is a unique perspective and not one I'd considered before," Father Alun said. "Do you believe this to be your calling?"

"I could never compare what Gareth and I do to what you do," Gwen said, a little embarrassed now. Yet again, she hadn't meant to speak so freely.

"But I could," Father Alun said.

There was that self-satisfied look again, but this time it didn't trouble Gwen because she'd come to recognize its source: Father Alun had reached a stage in his life where he was sure of himself, the world, and his place in it. Gwen surely couldn't begrudge him that feeling of security. She'd had it only since she'd married Gareth.

Then she frowned. "Is that the sound of hooves I hear?"

Father Alun glanced up at her, his eyes questioning, and then he stood up quickly. The drumming of hooves on the road was definitely getting closer, and the rhythm of it indicated it wasn't just one horse coming, but a company of riders.

"Get back in the church," Father Alun said.

"And leave you out here alone?"

"I am a man of God. Whoever these men are, you should not be the one to face them. Get inside!"

Gwen obeyed his voice of command, flying through the door and across the nave towards Gareth, but she stopped halfway across the floor, barely managing not to heave up the last meal she'd eaten at the renewed assault on her senses. The smell seemed much worse after the fresh scents of the garden outside.

Gareth, concern evident on his face, flipped the sheet over the whole of the woman's body and met Gwen a few paces from the table. "What is it?"

"Horsemen are coming. At least four from the sound of the hooves on the road. Father Alun sent me inside."

Gareth took a last look at the body and then moved towards the middle of the nave. Even though Gwen had meant to slam the door shut, it was heavy, with stiff hinges, so she hadn't managed it. A four-inch gap remained between the door and the frame. That, as it turned out, was just as well. The open door meant they could hear Father Alun greeting the newcomers. His voice was calm, even familiar in its manner, which eased Gwen's breathing some. A man with a gruff voice replied to him, though in words Gwen couldn't make out at this distance.

Gareth angled his body so he stood in front of Gwen and waited fifteen feet from the door, his hand on the hilt of his sword.

"Do you recognize the voice?" Gwen said in an undertone.

"No. But I hear the authority in it."

The chapel had no back door. There was no place to which they could flee, and no time to do it anyway. The door swung open to reveal a soldier dressed entirely in black, with black hair and beard in the fashion of the English. He wore a sword belted at his waist and a long flowing black cloak. He hesitated in the doorway for a heartbeat, taking in the scene—and probably the smell—and then his eyes focused on Gareth and Gwen.

He took two steps inside and said in a loud voice that echoed around the chapel, "Father Alun tells me that you are Sir Gareth ap Rhys, of the court of Owain Gwynedd."

Gareth squared his shoulders, his hand remained on his sword hilt, though he hadn't drawn the weapon. "I am."

"You will come with me."

Father Alun came through the doorway behind the man and tugged on his arm. "Sir Pedr. Let me explain why they're here."

The man shrugged him off, instead gesturing with one hand to indicate that Gareth should come forward. Gareth didn't move, and Gwen stayed where she was, slightly behind Gareth's left shoulder. She was surprised her breathing remained steady.

"Who are you?" Gareth said.

"My name is Pedr ap Gruffydd. I serve Lord Morgan, of Bryn y Ddu. I am tasked with bringing you to his seat."

"Why?" Gareth said.

Pedr hesitated. "I have not been given leave to answer that."

"And if I refuse to come?" Gareth said.

"Refusal is not an option."

"Of course it is," Gareth said.

Gwen couldn't see Gareth's face and couldn't tell what he was thinking, other than that his shoulders remained relaxed. Gwen recognized his stance. He was prepared for a fight.

Pedr put his hand on the hilt of his own sword and gestured that the five men who'd come with him should enter the nave. They circled around Gareth and Gwen, and while none of them had pulled their swords from their sheaths either, Gareth and Gwen were at a woeful disadvantage. Gareth was an excellent swordsman, but he couldn't fight six men at once.

Father Alun, his hands fluttering, rushed forward and set himself between Gareth and Pedr. Three more soldiers crowded through the chapel door after the priest. Gareth recognized the impossibility of his position, and the muscles in his jaw clenched. He slowly moved his hand from the hilt of his sword. For Gwen's part, she gripped the hilt of her belt knife as it lay in its sheath at her waist, though like Gareth, she didn't draw it.

"I don't want violence, especially not in a church," Pedr said. "If you come quietly, I won't be forced to tie your hands."

"I'm under arrest?" Gareth said.

Pedr nodded curtly. "Lord Morgan has charged me with the task of bringing you to his seat." He held up one hand. "Please don't make this more difficult than it already is."

Gwen found it ironic that Pedr could ask Gareth not to make life difficult for *him,* as if that should be where Gareth's sympathies should lie. In this case, however, making life difficult for Pedr would certainly make it even more difficult for Gwen and Gareth.

Then Pedr looked beyond Gareth to Gwen, as if seeing her for the first time. "If this is your lady wife, Sir Gareth, my lord requests her presence too."

Gareth edged sideways to shield Gwen more fully from Pedr's view. "My wife needn't be a part of this."

"My lord disagrees." He took another step forward, and this time he brought up one hand appeasingly. "I give you my word that she will come to no harm. I swear it on my mother's grave."

Father Alun had remained standing between Pedr and Gareth, but at this oath, he dropped his arms and turned to Gareth. "I know Sir Pedr. You can believe what he says." He leaned closer and spoke in an undertone. "Sir Pedr is very loyal to Lord Morgan. If he was bidden to bring you, that is what he believes he must do."

"Regardless of whether or not I want to come." Gareth made a guttural sound deep in his throat. "It seems my standing as the captain of Prince Hywel's *teulu* bears no weight with him."

Father Alun was back to anxious. "I assure you that Pedr isn't loyal to Ranulf of Chester."

"That may be true," Gareth said, "but it doesn't explain what possible grounds Morgan has for my arrest."

Gwen rubbed her forefinger on the back of Gareth's elbow and said in a whisper, "I don't think we have a choice but to go with him, Gareth."

"I know." He looked down at Gwen. "We have few choices, and none of them are good."

"Every villager saw us ride past," Gwen said. "Pedr named you directly. He knows who you are, which means he knows why we're here. At the very least, by speaking to Lord Morgan we might learn something about the woman and why she was buried in his grandfather's grave."

"I will learn nothing if I'm locked in a cell."

Father Alun was six inches shorter than either man, and Gareth met Pedr's gaze over the top of his head.

"There is so much more going on here than we know right now," Gwen added in an undertone.

After another moment's reflection, Gareth nodded his assent.

"Bring him." Pedr spun on his heel and strode for the door. The soldiers in the nave closed in on Gareth and Gwen, herding them before them.

Father Alun walked beside Gareth, wringing his hands. "This is all my fault."

Gareth stopped on the threshold of the chapel and put a hand on the priest's shoulder. "You didn't kill this woman. You only sought justice for her, which was the right thing to do. You are not to blame for Lord Morgan's betrayal."

"We'll be all right." Gwen said, trying to speak confidently even if she didn't feel it inside.

Lord Morgan was a completely unknown quantity. She couldn't imagine what he thought Gareth could have done to justify his arrest. King Owain ruled here. Arresting one of his sworn liegemen was hardly the best way to go about currying favor. The combination of death and fear curling in her belly was nauseating.

Stepping out of the door, she took in a breath of fresh air, just as she had earlier when she'd left the chapel on Gareth's orders. Pedr and his men waited a few feet away with their horses, next to where Gareth and Gwen had left theirs.

"What should I do with the body?" Father Alun glanced through the still open door of the chapel to the table where the woman lay under her shroud.

"I was all but finished with my examination," Gareth said. "If we haven't straightened this out with Lord Morgan by morning and returned to finish what we started, bury her as you planned."

Pedr, who'd moved a few steps closer in order to hear the tail end of Gareth's and Father Alun's conversation, said, "He won't be back." He waved an arm to indicate that she and Gareth should proceed to where they'd left their horses.

Gwen gave Father Alun's an imploring look. "Pray for us."

"I will be on my knees all night," he assured her, "for all of you."

7

Gareth

Gareth had almost fought Pedr. He'd been a hair's-breadth away from it, in fact, and he would have, even if that had then meant he'd have been taken before Lord Morgan in irons. Gwen's presence and the tensions coiling and twisting in that nave had forced him to reconsider. The nerves of every fighting man in the region had been on edge this autumn, which had led to arguments among friends in the encampment and actual sparring in some cases. Under such circumstances, Pedr's men might have simply run him through.

As it was, Pedr hadn't harmed either him or Gwen. He'd even stood at Gareth's stirrup and presented to Gwen his interlaced fingers to boost her onto Braith's back behind Gareth. She was riding pillion, which had been Gareth's choice as well as Pedr's. Gareth didn't want to risk being separated from Gwen, and Pedr wanted them tightly contained.

"Can we run?" Gwen asked in a low voice.

"Aren't you curious as to what this is all about?" Gareth said.

"Of course I am, but not enough to risk your life!" Gwen said.

"Leaving presents as much a risk as staying." Gareth tipped his head to indicate the man riding just to the right of them. "One shot from that bow, and either you, me, or Braith is dead."

He felt Gwen nod her understanding into his back.

Two of the men riding behind them held torches that threw out enough light to see the road and the ditches on either side. Gareth couldn't see anything else, however. The cloud cover over their heads was absolute, hiding the moon and stars. Again, if he were alone, he might have chosen to follow the riskier path, to urge Braith off the road despite the danger of being shot or the fact that he'd be riding blind.

Gwen's arms were tight and warm around Gareth's waist, and he patted the back of her hand. "It's going to be all right." With the cold and wind—and snow coming before the dawn—this wasn't the night to take Gwen into the hills unless he had no other choice.

"How do you know?" Gwen said.

"Because it has to be," he said. "I have done nothing to warrant arrest."

"What if Morgan's intent is to sell you to Ranulf?" Gwen said.

"That, to me, is the most likely scenario," Gareth said, "but I do not fear death at Ranulf's hands. He has no more reason to harm me than Morgan does. At worst, I might rot a while in a prison cell."

"That's supposed to be comforting?" But then Gwen pressed her cheek into his back, and he felt that she was comforted.

"As you've said in the past, it's a matter of tugging on a loose thread until the whole plot unravels at our feet," Gareth said. "We have to start somewhere. It might as well be here."

"I just wish Pedr and his men weren't so menacing," Gwen said.

More than anything Gareth wanted to assuage Gwen's fears and ease the anxiety he felt in her. Whether or not he had any real reason for optimism, Gwen would gain nothing—and jeopardize her ability to think clearly—by allowing those fears to cloud her mind. "Whatever happens, stay close to me."

Gareth would have expected the village to be deserted now that it was full dark, but a few women poked their heads out of their houses, and the tables in front of the tavern were even busier than they'd been when he and Gwen had arrived. He had to think the conversations would focus as much on their presence—and his subsequent arrest—as on the death of the woman.

Gareth tried to maintain a certain space between Braith and the men who hemmed them in, but it quickly became clear that they slowed as he slowed, and sped up as he did, with hardly a pause. They were a well-trained troop. Their sword sheaths had a sheen to the leather that meant they'd been much handled, and the men closest to him had an aura about them that indicated they would have been perfectly happy had the evening turned out differently and Pedr really had run him through.

All in all, Gareth was pleased to still be alive and upright. Although Pedr had taken his weapons, his hands weren't bound. As long as that was the case, he could protect Gwen or die trying.

Once through the village, they rode directly south towards the Alyn River, at twice the speed at which they'd ridden through the village. Gareth was very aware of his surroundings: his breath fogging in the air in front of him; the staccato of the horses' hooves; Gwen's arms cinched around his waist; and the lights shining from a settlement above them that he guessed to be Morgan's fort. Father Alun had mentioned that the stronghold overlooked the ford.

The horses slowed as the road dipped down to the river. Even though Gareth could hear water running over stones, he couldn't see the river until they were nearly in it.

Pedr headed across the ford, and Braith entered the water right behind him, following where Pedr's horse had put its feet. The ford was improved with flat stones, which widened the water's run, but also made it so shallow that they crossed with the water hardly rising past Braith's hocks. The road then curved to the right and began winding its way up to the settlement a quarter of a mile away on a rise.

Cleverly, the road wound back and forth across the face of the hill, crossing and recrossing in front of the fort's gatehouse, so the riders were always under the eyes of the soldiers watching from the wall-walk. The cart tracks in which Braith trotted were well worn. People had lived and worked in this region for generations, and Morgan's family had ruled them from this spot when Wales had belonged only to the Welsh.

Unlike the motte and bailey castle the Normans had built at Mold, Morgan's fort was more than a military stronghold. The palisade and buildings spread out across a flat area partway up the much higher hill that rose up behind it. Gareth had noticed it in the distance when they'd arrived in Cilcain earlier in the day.

A guard poked his head above the gate to observe them—and then admit them. As they passed through the opening into the courtyard, Gareth felt the eyes of everyone in the place on him and Gwen. The palisade surrounded an inner courtyard which, based purely on its size, provided a home to far more people than Morgan's immediate family.

Gwen squeezed him hard.

"Just follow my lead." Gareth swung his right leg over Braith's head and dropped to the ground.

"I wouldn't dream of doing anything else," Gwen said.

The instant Gareth's feet hit the earth of the courtyard, four of Pedr's men hemmed him in again, though they did allow him to reach up and help Gwen off Braith's back.

Upon entering the courtyard, Pedr had been met by an older man in a long robe, of the style stewards had worn before the Normans had come to Wales. While Gareth waited, they spoke urgently with one another, though in an undertone, so Gareth couldn't make out what they were saying.

Then Pedr turned to Gareth and Gwen. "This way." He marched off towards the hall after the steward, who led the way.

Like the rest of the fort, the main hall had a well-used look to it, indicating its long service to Morgan's family. Large and single-roomed, with a hole in the roof to let out the smoke from a central fireplace, its only concession to time was the way additional buildings had been added onto it over the years. Without a chamber for his exclusive use off the back or the side of the main building, a lord had no place to conduct his private business without clearing the hall of onlookers first. With abundant forests within hailing distance, wood was a cheap source of building material, not only for the hall itself but for little huts and craft halls that lined the inner side of the palisade.

Pedr waited on the stoop for Gareth and Gwen to reach the door. Then, Gareth's elbow in a tight grip, he directed them through it and into the hall. Gareth took Gwen's hand in his left, in part to stop himself from moving his hand to his hip to rest it on the hilt of a sword that was no longer there.

To compensate for his lack of weapon, he took long strides, almost dragging Pedr with him instead of the other way around. Entering Morgan's hall as a wanted man and surrounded by angry soldiers was, in equal parts, absurd and humiliating. It had been a long time since Gareth had entered a strange lord's home with this much dismay.

Regardless of how Gareth felt about it, however, he and Gwen were outnumbered fifty to one. A buzz of conversation had emanated from the hall at their arrival, but as Gareth and Gwen passed among them, the people present fell silent, ceasing to eat, drink, or talk. With Gwen's hand in his, Gareth walked purposefully towards the far end of the building where Morgan's chair rested. By the time he and Gwen reached the central fireplace, the only sound in the hall came from the flames themselves, where wood that had too much moisture in it crackled and popped.

The steward led them around the fire and then stopped ten paces away from Morgan's chair. He bent his head. Pedr did the same. Gareth came to a halt when they did, and it wasn't until the pair parted, one to each side of Morgan's chair, that Gareth was able to see Morgan's face clearly. He almost laughed—with relief and surprise—because he knew Morgan, though back when they'd met, Morgan hadn't been the lord of a stronghold such as this, but hardly more than a boy.

It wasn't a boy who faced him now.

Although Father Alun had said Morgan and Gareth were of an age, Gareth knew Morgan to be several years younger. The young lord was what the English called 'black Welsh': black hair, olive skin, and eyes so brown they were nearly black too.

Gareth never liked to be reminded of the days after Prince Cadwaladr had thrown him out of Aberystwyth. Because of it, he'd lost Gwen and his livelihood. He'd taken to wandering Wales in search of someone who needed a hired sword. He hadn't cared overmuch, at first anyway, about the tasks he was set, since he hadn't thought any could be worse than those Cadwaladr had given him. For nine months, Gareth served a lord by the name of Bergam whose son's escapades had gone far beyond youthful hijinks.

The last time he had seen Lord Morgan, Gareth had been dragging his charge out of the hall at a lord's fort in northern Powys. The young man in question had drunk too much, which was usual for him, but in doing so had taken it upon himself to proposition Morgan's sister. Gareth hadn't known exactly where Morgan was from or the name of his father. Even had he known, he might not have connected the two so many years later.

Gareth decided to take the initiative. "Lord Morgan. We meet again."

Gwen glanced up at Gareth in surprise, but he kept his eyes fixed on Morgan's. The hall was completely silent, and Gareth could feel the eyes of every soul in the room boring into his back.

"You remember, then. The circumstances of this meeting appear to be equally inauspicious." Lord Morgan rose from his chair. "Gareth ap Rhys, I arrest you in the name of King Owain Gwynedd."

Gareth released an involuntary laugh. "What's the charge?"

"Treason!"

Initially Gwen's jaw had dropped at the accusation, but now she said, "Don't be absurd."

Gareth was glad to hear the same mocking laughter he felt echoing in her voice, rather than dismay or fear. They were in tune tonight in that regard.

"Gareth and I rode from King Owain's headquarters a few hours ago. If he had wanted Gareth arrested he would have done it then."

"He doesn't know what I know," Morgan said.

"And what is that, exactly?" Gwen stood with her hands on her hips, glaring at the man.

"Gareth has been conspiring with Earl Ranulf against King Owain!" Morgan said.

"That is a lie."

Morgan took a step back, clearly taken by surprise by Gwen's forceful tone. He tried to look stern. "It is common knowledge in the hall—"

"Who accuses him of treason?" Gwen swung around, her eyes searching among the onlookers.

"Gwen—" Gareth would have preferred to confer privately with Morgan, to reason with him and sort out what was clearly a misunderstanding, but Gwen's color was high, and she was furious.

Years ago, King Owain had made what in retrospect was an absurd accusation against Gareth, and even Prince Hywel had given way before him, accepting what he couldn't change until he found proof of Gareth's innocence. Gwen and Gareth had been younger then and less experienced, and that had been in King Owain's court, not Morgan's. Gwen might yield to King Owain, but Lord Morgan was another matter entirely.

Morgan put out an appeasing hand to Gwen. "Lady Gwen—
"

She actually had the audacity to slap his hand away. "Don't Lady Gwen me! You are accusing my husband of treason! You have arrested him on what grounds? Rumor!" She glared at Pedr, whose hand had come down on Gareth's shoulder to prevent him from running.

Pedr appeared unmoved by Gwen's anger, but Morgan recoiled in the face of her wrath. Gareth could see that it had been with fire in his belly and good intentions that Morgan had sent Pedr to Cilcain to arrest him, but now that Gareth and Gwen were before him, he had to be rethinking that decision. He was definitely over his head with Gwen.

"I challenge whoever has said these things about my husband to come forward and speak them to his face!"

Nobody in the hall moved. No man rose to his feet. Gareth knew as surely as he was a Welshman that Morgan could have no actual proof, of course, but it may not have occurred to Morgan himself until just now.

Gwen realized it too, and she swung back around to Morgan. "How did you know Gareth was in Cilcain?"

That Lord Morgan could answer. "One of my men saw him ride through the village this afternoon with Father Alun. I realized at that point that the good father didn't know he'd brought a viper into our midst, so it was my duty to remove him."

During Gwen's tirade, the steward had moved closer to Lord Morgan and had been subtly trying to attract his lord's attention without success. Now, he tugged on Morgan's elbow, and Morgan finally turned to him. "What!"

The steward leaned in to whisper in Morgan's ear.

At first, Lord Morgan's face went completely blank, but then he said in a far more moderated tone, "Say that again?"

The steward cleared his throat. "It's about the body that was found earlier today, my lord."

Morgan moved his hand impatiently. "What does the dead man have to do with Gareth?"

The steward didn't retreat. "My lord—" he gestured in Gareth's direction, "—he looks just like him."

8

Gareth

"Obviously I myself didn't look into his face before this moment," Morgan said. "I took my steward at his word that the dead man wasn't from around here, thinking Einion would know more about it than I."

As with the woman in the chapel at Cilcain, this man had been washed and dried for burial, though he didn't yet wear his burial gown.

It could be me on that table. That's all Gareth could think of as he stared down at the dead man's face. When Gareth himself died, he wouldn't care what became of his remains, but to know that Gwen would have to stand over him, in the same way they were standing over this possible brother to Gareth now, brought bile to the back of his throat.

Beyond this initial non-apology, it was almost as if Morgan didn't know what to do with himself. He kept opening his mouth to speak and then closing it without saying anything. For his part, Gareth was doing his best to ignore the fact that he was supposed to be under arrest.

Morgan seemed ready to ignore it too. “Einion tells me he was run through.” The lord reached for the sheet, but before he could throw it off the man’s body onto the floor, Gareth caught his wrist and stopped him.

“What?” Morgan said.

Gareth’s eyes flicked to Gwen, who was chewing on her lower lip, her arms folded defensively across her chest.

“My apologies.” Morgan relinquished the sheet and stepped back from the table.

With his back to Gwen, Gareth lifted the cloth so he could look under it without exposing the whole of the body to Gwen’s view. The wound to the man’s gut was deep and wide. Gareth didn’t need to inspect it closely to agree that it had been made by a sword, not a knife, driven into the man’s belly and pulled out without ceremony or stealth. The wound was clean and no longer bleeding, of course, so Gareth decorously folded back the sheet, exposing the wound but not the man’s body below the waist.

At the sight of it, Gwen stopped chewing on her lower lip, and her expression cleared. “But this could mean he wasn’t murdered. We are in the midst of a war, after all.”

“The body was found by a man searching with his dog for a lost lamb. It was buried in the ground, but not buried deep,” Morgan said. “You don’t bury a man you come upon in war. You kill him and leave him where he lies, thankful you have lived to fight another day.”

Gwen nodded her acknowledgement of Morgan's assessment, pursing her lips as she studied the dead man. She appeared far less upset than she could have been.

"He looks exactly like you," Gwen said, "except for something around the eyes. I would have liked to have seen him when he was alive. He could be you sleeping there." She looked up at Gareth. "He has a bump on the bridge of his nose. You don't. Yours is straight."

"I have been fortunate enough never to have had my nose broken, even with all the fights I've been in," Gareth said, trying to keep the mood light, even if it might be a lost cause.

Gwen seemed to be endeavoring to do the same. She leaned closer to study the man's face. "A beard hides many imperfections too."

Gareth rubbed his stubble-covered jaw. He'd shaved off his beard only three days ago because he wanted to keep the lice, which were rampant in the camp, at bay, and they seemed attracted to his beard no matter how often he dunked his head in the washing trough. Gareth had cropped his hair short then too, unlike this man, who'd allowed it to grow long enough to pull back and tie at the base of his neck.

Three days ago, however, he would have looked identical to Gareth, just as a few tweaks to the false Gwen could have confused anyone who didn't know Gwen well. This man's similarity to Gareth was even more uncanny.

Gareth's head came up, sensing menace in every flickering shadow the candles threw on the walls of the small chapel. Unease curled in his belly, beyond the discomfort associated with seeing his dead twin on the table. Someone had murdered two people who looked like him and Gwen. What would he do when he found out he'd killed the wrong people?

Fortunately, Gwen's thoughts hadn't yet stretched that far.

She lifted the man's arm an inch or two, before laying it back down on the table. "The feel of him is similar to the woman. If I had to guess, I'd say she died first, if only by a few hours."

Gareth picked up the man's wrist as Gwen had done. The body had turned cold and was stiff with rigor. If the body were cold and not stiff, it would indicate he'd been dead for more than two days.

He glanced at Morgan. "You said the body was found by a sheepdog. Where was this?"

"Not far from here, upriver," Morgan said.

"Am I correct in remembering that the body was found today?" Gwen said.

Morgan turned to look at his steward, who'd come with them to the chapel. "Einion?"

Now that he'd been called upon to speak, Einion took a step forward. "The body was discovered shortly after noon. The herdsman who found him sent his son to me immediately, and my men arrived back here with the body about two hours before sunset."

That was more than an hour before Gareth and Gwen had arrived in Cilcain.

Einion gestured to the dead man. "I thought it best to wash the body in preparation for burial, given the time that had already passed since his death."

Gareth nodded, not questioning the steward's decision. The man had been murdered, but most people didn't know that a murder investigation went better if the body was left where it was found. In this case, both bodies had been moved, but at least he and Gwen would be able to return to the initial burial sites.

"It was the arrival of the body which prompted me to send a man into Cilcain to find the priest," Morgan said. "Instead, Father Alun's housekeeper told him of the murdered woman discovered in the graveyard, and that Father Alun had ridden to King Owain's camp looking for you. I posted one of my men at the tavern under orders to inform me the moment you arrived."

Gareth gave a low grunt. When they'd ridden through the village, he'd feared exactly that—except he'd been afraid the informer would run to Ranulf at Mold Castle. Only a few hours ago, being detected by the Earl of Chester was his most pressing concern. It was odd how so much could change so quickly.

"And you did that not because you wanted Gareth to examine the body of a murdered man, but so you could arrest him," Gwen said, not yet willing to forgive the young lord.

Morgan looked down at his feet. "I wish now that I had asked more questions before I sent Pedr to the chapel."

"You no longer believe that Gareth has committed treason?" Gwen said.

Morgan raised his head. "Let me just say that my earlier certainty has given way to doubt."

That might be all the apology Gareth was going to get. The transformation from arrested man to investigator had been abrupt, but Gareth wasn't going to rub Morgan's nose in his mistake. He didn't want to make worse the extent to which Morgan was going to lose face in front of his people for having made a poor decision, even if at present Einion was the only one to witness the reversal.

Then Morgan's expression turned to one of interest. "You have come a long way from protecting that spoiled boy you used to mind, Sir Gareth."

"I can't disagree," Gareth said.

"I have not been misled in my understanding that you and your lady wife uncover the whys and wherefores of murder, have I?"

It was Gwen who answered. "You have not. After all, that was why Father Alun came to King Owain's camp to fetch us in the first place."

"Excellent." Morgan bobbed his head. "Since you're here, I have a murder that needs solving, and it seems that you are the man to do it."

Gwen reached for Gareth's hand and squeezed it. "What's going on here, Gareth? How can this man look so much like you?"

"And what terrible crime has he committed such that rumors of my treason have spread throughout Cilcain," Gareth said.

Morgan looked from Gareth to Gwen. "You have never seen him before, then?"

"He wasn't my brother, my cousin, nor any relation to me at all as far as I know," Gareth said. "What concerns us is the juxtaposition of your accusation, this body, and the remains of the woman currently in the chapel in Cilcain."

Gwen didn't make Lord Morgan ask what Gareth meant. "The dead woman there looks like me."

Morgan's jaw dropped. "The housekeeper said a woman had been murdered. Are you saying that we have the body here of a man who resembles you, Sir Gareth, and in Cilcain is the body of a woman who resembles Gwen?"

"That is exactly what we're saying." Gareth said.

"Such a circumstance cannot be coincidence," Morgan said.

"No," Gwen said. "They had to have been together. Nothing else makes sense."

Gareth licked his lips, hoping he could add what came next without offending Morgan. "Are you aware that the woman was buried over the top of your grandfather's remains?"

If Morgan had been shocked before, now his face reddened in sudden anger. "I did not know that. Someone defiled my grandfather's grave with murder?"

Gareth held up a hand to him in an attempt at appeasement. "Like the man here, she was buried less than two feet down. Your grandfather's body wasn't disturbed, either by the burial of the dead woman or by her removal. Father Alun made sure of it."

Morgan swallowed hard. “None of my people reported this.”

Gareth couldn’t blame them for that. None of Morgan’s men would have wanted to be the one to inform him of the desecration, though it could also be that only Father Alun, the gravediggers, and his housekeeper knew the truth. Rumor could spread quickly in a small town, but not everybody gossiped about the same things.

“I’m sorry.” Gwen took a step towards Morgan. “You can see now why we are so deeply concerned about what has happened here—and what may still be happening. And why any accusation of treason against my husband must be mistaken—and will only impede the uncovering of the truth.”

Gareth made another appeasing motion with one hand. “If it is acceptable to you, my lord, I should inspect this body before any more time passes.”

“Yes, of course.” Morgan flicked a finger at Einion. “Some wine wouldn’t go amiss.”

The steward bowed and departed with a quickness to his step that hadn’t been there earlier, relieved perhaps to have something to do, and that his lord had been saved so quickly from a grave mistake.

“May we see the man’s clothing?” Gwen said.

“Einion had everything laundered,” Morgan said. “I believe the clothes remain on the washing line.”

Gareth grunted his acceptance of that which didn’t surprise him.

Correctly interpreting Gareth's grunt as muted disapproval, Morgan added, somewhat defensively, "His clothing had to be stripped from him in order to wash the body. It reeked of odors. Lady Gwen, if you would follow me?"

"Thank you." Gwen headed towards the chapel door with Morgan.

Before they could depart, however, Gareth said, "Lord Morgan, I would appreciate the return of my sword."

"Of course, Sir Gareth. I will see to that as well."

As Morgan and Gwen disappeared, Gareth took in a relieved breath. Lord Morgan's doubts had been dispelled once he'd seen the body, but without it, Gareth would have spent the night in a cell or in a back room of the stable. It had been a near thing—and while it could be no coincidence that the false Gareth and Gwen had died on the same day, Gareth could bless coincidence that they'd been found on the same day too.

Gareth moved around the dead man. He wanted to have most of his examination completed before Gwen returned, for both their sakes. She'd examined dead men many times, of course, but if he could spare her the task, he would.

He flipped back the sheet to reveal the full body, naked except for a loin cloth. Other than an old scar, long since healed, that ran along the length of his left calf, the man was undamaged below the waist. Gareth covered the man's lower half again and focused on the wound itself.

A sword was an unusual murder weapon because it implied several things. In particular: first, the murderer hadn't tried to get close enough to the victim to kill him with a knife; second, he possibly hadn't known the victim well enough to get that close to him; and third, the murderer possessed a high enough station in life to have borne a sword.

Most murders were crimes of passion, done on the spur of the moment to a loved one or to a companion whom the murderer knew well. Nothing could make a man angrier than the behavior—or the tongue—of a family member. Those murders were of a type that Gareth and Gwen rarely investigated because the guilty party tended to be easily found.

Murders such as those were difficult to cover up because all paths led directly to the killer. In fact, much of the time, there were witnesses to the act. And even those who got away with the crime initially were often beset with guilt and shame. Murder had that effect on normal people.

The deaths of this woman and man, however, were of a different type. This culprit had buried the victims—clumsily, to be sure—but he'd buried them nonetheless. Gareth hadn't yet seen the site of the man's burial, but to have killed a man with a sword and buried him far out in the woods implied a degree of organization that put this murder in a different category from most. And that was before Gareth took into account that the man looked like him.

In addition, many men-at-arms didn't bear swords. Gareth's own sword was both his livelihood and his most treasured possession. He'd inherited it from his uncle, who, after Gareth's parents had died, had trained him to be a knight. The sword's value was greater than that of the whole village of Cilcain. Gareth had learned to use it as the tool of his trade, but he wore it proudly because it was his station to do so.

He couldn't remember the last time he'd left it off when he dressed in the morning, even on days he didn't wear armor. He felt naked without it and missed its comforting weight at his side. Normally, he kept his sword within arm's reach at all times, even at night while he slept.

The man who'd murdered Gareth's lookalike had done so with a sword, and it meant that the way Gareth himself lived and everything he knew could be reflected in that man's life as well. Unfortunately, while murder by sword limited the range of murderers to noblemen, knights, and men-at-arms, this region of Wales was teeming with all three this autumn. Discovering the killer's identity wouldn't be quite like finding a needle in a haystack, but it wasn't far off from culling the world of possibilities from 'everyone' to 'men'.

From the wound in the man's gut, Gareth worked upward, examining his skin for old wounds and new. A full beard covered his neck, and as Gareth tipped the head from one side to the other, he leaned closer, noticing red marks and bruises—

"Gareth."

He turned to his wife, who'd reentered the chapel, a stack of clothing in her arms. As he watched, she laid out each item on the floor in front of her. Her tone when she'd spoken had been one of both warning and concern—enough so that he left the body and crouched beside her.

"What has you so concerned?"

She gestured to the clothing before her. "These are yours."

"What do you mean, they're mine? They can't be—" He cut himself off as the individual items came into focus. That was his shirt. Those were his spare tunic and surcoat with the crest of Gwynedd emblazoned on it. He'd lost them all in the river over a month ago when the army had moved from Powys to the current encampment in eastern Gwynedd.

"Did I hear you say that these were Gareth's clothes?" Morgan was back too, thankfully bringing Gareth's weapons with him. He was followed by Einion with a carafe of wine and three cups. "One more surprise in an evening of surprises."

"A surprise that I, for one, could have done without." Gareth accepted his sword from Morgan, unwound the belt from around the scabbard, and then settled it around his waist.

Morgan's eyes narrowed as he watched the practiced movements of Gareth's hands. "We don't have to ask why this man would steal your clothes. The answer is simple: to better transform himself into you."

Gwen sat back on her heels. "When I first saw the body, I thought the man and woman had been killed because the killer meant to murder Gareth and me, and he killed these two by mistake."

That had been Gareth's first thought as well. He'd been hoping Gwen's mind hadn't yet arrived at that conclusion, but it had only ever been a faint hope.

"But now that supposition may be wrong. Not only did this man look like Gareth, he was *trying* to look like Gareth."

"Meaning that he meant for me—or someone like me—to accuse you of his own wrongdoing, Sir Gareth," Morgan said. "Either this man impersonated you of his own volition or because someone paid him to do so." He paused. "And then that person killed the false Gareth when he had no more need of him."

Gareth hadn't spoken more than two sentences to Morgan in conversation all those years ago when they'd first encountered each other, but he was pleased to realize now that Morgan had grown into a man of some intelligence and one not blinded by pride. His conclusion, while premature given the early state of the investigation, was a terrible and fascinating one which Gareth hadn't yet reached.

"Perhaps," Gareth said. "What wrongdoing is that, however? In the hall, you accused me of treason, that I'd conspired with Ranulf. How did you hear of this in the first place, Lord Morgan?"

"Men were speaking of you in my hall." Morgan studied his feet, indicating his reluctance to say more, but then he looked up and spoke anyway, "Two nights ago, I overheard several of my men talking around the fire. They were far into their cups, which, to my mind, made what they were talking about both less and more likely to be the truth." He tipped back his head to look at the ceiling, rather than Gareth's eyes, and took in a breath. "They said you'd been bought."

Gareth didn't even blink. He'd been impersonated and accused of treason. It didn't take a great stretch of imagination to assume that the false Gareth had been doing something to which the real Gareth would object. Despite the inevitability of Morgan's words, Gareth felt his anger rising. With effort, he tamped it down, though he didn't trust himself to reply. To do so would give credence to his emotions, which he couldn't allow himself just yet.

Thankfully, Gwen knew him well enough to speak instead. "Were they certain it was Earl Ranulf who'd bought Gareth, and did they say what he'd paid him to do?"

"The men didn't tell me that," Morgan said. "They were drunk at the time, and if they had known specific details, they might have blurted them out in an unguarded moment. As it was, when I asked them to elaborate, they couldn't tell me anything more."

Morgan was looking extremely uncomfortable with the way their conversation had gone, though he had to have known that once he recanted his original accusation, Gareth and Gwen would have questions.

"When we return to the hall, can you point me towards the men in question?" Gareth said.

"Of course," Morgan said, though both of them knew that with or without Morgan hovering over them, they were unlikely to tell Gareth to his face what they knew. If they were drunk enough two nights ago, they might not even be aware that they'd said anything about Gareth at all, and that their words had been the source of Morgan's accusations against Gareth.

"Thank you for telling me," Gareth said, "and I appreciate your willingness to reconsider my arrest."

"I'm sorry for all of it. Truth be told, if not for the war and the proximity of King Owain's forces, I might have dismissed their words as drunken ramblings. I was a fool to think that arresting you would bring me favor in King Owain's court."

"We should be grateful you overheard them," Gwen said. "In fact, we should count our blessings for the rest of our lives that all of this has fallen out as it has. Imagine if we hadn't found the bodies of the false Gwen and Gareth. Even if Prince Hywel or those closest to us never believed Gareth had betrayed them, Gareth could have spent the rest of his life trying to live down what this man here has done in his name. He still might, if there are more men like those in your hall."

"And more lords like me, who act before they think," Morgan said.

"Gwen, it's what they've done in *our* names," Gareth said.

Gwen took in a sharp breath.

Gareth looked again to Lord Morgan. "I realize this is a great deal to ask, but will you speak to the people of your error, and why you made it?"

"It is the least I can do." Morgan ground his teeth. "I am angry at whoever arranged for such a nefarious scheme. Impersonation and murder ..." He shook his head.

Gareth's mind churned with uncomfortable possibilities. He wanted to assume that he and Gwen were safe within Morgan's fort, but he still felt an unnamed menace pressing on him from beyond the walls.

Gwen had both arms wrapped around her middle, hugging herself, and Gareth bent down to wrap his arm around her too and pull her close to him.

"Whatever they planned, whatever ruse they were employing, it ended with their deaths," Lord Morgan said. "The one who killed them either did so because he mistook them for you, or because he no longer wanted anyone to mistake them for you."

Gwen rose to her feet, a little stiffly due to the cold stones on which she'd been kneeling. "Either way, Lord Morgan, it's a very uncomfortable thought."

9

Gwen

"Before we go too far down either road, a moment ago I found something on his body that might better direct our inquiries." Gareth touched Gwen's shoulder, and she followed him back to the table where the body lay.

Gareth had recovered the man with the sheet while he'd inspected the clothing Gwen had brought inside the chapel; now, he pulled the cloth away again and tipped the man's chin to one side, exposing his neck. Within and underneath his bushy beard, he bore a series of long scratches.

Gwen gazed at them and then looked up at her husband. "Those look to me like they could have come from fingernails."

"That was my thought," Gareth said. "Remember the way the woman's nails were broken and chipped?"

"This man killed the woman found in the graveyard?" Morgan had trailed after them to the table and was now staring down at the wounds on the man's neck.

"We have no evidence he murdered her, only that they may have fought," Gareth said.

"But then—" Morgan began.

Gareth tipped his head in acknowledgement of Morgan's puzzlement. "It does raise the possibility that he was responsible for her death. That then leads to a conclusion that someone else would have had to have murdered him, changing our scenario and making it less likely that anyone could have murdered him because he mistook him for me."

"I have not only two murders but two *murderers* in Cilcain?" Morgan said. "How can that be? In all the years my family has ruled these lands, we've never had even one."

Gwen was just as unhappy as Morgan appeared to be at the idea of one killer murdering another. She had felt vulnerable many times in her life. Bad things had happened to her, from the death of her mother at her brother's birth, to the loss of Gareth when she was sixteen, to her abduction by Prince Cadwaladr before she married Gareth. Tonight's threat, however, had a newness to it—and peril—that she'd never felt before.

It wasn't that finding a dead couple impersonating her and Gareth was worse than when her mother had died—how could it be?—but it was a threat that was all potential, to an end which she was having trouble envisioning or speculating upon. Gwen had felt something like this in the first throes of Tangwen's birth—waiting for what was to come and knowing it could be death—and not being able to do a thing about it.

When Gwen had first seen the woman's face, her first thought had been anger at whoever had killed her before they could meet. Now, however, she had to accept that this unknown woman had felt nothing for her, or at least not enough to change her course.

Since the woman had lost her life to this ruse, Gwen couldn't sustain her anger, but as a result, all she was left with were feelings of helplessness and fear. Who knew what this couple had done while they were pretending to be Gareth and Gwen?

"I haven't ever encountered an investigation quite like this either," Gareth said.

"I should hope not!" Morgan said. "Did you discover anything about the woman that can help us identify her?"

Gwen almost laughed at the 'us'. *Almost.*

Gareth suppressed a smile too. "I can't say for certain how close in age she is to Gwen. It is almost impossible to determine the age of a woman who is between sixteen and twenty-five. There wasn't anything more in her clothing, was there, Gwen?"

"Whoever killed her took her purse," Gwen said, "or she didn't have one on her."

"This man here didn't either," Morgan said.

"The one who killed him could have taken them both with him." Gareth flipped the sheet back over the man's face. "Tomorrow I'd like to visit the site where he died to see if the killer left anything for us to find. Tonight I would like to speak to the husbandman who found him."

Morgan made a noncommittal motion with his head.

"No?" Gareth said.

"At this hour of the evening, you might not get much out of him that makes sense," Morgan said. "I keep an eye on him, for his son's sake, but he lost his wife last winter and hasn't been the same since."

Gwen understood that all too well. After the loss of her mother, her father had drowned his sorrows in drink for a time, before gradually coming to his senses. Now, with the birth of Tangwen, Meilyr seemed a different man entirely, more like he'd been when Gwen herself was a child.

"Are we done here for now, Gareth?" she said.

At Gareth's assent, the three of them returned to the hall, where they found Father Alun just arriving. He'd decided to do more than pray and had ridden his mule to the fort, leading Gwen's horse.

"I am pleased to find you well," Father Alun said as he took Gwen's hand.

Gwen smiled to see the priest, some of her anxiety dissipating in the warmth of the hall. "It was a misunderstanding that has been resolved. No more need be said about it than that."

Gwen had been very angry when Morgan first accused Gareth—so angry she had been nearly shaking with it. But allowing it to consume her for more than a short while gave the man who'd arranged all this too much power over her.

Morgan invited Gareth, Gwen, and Father Alun to sit at the high table with him, and when food was placed in front of her, Gwen suddenly discovered she was hungry. The sickness in the pit of her stomach that had nagged her since she'd learned of the woman's death fell away, and their visit to Morgan's hall, which had begun in suspicion and fear, began to turn into a friendly party—or as friendly as it could be given that they had two dead bodies on their hands.

Under the influence of food and drink, Father Alun turned talkative. "Could I ask what you've discovered about the death of the woman in my chapel?"

"You can ask," Gareth said. "Neither our latest findings, nor the conclusions we have drawn from them, are at all comforting." Then Gareth related what they'd learned since they'd last spoken to the priest. "It is possible that the dead man in Lord Morgan's chapel had a hand in the death of the woman in yours. Who killed him, however, remains a mystery."

Father Alun leaned in, his expression grave. "I see an odd combination of ruthlessness and blunder in the way this pair were murdered and buried."

"What do you mean by that?" Morgan said.

Father Alun tapped a finger to his chin. "It seems to me that in regards to the actual murders, both deaths were brutally—and ruthlessly—accomplished, but when it came time to dispose of the bodies, it's as if the killer stumbled in his mind, or was suddenly afraid of being found out, where before he'd been single-minded in his resolve. It's almost as if he was thinking too hard about the problem, instead of applying the same ruthlessness to their burials as he did to their deaths."

Gareth took Gwen's hand and sat back in his chair, indicating to Gwen that they should let Alun and Morgan talk. If Hywel were here, he would have stopped the speculation and the assumptions, but this wasn't Gwen and Gareth letting their imaginations run wild. In some instances, fresh eyes on the investigation could be a good thing.

Morgan pushed back his chair and moved to pace in front of the fire. "It's clear to me that if the girl was murdered at the second killer's behest, than the death of her killer was a matter of tying up loose ends."

Lord Morgan turned to query Gareth. "Is this how you see it too?"

"You both have far too devious minds," Gareth said.

Gwen heard a touch of admiration in his voice, and she agreed with Gareth that both of them had taken on the problem with an unseemly eagerness. But that wasn't to say they were wrong.

Morgan canted his head. "I'll take that as a compliment, coming from you."

Gareth straightened in his chair. "As to your analysis of the murders, your guesses are as good as mine. We won't know the truth until we learn far more than we have yet discovered. It would be most helpful to put a name to either victim."

"I'm sorry these people chose Cilcain for their foul deeds." Father Alun gave a shiver of distaste.

"No, that's where you're wrong," Morgan said. "As Gwen said earlier, we should be glad the murders happened here, because that meant Gareth and Gwen were only a short ride away. Without their expertise, how would we even have begun to go about this investigation? Certainly our chances of discovering who murdered the dead couple would have been much diminished, and we would have been further hampered by the mistaken idea that Gareth and Gwen themselves were the victims."

Gwen just managed not to shake her head at Morgan's complete reversal of his earlier position. Not that she didn't appreciate it. "It's—"

She broke off with a glance at her husband, who ended up finishing her sentence for her.

"It's what we do," Gareth said.

"Sir Gareth, we must consider why someone would want to ruin your reputation," Morgan said.

"I have angered many men in my life—more so in the last few years," Gareth said.

"Creating a false Gareth and Gwen can't be for such a simple reason, Lord Morgan. My husband is a remarkable man, but the man who did this put an enormous effort into the endeavor, and I can't see how anyone could hate Gareth so much for something so intangible. At the very least, the killer risked having the results easily refuted with proof that Gareth was somewhere else when whatever heinous deed he was supposed to have perpetrated was occurring."

While she and Gareth had made enemies over the years, most of those they'd mightily offended had received justice at the hands of a lord or the king. And many were dead. The only possibility she could think of was that, as had been the case with the attempted murder of King Owain several years ago, the person coming after them was a child or relative of one of these people, who had taught him to hate.

Father Alun nodded. "I find it more likely that ruining Gareth's reputation was an ancillary goal for the killer instead of the main one. It could even be that impersonating Gareth and Gwen was a means to an end only."

"What end?" Lord Morgan said.

"What if tarnishing Gareth's reputation is in the service of creating distrust between him and his lord and ensuring Gareth's removal from Prince Hywel's side?" Father Alun said.

Gareth's jaw turned rigid, and it looked like he was finding it impossible to speak around it. Gwen wanted to deny Father Alun's conclusions, but she found it impossible to do so.

Morgan nodded as he thought. "Thus leaving room for another, who does not have your lord's best interests at heart. I don't like the sound of that."

Gareth finally managed to unstick his jaw. "Nor do I."

10

Gareth

Gareth had noted the absence of an inn in Cilcain but hadn't worried about having no real place to sleep. Welsh hospitality being what it was, he'd assumed that he and Gwen would find a place to lay their heads eventually. And then after his arrest he'd feared Gwen would be left unprotected and alone in Lord Morgan's hall while he spent the night in a cell.

As it turned out, Lord Morgan had given them a pallet in a corner of the hall. Gareth and Gwen were warm under thick blankets and were able to whisper to one another without fear of being overheard. Although the day had been relatively fine, if cold, the wind was howling on the other side of the wall a foot from Gareth's back as he lay on his side facing Gwen.

"Do you remember last summer when that poor cloth apprentice was murdered and put into the millpond?" Gwen said.

"Of course," Gareth said. "It isn't something I'm likely to forget any time soon."

Gwen gave him a playful poke to the belly. "Let me finish. Do you remember my comment that I thought Prince Rhun was a little too fascinated by the investigation?"

Gareth caught Gwen's hand before she could poke him again. "Father Alun and Lord Morgan are the same."

"Yes," she said, "which is why I didn't pursue the last thought I had any further while we were with them."

"Which thought was that?" Gareth's eyes had been on the verge of closing when Gwen had started talking, and he was trying to wake up again without actually having to think. Gareth kissed his wife's hand, stalling for time. He really would rather not think or talk, but Gwen was wide awake, her mind churning, which meant this was important.

"About the man or men behind all this," Gwen said. "Who murdered the false Gareth—and possibly ordered him to murder the false Gwen—and who was our false Gareth and Gwen supposed to fool? I am concerned about where our victims were in the days before their murders."

"I care very much about the identity of the former, but it's the latter person who has my stomach in a knot," Gareth said. "It was foolish of me to hope that your mind wouldn't wander in the same direction as mine."

"What do you think they might have been doing?" Gwen said.

"I have no idea." Gareth yawned. "Hopefully not killing somebody else."

"How about the first person then?" Gwen said. "Who would come up with the mad idea of having two people impersonate us?"

Gareth shook his head, trying to dispense with the last of the fog in his brain. "If you were to think of a man of our acquaintance who is capable of concocting an unnecessarily complicated plot that ends in murder, what is the first name that comes to mind?"

Gwen was silent for a moment. "You know the answer as well as I: Prince Cadwaladr. I haven't wanted to say his name, because he hasn't done anything truly hideous recently—"

"—that we know of," Gareth said.

"That we know of," Gwen amended, "and his name is always the first to come to my mind when trouble strikes. Although he ordered the death of King Anarawd, we've had to look elsewhere these last three years for the person responsible for the murders we've encountered—and we were right to."

"I know." Gareth adjusted his position so he could see his wife's face better in the flickering firelight. "And we're going to proceed along the same lines here." He raised his right hand. "A pact."

Gwen raised her left hand to clasp his.

"We won't mention Cadwaladr's name again unless all options narrow to him," Gareth said.

Gwen's expression cleared. "Agreed."

The wind died sometime in the night, having brought storm clouds and a few inches of snow to eastern Gwynedd, a rare event for the end of November—or any month in Wales for that matter. Some years, it snowed merely enough to whitewash the grass. The only inhabitants of the fort who appeared pleased with the change in the weather were those whose job it was to fill the ice house against a hot summer, boys under twelve, and Father Alun. He stood beside Gareth at the entrance to the hall, smiling as he rubbed his hands together to warm them.

"Why are you so happy?" Gareth said.

A stray snowball from the flurry of missiles the rambunctious youngsters were throwing about the courtyard hit Gareth's hip. He brushed the snow off his cloak and sent a glare in the direction of the boy who'd thrown it.

The boy's eyes went wide as he realized his mistake. "Sorry, my lord!"

"Not as sorry as you're going to be!" Gareth bent to scoop a handful of snow from the stoop, formed a ball, and sent it whizzing back across the courtyard at the boy. "Take that, you rascal!"

The boy dodged it expertly, laughing. Gareth wasn't so old he couldn't remember how much he'd loved playing in the snow with his friends. He was sorry he wasn't at Aber today because he would have liked to have been the one to introduce his daughter to her first real snow.

"Today will be a day men stay home if they can or crouch around the campfire if they can't," Father Alun said, as if the brief interruption hadn't happened. "The war will be held in abeyance for a day until the snow clears."

"Only a day?" Gareth checked the sky. Snow fell from it, though perhaps less thickly than even a half-hour earlier.

"It is November," Father Alun said. "The snow will stop in the next hour and will have mostly melted by mid-afternoon. Mark my words."

"Then we'd better get going before the trail becomes muck." Gareth turned back to the door, thinking to return to the hall to see what was keeping Gwen, but then she came through it, wrapped to her eyes in wool.

"Oh." She pulled down the scarf that protected her cheeks and chin. "It isn't as cold as I thought. I think this might melt soon."

Gareth shook his head, laughing and looking from Gwen to Father Alun, who held out his elbow to her. "My thoughts exactly, my dear." They walked forward from the doorway so they wouldn't block the passage of other people who wanted to enter or exit the hall.

"Where should we go first?" Gwen said.

Gareth gestured to the boy who was leading their horses from the stable. "We need to visit the site where the false Gareth was buried. When I talked to him last night, the man who found his body wasn't terribly coherent, but he did say that he'd meet us where the road forks. This journey will serve the dual purpose of letting us see where the man died and was buried and allowing us to question our guide.

Father Alun nodded. "Bran knows that if he sets foot in the hall before nightfall, the drink will call him."

"He was quite drunk last night," Gwen said. "It'll be a wonder if he's able to walk this morning."

"It is a matter of pride with him." Father Alun picked at his lower lip with one finger. "I must do better about finding him a wife."

And with that, Father Alun set off across the courtyard to the stable where he'd left his mule. He'd spent the night at the fort too, rolled in a blanket on the opposite end of the hall from Gareth and Gwen. Gareth couldn't blame him for staying. His house was cold and lonely in comparison to the fellowship found in Lord Morgan's fort.

"Are we ready?"

Gareth and Gwen turned at the voice. Morgan himself appeared beside them, still shrugging into his cloak. He settled it around his shoulders and then pinned the broach at his throat.

"My lord, I didn't realize you intended to ride with us," Gareth said. "Your duties—"

"Can wait," Morgan said. "This is important."

"Yes, my lord," Gareth said, somewhat puzzled still at Morgan's continued presence.

And yet he'd heard in the hall last night that, like Bran, Morgan had lost his wife to childbirth. The child had lived, but Gareth could see how the days grew painfully long without his wife. Gareth had kept busy fighting this war during the three months he'd been parted from Gwen. Many nights he was so tired he fell asleep instantly, but on those occasions he couldn't, and he allowed himself to think about Gwen and Tangwen, the hours until dawn were endless.

Lord Morgan's inclusion in the company required an additional three men as guards. King Owain never went anywhere without at least twenty, so three were hardly any trouble at all. Leaving Einion watching stolidly from the entrance to the fort, they rode out from the gatehouse and down the hill towards the ford.

Even with the snow, which had all but stopped by now, daylight afforded a fine view of the surrounding countryside, down to the river and across it to Cilcain. Eastern Wales beyond the Clwyd range sloped gently down to the Dee Estuary and to Chester. In winter, with the trees mostly bare, the air crisp and clear, and everything coated in a layer of white, a man could see for miles. Gareth liked it because it meant he could see the enemy coming before he was upon him.

When it wasn't covered with snow, the English liked the landscape too because they could march their huge armies across the fields and meadows without obstruction—and without having to worry about where the Welsh were hiding. The Welsh, in turn, had a long history of responding to English military action by retreating into their mountains, and woe betide the foreign soldiers who followed them there. By Norman standards, Welshmen had no honor. They thought nothing about ambushing their enemy from behind any tree, boulder, or hillock, shooting their arrows from afar and at no danger to themselves.

The Normans hated the ambushes but hadn't yet adopted the bow with any regularity, though certainly some lords had men who could use it, particularly in the north of England. It was terribly short-sighted of them, but Gareth feared the day Englishmen trained to use it on the scale the Welsh did because the Welsh would have lost one of the few advantages they had.

Where the road down to the river divided—one path heading to the ford of the river and the other northwest upstream—they found Bran waiting for them. He gave no greeting, but turned his back at the sight of them and started walking. He didn't have a horse, but that didn't stop him from setting off at a quicker pace than Gareth was riding.

Gareth spurred Braith to catch up, and when he got close, he dismounted so he could walk beside the herdsman. "Tell me what you saw."

He intentionally spoke bluntly, having learned last night from Lord Morgan—and confirmed by Bran's behavior if he hadn't been sure of it already—that the man didn't like to waste words and took offense when anyone else did. Short and abrupt answers were normal for him whether drunk or sober.

Bran was a few inches shorter than Gareth, but he was just as muscular, with heavily calloused hands from laboring daily among his herds and on his farm. He pushed back his hood, revealing dark brown hair that had been cropped close to his head like Gareth's. He was fifteen years older than Gareth, however, so his hair was also receding from his forehead and balding at the back of his head, with more gray in it than Gareth had. In fact, his mustache was almost entirely white and stood out clearly against the man's tanned face. Gareth's face was tanned too despite the long, rainy autumn, simply from spending so much time outdoors.

"The body lay in the dirt," Bran said, startling Gareth by stringing six words together at the same time.

"It was partly buried, I hear," Gareth said.

Bran gave him a curt nod. "The dog found him." He gestured to his sheepdog, which trotted at his master's heels, his tongue hanging out. The dog was enjoying the snow as much as the children.

"He's beautiful," Gareth said, and meant it.

All Welshmen appreciated a good sheepdog, and this one appeared particularly intelligent and alert, either observing his surroundings while trotting along the trail or bounding ahead, his nose to the ground and sniffing everything in sight.

"Why were you on the trail?" Gareth said.

"Lost lamb."

"A lamb had become lost in a thicket?"

Bran nodded.

"Did you find it?"

Bran grunted, which Gareth took to be a yes.

"So am I to gather that you were returning home when you found the body?"

Again the grunt, and then Bran whistled to his dog, who'd run farther ahead than Bran wanted. The dog responded instantly and returned to Bran's side.

Gareth waited until he had Bran's attention again. The trail was rising steadily towards the mountains, and Gareth was starting to huff with the effort of keeping pace with Bran. "Did you see anything unusual around the body, something you noticed either before you discovered it or after? I'm particularly thinking of boot or hoof prints and the like."

Bran started to shake his head, but then he arrested the movement and tipped his head to one side, thinking. "Yes." It was a real assent, and Bran's eyes flashed with something that looked like interest for the first time too. Up until now, his participation had been the result of duty—his allegiance to Lord Morgan—rather than because he cared about his role in finding either the body or the killer.

"Will you show me?"

Nod.

After another half-mile of walking upstream, by which point Gareth was sweating heavily in his mail shirt and thick padding, Bran came to a halt in the shelter of a wood which lined the trail on both sides. The river rushed by thirty yards to the northeast of their position.

Bran stepped off the path a few yards, his eyes on the ground, and then pointed to the base of a tree. Snow had filled in the whole area, but indentations remained beneath it, which the snow couldn't entirely mask. Gareth put out a hand to keep the others from coming any closer. Leaving his reins with Gwen, who'd dismounted too, he crouched low to the ground and gently swept aside the snow with his gloved hand.

"What do you see, Gareth?" Gwen said from behind him.

"Tracks." Gareth swiveled on his heel to look at his wife. "At least three horses, I'd say, same as the graveyard, plus a number of boot prints. They seem to extend over a broad area."

"Can you tell if they're the same as those near the chapel?" Morgan said from his seat on his horse. "You said you were looking for a man with large feet."

Gareth gave Gwen a wry look before directing his response to Cilcain's lord. "Because the earth here was wet from all the rain we've had, the men who walked here left particularly distinct prints. And then we were very lucky that the colder weather came when it did because they're better-preserved than they could have been."

While he'd explained the situation to Lord Morgan, Gwen had started to move away from him, somewhat bent over with her eyes fixed on the ground. "Gareth, I think I see two sets of footprints going this way. The trail is too hard-packed and snow-covered to read where they went once they reached it."

"Can you hand me the rope?" Gareth said.

Gwen loosened the ties on Gareth's saddlebag and took out the length of rope he kept there for measuring. Taking it from Gwen, he set it in the boot print and marked the fibers with a piece of charcoal to indicate how long and wide the print was.

"Lucky that Bran noticed these were here." Gareth nodded towards the herdsman, who stood impassively by the tree near where Gareth was crouched, his dog to heel at his left ankle. "We might have missed these in the snow."

Lord Morgan shook his head. "It's amazing you can keep all this straight in your head."

"Most people don't think about details of murder unless they have to," Gwen said. "Believe me, there are times when I wish I didn't know what I do."

"I don't believe that," Morgan said flatly.

Gareth glanced up at him, surprised at Morgan's tone and that his words had been spoken without humor.

Morgan's face was perfectly serious. "I have no doubt you're going to find out who did this. Not only that, your honor is such that nobody will be able to believe for long that you have betrayed either it or King Owain.

They'd come a long way from accusations of treason in a very short time.

11

Gareth

All things being equal, Gareth was glad for that, but it was a miracle that he was managing to keep his voice level as he went about the business of investigating these murders. Ever since Morgan had shouted 'treason!' to the hall, Gareth's anger had been on a slow boil. He was struggling to prevent it from bubbling over, and the out-of-control nature of it shocked him. His hands shook with it.

What he really needed to do was to move, to shout, to brandish his fist at the sky in frustration.

"We should see the place where the body was buried," Gwen said, "and if we think we've missed something, we can stop here again on the way back, since we have to pass this way on our return journey."

Gareth nodded his assent, still not trusting his voice, and rose to his feet. As he walked with her back to the horses, Morgan's assertion continued to resonate in his head.

There had been a time when his honor had been all he'd had left. Because of honor, he'd walked away from his companions, from Gwen, from everything he'd spent his life training for, even as he'd cursed himself for refusing to swallow down his conscience so he could have the life he wanted. Gwen had never chastised him for putting his honor ahead of her. She'd loved him for it, even as she'd lost him.

Humbled by her sacrifice, in the five years without her he'd endeavored to ensure that he hadn't walked away from his service to Prince Cadwaladr only to lose his soul to some other honorless lord. At the time he'd met Morgan in Powys, Gareth had been serving such a man. And then Gareth *had* resigned his position again rather than obey one more order he couldn't stomach.

As when he'd been thrown out of Aberystwyth, he hadn't known if he'd ever be accepted by another lord again. He'd known what he had to do, however, regardless of the consequences. Whatever the price, he'd paid it with his eyes open.

And miracle of miracles, after he'd left Lord Bergam, Prince Hywel had found him and hired him *because* of his sense of honor. Then Gareth had found Gwen again on the road from Dolwyddelan, and he was damned if he was going to allow another man's actions to take his life from him for a third time, especially when he'd done nothing wrong.

He was going to fight this to his last breath.

Unaware—or at least acknowledging—of the turmoil inside Gareth, Bran led the company another hundred yards up upriver to another location, nearer to the bank, which dropped steeply down to the fast flowing water below. He came to a halt at a gaping hollow. When Lord Morgan's men had recovered the body from the ground yesterday, they hadn't filled in the makeshift grave again. Snow had blown in, prettying up the scene, but thanks to the mist coming off the river, it was starting to melt.

Seen through the eyes of the killer, it wasn't a bad place to bury a body. As where the horses had been picketed, the ground here was soft and would have been softer two days ago, so easy to dig into. Had the false Gareth not been discovered, by the time the late winter rains flooded the banks and brought the remains of the body out of the ground where he'd been buried, the bones would have been unidentifiable and the killer long gone. He was long gone enough as it was.

The killer's mistake, beyond the murder itself, was choosing to bury the man so close to the trail. Gareth could have discovered the burial site simply by walking past, just as Bran had done. Likely, it had been dark when the false Gareth had died, so Gareth could see how what was clear in daylight might have been less clear in the dark. But the burial was still sloppily done.

Beside him, Gwen sighed. "Another grave."

Gareth reached up to help her dismount. "Despite Lord Morgan's confidence in you as well as me, you don't have to do this anymore, Gwen."

"I don't want to stop." She shook her head. "I'm just tired."

This time, all the riders, including Morgan's soldiers, dismounted to have a look at the grave. There wasn't much to see, but Gareth crouched next to the hole anyway, trying not to disturb it more than the men had yesterday. To their credit, they'd scattered the dirt, picking through it in case some of the man's possessions had been discarded in it. Gareth brushed the layer of the snow aside but revealed only more dirt.

As at the graveyard, Gwen took it upon herself to walk in ever-widening circles around the site to see if she could find evidence of the killer. Morgan joined her, having watched her technique back where the horses had been tied.

Gareth glanced at them out of the corner of his eye, noting when they paused a dozen paces away from him, close to the trail. "Did you find something?"

"Boot prints again," Morgan said.

"We shouldn't be surprised by that," Gareth said. "Are they large like the others?"

"It's hard to tell, but I think these are normal-sized feet," Morgan said.

Gwen peered at the ground. "I think this is blood."

That news had Gareth moving swiftly towards his wife and looking to where she pointed. The leaves here were particularly thick, since they were standing under an ancient oak tree. And while snow covered everything, there was only a light dusting here, making the blood obvious now that they knew what they were looking at. Plentiful too.

Gareth thought he could even smell the faint salty twang of it, though that was probably just his imagination. The leaves throughout the area were discolored under the snow, and when he and Gwen carefully brushed a few off and picked them up by their stems, an area of darker ground underneath where the blood had soaked into the earth was revealed.

"He was killed here." Gareth frowned as drops of rain pattered onto the leaves beside him. The air had warmed since they'd left the fort, but he hadn't thought it was warm enough to turn the snow to rain. The snow hadn't even melted on the trail yet.

He glanced up at the sky, noting the dark clouds, and then he returned his attention to what lay before him. It was good they'd pursued this lead first thing this morning, because even if the snow hadn't erased the details of the crime, the rain that was coming surely would.

"Why leave the horses so far down the trail from where the false Gareth was buried?" Morgan said.

"I know the answer to that," Gwen said. "Imagine this: the riders stop to rest, and the killer asks our dead man to walk with him a ways out of earshot of the rest of the men."

"In order to kill him!" Morgan tapped a gloved finger to his lips as he thought. "He didn't want to scare the horses with the smell of blood, and he needed to get the man alone. I wonder what he said to lure him away."

"He could have promised him something," Gwen said.

Morgan nodded. "The killer could have suggested he had a secret he would only share with our dead man. Perhaps the killer told him that he distrusted one of the other men in their party and wished to confide his suspicions to someone."

"Gold could have done it too," Gareth said.

"The false Gareth wouldn't have gone with him if he thought he was dispensable." Morgan's eyes narrowed. "Ensuring that my people know the truth isn't enough, Sir Gareth. You must ride for your camp immediately. The killer was heading that way, and even now could be standing at King Owain's side, telling him lies about you."

Gareth looked back down the trail. "We have an investigation in progress."

"Don't be stubborn," Morgan said. "Riding to King Owain's camp is a journey of a few miles. If our killer has reached the king or Prince Hywel before you, and is even now insinuating himself into his inner circle, he will have given himself away, won't he? And if he hasn't, you can lay all that you know at your lord's feet. That way, if Prince Hywel and King Owain do hear rumor of your fall from grace, they will already be on the alert and be prepared to follow those rumors to their source."

Gwen put a hand on Gareth's arm. "A few hours away from the investigation in order to avert disaster at home is surely worth the time and effort involved."

Morgan barked a laugh. "And you can also look for a man with big feet."

That last was meant as a jest. Gareth obliged Lord Morgan by giving him a twitch of a smile. "We give way." Cilcain's lord had a habit of making sense, even if he was prone to bouts of wild speculation, and Gareth regretted speaking so little with him all those years ago, though at the time their stations in life had been much further apart than they were now. "Gwen and I will go. If all is well, we will be back before sunset."

"If we do not return, try not to assume the worst," Gwen said. "It may be that Gareth was needed for something else."

"In which case, you should bury the false Gareth and Gwen without us," Gareth said.

"It will be done," Lord Morgan said. "In the interim, I will do what I can to discover if anyone saw them. At the very least, my men can question my people and the villagers. They all know what you look like now, and your recent visit may prod their memories about seeing your look-alikes a few days back."

"You should know that I did not reach this region until yesterday," Gwen said. "Gareth, on the other hand, has been scouting this area for weeks. If he was seen with me, then it would have been the false Gareth and the false Gwen."

"I appreciate whatever efforts you can make," Gareth said, uncharacteristically content with foisting these tasks onto someone else. "The more people who know we've been impersonated, the easier it will be not only to put names to the victims, but to combat rumor and gossip about what they have done and what Gwen and I have done."

Morgan gave a jerk of his head in assent.

Gareth and Gwen mounted their horses and, instead of turning east towards Cilcain as Lord Morgan and his men did, continued up the trail into the western mountains. Once they were out of earshot, Gwen looked at her husband. "I want to trust Lord Morgan. But can we really? It would have been devious and clever of him to bury the woman over his own grandfather's grave. Both bodies were found on his land. He could be hiding in plain sight."

"I don't think so, but how can I know for certain?" Gareth said. "Gwen, we're looking for a man who knows how to wield a sword and are heading towards a place where everyone fits the description of our killer. We may not be able to trust anyone."

12

Gwen

Her husband was eyeing her, worried as usual about how she was feeling. The trail was narrow here, barely wide enough for them to ride side-by-side, which meant Gwen couldn't evade his eyes for long. It had started to rain in earnest too, and the water plunked onto her head from the branches above her.

"I know what you're thinking," she said.

"Do you?"

"You're wondering how I can be so detached about the death of a woman who resembled me."

Gareth gave her a small smile. "I was actually thinking about how beautiful you are, but I suppose, if you pressed me, I was wondering about that too. How are you doing?"

"My anger is sustaining me right now," Gwen said. "I felt sorry for her before and didn't think I was angry at all. Now, if I allow myself to think about who she might have been, and lose focus on what she did, I start to fall apart. How could she do what she did—to me and to us? How could she pretend to be me?"

Gareth reached out a hand to Gwen's knee and patted once. "I know how you're feeling, Gwen, because I'm angry too. When Lord Morgan spoke of how I could be bought, a red haze swam before my eyes. I wish I had answers, but I don't."

"I'm working on pitying her. Perhaps she didn't have the advantages I had growing up or a loving family."

"If your father was her father, she could have resented that he never acknowledged her."

"My father didn't know she existed," Gwen said. "I would swear to it. For all his faults, he would never abandon his own child."

"You can never truly know what is in another man's—or woman's—heart, Gwen," Gareth said. "Your father may not have known about her, but somehow this woman was twisted up inside enough not to care about you." He canted his head. "Then again, she may have thought whatever she was doing was relatively harmless—or she was paid well enough to convince herself of it. It's only because someone killed her that her actions have taken on a more sinister tone."

"So she pretended to be me on a lark?" Gwen wasn't any happier about that. She'd had a privileged childhood until she was ten, but her childhood had ended after the death of her mother. From that day onward, Gwen couldn't remember doing anything on a lark. Ever. At sixteen when she'd met Gareth, she'd been a serious young woman. For a brief time, he'd made her giddy and joyful. After he'd left, she'd been bitter and resentful, and the experience had hardened her a bit around the edges.

Gwen didn't enjoy thinking about that time, and she wondered what could have gone so wrong in the woman's upbringing that she could think any amount of gold made impersonating Gwen a good idea. Gwen didn't add that she hoped the woman *had* been well paid, because in the end she'd paid for what she'd done with her life.

They reached King Owain's headquarters by mid-afternoon, though not before enduring two hours of uncomfortable riding. That morning's snowfall had been heavier in the mountains between Cilcain and the abandoned monastery, which would have been bad enough to travel through, but because the rain had started to fall and the weather to warm, it wasn't long before the snow began to melt in earnest, turning the trail to mud. Thus, by the time Gareth and Gwen descended the path towards the monastery, Gwen was exhausted, freezing, and soaked through from head to foot.

She swept a sodden lock of hair out of her eyes, glad to know that she would soon be able to warm herself in front of a fire. She hadn't really taken in the monastery's setting when they'd come here the first time. Although the location was remote, it was beautiful in a way that only a Welsh valley could be beautiful. Even though it was approaching winter, the grass remained green from the fall rains, and late season roses bloomed white and pink where they grew against the stone walls.

Although some of the outbuildings had fallen into disrepair, the chapel, abbot's quarters, and cloister remained intact—and at the moment, inviting. It would be nice if, when the fighting finally ended, an offshoot convent or some enterprising monks settled here once again.

The two men standing in the shelter of the guardhouse came to attention at Gareth's approach, and Gareth lifted a hand to them as he led Gwen through the derelict gatehouse and into the courtyard.

Both guards braved the rain to hold the bridles of their horses. Gareth dismounted and then helped Gwen to the ground. She tried to put her feet down in a somewhat dry spot, but the entire courtyard had turned into a muddy puddle, and she landed with a splash and a squish. Her toes were so cold, however, that she hardly felt the sudden wash of water over them.

"Is King Owain in residence?" Gareth asked the guard, who was tugging on Braith's bridle to lead her to the stable.

"He is," the guard said, "but—" He broke off as Prince Rhun appeared in the doorway to the courtyard, having come from what had once been the abbot's quarters. He halted at the sight of Gareth and Gwen, and then he stepped back into the shelter of the cloister, motioning for them to come to him.

Gareth and Gwen obeyed, trudging through the muddy courtyard to reach him. Gwen held up the hem of her dress, but in her head she was already relegating this dress to the bottom of her trunk, to be worn from now on only on days precisely like today. They stepped through the doorway into the sheltered walkway that surrounded the well at the center of the cloister, though it was only moderately less chilly out of the rain than it had been in it.

Rhun frowned. “I didn’t expect you back so soon.” The prince wore his cloak, boots, and gloves, as if he’d just arrived or was just leaving.

Gwen looked past the prince, wondering how far away a fire might be.

Rhun didn’t seem ready to take them to one yet. “Have you solved the case already?”

Gwen pushed back the hood of her cloak and shook out her hair, spraying drops of water on the flagstones. “Not quite.”

A tinge of humor echoed in her tone. She hadn’t expected to feel amusement, but now that they were here, and the rain wasn’t falling on her head, her spirits had risen. They hadn’t solved the murders, but they were safe and among friends. It wasn’t the best possible situation, but it was enough to be going on with.

“Our problems are greater than one murder, my lord,” Gareth said.

“It’s after noon now, isn’t it?” The cloister was open to the sky in the center, and Rhun took a quick step out from under the roof to check the quality of the light. Gwen could have told him that the sun wouldn’t shine again today. “Can whatever you have to tell me wait? We’ve had some trouble here too.”

At the same instant Gareth said, “What trouble?” Gwen said, “It would better for Gareth and me if it didn’t.”

Rhun placed his hands on his hips, looking from one to the other, not in a rude way, but simply assessing.

Before he could answer, Gwen added, "What has happened that you haven't the time to speak to us? Are you off somewhere?" Gwen was suddenly afraid that Rhun had heard a rumor about Gareth that put his trust into question.

But no, that wasn't it at all.

"My father is very ill," Rhun said finally. "I had a thought to bring a healer from the encampment to him, but now that you're here, Gwen, perhaps that won't be necessary."

"What's wrong with him?" Gwen said.

"It's his stomach," Rhun said. "In all my life, I have never seen him laid so low. All he can do is vomit or lie lethargically on his bed."

Gwen bit her lip. That wasn't like King Owain at all.

Rhun read her expression correctly. "You know what he's like—always full of energy. Even when he has a fever, he remains up and about. Now, while he continues to insist that when we move the camp closer to Mold he will come with us, he shows no ability to do anything but lie on the bed unmoving."

"The assault is about to begin?" Gareth said. "I thought we had more time."

"We did," Rhun said, "but after you left yesterday, all the lords and captains who have joined this war met and decided that now was the time."

"Please don't tell me that you're basing this on Father Alun's word?" Gwen said. "He's a kindly priest, but he knows nothing of war."

"Did you see any of Ranulf's soldiers in Cilcain?" Rhun said.

"No," Gareth said.

Rhun lifted one shoulder and dropped it. "Yes, Father Alun's news contributed to the decision, but it was a combination of several things: Lord Goronwy says dysentery is spreading among his men, not unlike what Father has; Chester's troops are definitely on the move, whether to refortify Mold or to attack us; and then there's the weather."

"It wasn't snowing yesterday," Gareth said.

"But those who task it is to judge the winds believed it would. And they were right. If we wait any longer to begin the offensive, we may face more weather like we woke up to this morning. The consensus is that we're running out of time. But now with Father ill—" Rhun gestured helplessly with one hand towards the inner recesses of the monastery and looked at Gwen, "—maybe he'll listen to you."

"To me?" Gwen said. "Why would he listen to me when he won't listen to you?"

"Because he likes you. I am his son. Words fall from my lips but he doesn't hear them."

Gwen had noticed a similar tendency in her father and her brother. Gwalchmai, in particular, was of an age where his sister couldn't possibly be right about anything. She hoped he would grow out of it soon, since she was in the awkward position of being both sister and mother to him. She wouldn't have thought, however, that King Owain and his favored son would have a similar relationship.

"I can try." She put out a hand to the prince, hating even to say what was in her mind and knowing it was only in her mind because she was so full of suspicion already. "Could-could the king have been poisoned?"

Rhun's hands clenched. "I don't want to think it. He never eats unless someone else has eaten first. If he was poisoned, I don't know how it could have happened." He turned on his heel and marched back into the recesses of the monastery. "I'll take you to him as soon as we get you out of those wet clothes."

"How long has he been ill?" Gwen said, hurrying to catch up. "You mentioned yesterday that he was unwell."

"I should have had you look at him before you left." Rhun looked over his shoulder at Gwen. "He was too ill even to receive King Stephen's letter."

Gwen frowned. That was very ill indeed.

"While Gwen sees to my father, perhaps you can tell us what has gone wrong with your investigation, Gareth."

"Us?" Gareth said.

But then the question was unnecessary because they'd turned a corner and arrived at the warming room. Hywel and Godfrid were seated in chairs near the fire, with Madoc and Cynan, Hywel's and Rhun's two younger brothers, close by at a corner table. They'd all been conferring together in low voices, but they looked up as Rhun, Gareth, and Gwen came through the door.

"Look who I found," Rhun said.

Hywel stood abruptly. "I wouldn't have thought you'd return so quickly. Did you solve the murder?" He put out a hand to Gareth, and the two men grasped forearms.

"Sadly, no," Gareth said. "In fact, that's why we're here."

A large fireplace took up part of one wall. Its smoke vented out the back, along with a portion of its heat (unfortunately), but Gwen wouldn't have cared if the room had been full of smoke, just so long as it was warmer than outside. Her hands were frozen, and she moved straight to the fire, stripping off her gloves as she went. She dropped them to the hearth and held out her hands to the flames.

"Tell us!" Godfrid cleared the cups on the table out of the way with one hand while beckoning with the other that they all should sit.

Gwen stayed where she was by the fire, though she turned her back to it so she could see the men's faces. After a moment, she removed her cloak and hung it on a hook to the left of the fire so it would dry. The heat warmed the back of her dress, and she felt her shoulders relaxing for the first time since she and Gareth had left Lord Morgan's fort that morning.

"I was hoping Gwen could see to Father first, since she's here," Rhun said, not yet ready to sit either.

Hywel waved a hand at his elder brother. "I just checked on him. He's asleep, and Tudur said he'd come find me the instant he wakes, so let's hear what Gareth and Gwen have to say in the interim." He peered into Gwen's face. She hastily tried to smooth the pinched look she knew she was wearing, but she was clearly unsuccessful because Hywel added, "What's wrong? What has made you come back before the investigation is finished?"

Gareth glanced at Gwen. She canted her head to indicate that he had the floor, so he took up the task, laying out everything they'd discovered so far for the princes to examine: the dead woman who looked like Gwen; Gareth's arrest for his supposed treason; the appearance of the second body; plus all the bits and pieces, from the character of Father Alun, to the gravesites, to the reticent answers of Bran. He was careful not to interpret the evidence or assume anything.

Meanwhile, a servant brought food and drink for Gareth and Gwen. Now that Gwen was warm, she was hungry too, and she came forward from the fire to devour what was in front of her as Gareth talked.

When he'd finished, Hywel's face was a thundercloud. "You were right to return, both of you. I am shocked that Lord Morgan arrested you on such flimsy evidence merely to gain favor with Father."

"I assure you, no matter what the rumor, we wouldn't have believed it," Rhun said.

"What if someone told you they'd seen me in the company of one of Earl Ranulf's men?" Gareth said. "What then?"

Rhun's face fell.

Gwen nodded. "Regardless of who murdered whom, someone out there met the false Gareth and may well believe the real Gareth has been bought."

"I haven't been associated with prior murders, but it does seem likely that the killer of the false Gareth is a nobleman or knight and has the freedom to come and go to some degree as he pleases." Cynan said.

Stocky and blond and the spitting image of his father, though somewhat shorter in stature, Cynan was an unknown quantity to Gwen. It was practically the first time she'd heard his voice or participated in a conversation that included either him or Madoc, in part because this war was the first time King Owain had brought his two younger sons into his confidence.

Not as handsome as either Rhun or Hywel, Cynan did possess the bluest eyes Gwen had ever seen. Madoc, his blood brother, sat beside him. Two years younger than Cynan, he had darker hair and brown eyes, but exactly the same shape and features. Except for their coloring, the two could have been twins.

"From the tracks you found, the killer rides a horse as well," Hywel said. "It's easy to forget, living at Aber as we do, or now with the army, how few of our people have the wherewithal to own a horse that can be ridden."

"One wonders what has become of my belongings," Rhun said. "They fell into the river at the same time as Gareth's."

"Are we going to find the body of a false Rhun in another day or two?" Cynan said.

Gareth rubbed at his forehead as if his head ached there. Gwen's certainly did.

"We haven't even figured out why the false Gareth and Gwen were in Cilcain, much less where they'd been and what they'd been doing. We need to get out there and find more evidence." Gareth half rose to his feet.

"Wait, Gareth." Godfrid waved him down. "Who knew besides we few that Gareth and Gwen had gone to Cilcain?"

"Nobody but us and the guards on gatehouse duty yesterday," Hywel said, "unless you told someone."

"I wouldn't," Godfrid said.

Hywel nodded. "Rhun and I swore the guards to secrecy and agreed not to speak of it to anyone outside our immediate circle. The fewer people who knew of their mission the better."

Godfrid raised his eyebrows. "You already didn't trust someone in your own camp?"

Hywel shrugged. "My concerns were unspecific. I felt I was sending Gareth and Gwen into danger, and when I do that, I don't gossip about it."

"So none of the lords with whom we met yesterday afternoon knew that Gareth and Gwen had ridden east?" Cynan said.

"No," Hywel said. "What are you thinking?"

"The killer might not yet know that the bodies have been found. And if he thought he killed the real Gareth and Gwen, he wouldn't know yet that he killed the wrong people," Cynan said, proving that his mind was as capable as the others, even if he spoke less often.

Madoc still hadn't spoken at all, and for all that his brown eyes surveyed the room with serenity, Hywel reported that this younger brother was by far the wilder and more adventurous of the two.

"Did you notice anyone acting nervous or anxious, my lords?" Gareth said. "More so than might be expected when war is under discussion?"

The other men in the room turned thoughtful. It was one thing to speculate on the identity of the killer. It was quite another to think about being in the same council with him yesterday.

"No," Godfrid concluded finally. "I didn't. Did any of you?"

Heads shook all around.

"Three days ago, when the murders happened, we had not yet decided to advance towards Mold," Madoc said, finally breaking his silence. "The decision to do so could be making the killer very nervous."

"Or emboldening him, Madoc," Cynan said.

"Why do you say that?" Godfrid said.

"The army is going to march right through Cilcain," Cynan said. "It will cause chaos in the village and all around the countryside, from now until Mold falls or we go home. The more upheaval the war causes, the less likely anyone would be to notice an irregular burial in the graveyard or a dead body on a mountain trail."

"When are we to move out?" Gareth said.

"Within the hour, actually," Rhun said.

"If father hadn't fallen ill, we would have moved already." Hywel gestured to the other men in the room. "As it was, we put it off for a few hours in the hope that his health would improve."

"I probably should see him now," Gwen said. "If he's asleep, I can at least assess his fever and speak to his manservant."

"I grow more worried for him with every hour that passes," Rhun said.

Gwen pressed her lips together, worried also. Nausea and diarrhea were the scourge of all armies. Even sleeping well at the monastery and eating better food than his men hadn't been enough to keep the sickness at bay.

"I should have something in my box that can help him," Gwen said, looking at Gareth.

"I'll get it." Gareth stood and left the room.

"We would be grateful for whatever you can do for him," Hywel said.

"As I said, he needs someone other than his sons to tell him what he doesn't want to hear." Rhun paused before adding, "If he can even understand you."

Gwen stared at Rhun. "My lord, if he's that ill, we shouldn't have been sitting here discussing Gareth's and my problems. I can't promise I can help him, but—"

A shout came from beyond the walls, along with the faint clash of steel. As one, the men shot to their feet and ran from the room, Hywel in the lead. It had been Gareth who'd shouted, but while Gwen rose to her feet immediately, there was no point in her leading the way to the sound if it was men with swords Gareth needed.

Gwen followed on the heels of the men, her heart in her throat and her fear a knot in her stomach. Gareth was a knight. He lived by the sword, but that didn't mean he couldn't die by it too.

By the time Gwen arrived in the courtyard, however, the fighting—what there had been of it—had ceased. Prince Hywel himself stood between Gareth and another man dressed in worn traveling clothes and a thick wool cloak upon which water beaded. The heavy rain of earlier had eased with the waning of the day, turning into a drizzle that could go on for hours. The stranger was perhaps a year or two younger than Gwen and was breathing hard with exertion.

He pointed his sword at Gareth, his dark eyes flashing with hatred, and spoke in near-perfect Welsh. "Stand aside! That man is a thief and a brigand!"

13

Gwen

"No, he isn't." Hywel's voice held amusement, which was typical of the man. It was his earlier anger that had been unusual.

"He is wanted by the sheriff of Shrewsbury!"

"You speak our language, so you should be Welsh enough to know that we don't abide by English law here," Hywel said, speaking for every Welshman in the courtyard, whose hackles had risen at the newcomer's words.

Everyone but the stranger knew that Gareth wasn't the man he wanted, but his immediate innocence was instantly put aside to defend the integrity of their homeland. The guards at the gatehouse stepped closer, their own swords out and ready. Godfrid, Cynan, and Madoc moved to block any escape.

The man ducked his head, suddenly uncertain. "I thought this land belonged to the Earl of Chester—"

"Not anymore. He has no power here." Rhun came forward, halting out of sword reach of the stranger.

The man wore no helmet, and his brown hair was plastered to his forehead from the rain. His clothing was that of a man-at-arms, though the sword he held was finely wrought. He was either of higher rank than he looked or a well-trusted emissary.

"Put up your sword," Hywel said.

Grossly outnumbered, the man flicked his eyes nervously from Hywel to Rhun and back again, only now noticing their fine clothing, swords, and armor. He swallowed hard and, after another moment's hesitation, obeyed.

Having sheathed his sword, he spread his hands wide. "May I ask to whom I have the honor of speaking?"

"I am Prince Hywel of Gwynedd, and this is my brother, Prince Rhun, the *edling*."

The man expelled a breath, and then he bowed deeply. "John Fletcher of Shrewsbury at your service." He lifted his head, glancing first at Gareth, who hadn't moved to put away his sword as yet, and then he straightened. "My lords, I may have crossed the border into Wales in error, but this man is still a highwayman. You should know that you have a serpent in your midst."

"Did this thieving and brigandry occur in Shrewsbury too?" Hywel said.

"It did," John said. "A month ago."

Hywel turned slightly to look at Gareth. "Have you been to Shrewsbury in the last year?"

"You know I haven't."

"Sir Gareth is the captain of my guard," Hywel said. "He has hardly left my side in five years of service, except at my direction and to places he has then proven to have reached. He has not been to Shrewsbury, and there was never a time in the last year he could have ridden there and returned without my noticing his absence. This is not the man you're looking for."

"But—" The stranger's determined expression had been faltering as the prince talked, and now real puzzlement entered John's eyes. "Did you say, 'Sir Gareth'? Not the Sir Gareth who saved the life of Henry Plantagenet, the son of Empress Maud?"

"The very same," Hywel said.

The man put a hand to the top of his head. "I am at a loss." Placing his heels together, he bowed, but this time in Gareth's direction. "My lord, I apologize for mistaking you for someone else." He squinted too, his expression still full of concern. "My eyes aren't what they used to be."

"Clearly," Hywel said.

Gareth finally lowered his sword and took one stride towards the stranger, his arm out. "I am Gareth ap Rhys, captain of Prince Hywel's *teulu*."

Hywel stepped aside so John could grasp Gareth's arm. "John Fletcher, undersheriff in Shrewsbury, sent to trace the whereabouts of one Cole Turner. For some time he's been wanted for crimes committed in England, but we had word only a few days ago that he'd been seen on the road north of Shrewsbury. I picked up his trail and followed him here."

"Are you saying that the trail led to this monastery?" Gareth said.

John shook his head. "I lost his scent a ways to the south, and I must have turned the wrong way in the rain because I didn't mean to enter Wales. What is this place?"

"King Owain, who rules these lands, has taken this abandoned monastery as his headquarters for his campaign against the Earl of Chester," Gareth said.

John licked his lips. "I hadn't realized your victories had brought you so far north and east, my lords." He released Gareth's arm and turned to the princes. "I request permission to explain my task to the king in order to pursue Cole into Gwynedd."

"That will not be necessary," Prince Rhun said.

John blinked in confusion. "Why not?"

Gareth made a slashing motion with one hand, not yet ready to answer that question. "I want to know more about this man who looks like me. It is obvious you have met him. Did you know him personally?"

"Not as a friend, mind you, but we caught him red-handed nearly a month ago on the high road to London, robbing a merchant. He escaped custody, however." John ground his teeth in frustration.

Gareth grimaced, which may have been a failed attempt at a smile. Gwen didn't feel like smiling either. It was of some comfort to know Cole's name, but that he'd been wanted for highway robbery only made her more concerned about what else he'd been doing in the last month, and how willing he might have been to do something far more heinous in Gareth's name.

"Then you may be pleased to learn that he is dead," Gareth said.

"Dead? How so?" John said.

"He was run through and left beside a trail that passes through the mountains to Cilcain. Lord Morgan's man found him, and he told us of Cole's death yesterday, though we didn't have a name for him until now. My wife and I examined the body ourselves." Gareth gestured that Gwen should come forward.

John had been looking into Gareth's face, but at Gwen's approach, he looked past him to her. His mouth opened. "What—how—"

Gwen felt a frisson of satisfaction at John's reaction.

Gareth smiled grimly too. "This is my wife, Gwen ferch Meilyr. From your expression, I don't have to guess that she looks familiar to you too."

John made a helpless gesture with both hands. "Indeed, though now that I look more closely at both of you, I realize that I was mistaken on her behalf as well as yours."

"Who did you think I was?" Gwen said.

"You look very much like the daughter of one of our merchants in Shrewsbury, a young woman named Adeline," John said.

"Is she, by chance, missing, having been last seen in the company of Cole Turner?" Gwen said.

John couldn't keep his eyes off Gwen's face. "How do you know about her?"

Before Gwen could answer, Hywel intervened. "May we see your credentials?"

"Of course." John pulled a folded piece of parchment from the recesses of his coat and handed it to the prince.

Hywel studied the paper. From where she was standing, Gwen could see the elaborate seal and signature at the end of the letter. Although she didn't recognize the sheriff of Shrewsbury's emblem on sight, Hywel obviously did, since he gave a brief nod to indicate that all was well.

"For all that your name is of Saxon origin, you speak Welsh with barely an accent." Hywel refolded the parchment and returned it to John. "How is that?"

"My mother is Welsh." John accepted the return of his credentials with a slight bow, and when he straightened, he proceeded to detail her ancestry for three generations. She was from Powys, and not of a family that Gwen knew.

"My task is not at an end, you understand?" John concluded. "Even if Cole is dead, I still seek the girl. I have word from those who saw them together that she went with him willingly on this journey north. If she's up here alone, however, now that Cole is dead, she may be lost or in distress."

Nobody replied for a few heartbeats, and then Gwen sighed, deciding that it might as well be she who answered him. "I'm afraid that as to the woman you are seeking, the news of her fate is similar to that of Cole's."

John stopped in the act of pocketing his credentials, his gaze moving sharply to Gwen's face. "Don't tell me she is dead too?"

Gareth put a hand on the undersheriff's shoulder, more familiarly than might be normal with a stranger, but this wasn't a normal piece of news. "I'm sorry, John. She is, indeed, dead. She was murdered, as Cole was."

John's face fell. "No." Blinking rapidly, he stepped away from Gareth, who dropped his hand. The other men didn't look at John directly, pretending not to notice his distress.

Gareth did him the service of continuing to speak, even if he was talking to the back of John's head. "Two nights ago, the killer left her body in the graveyard of the church in Cilcain."

John swung around to face Gareth again, and Gwen was glad to see he'd mastered himself and his eyes were clear. "You saw her body as well as Cole's?"

"Yes," Gareth said. "Her resemblance to Gwen was unmistakable."

"I'm so sorry," Gwen said. "You must have known her well."

"I thought I did," John said.

"Can you tell us how a merchant's daughter became a companion to a thief?" Gareth said.

John's expression turned stony, and when he spoke next, his voice was without inflection. "I have no idea how she became acquainted with Cole and ended up here, dead." He licked his lips. "Do you?"

"For all that she resembled me, we didn't know her name until this moment," Gwen said. "It seems she might have been a cousin I never knew I had."

"We are in the early stages of our investigation," Gareth said. "We haven't had the opportunity to question more than a handful of people about what they know. We were just about to return to Cilcain when you arrived and accosted me."

John took in another deep breath and let it out. "I would like to see her."

"She was to have been buried today," Gareth said gently, "as was Cole."

Gwen looked up at Gareth. "We woke to snow. Father Alun may have waited for the ground to soften before ordering out the gravediggers."

Hywel nodded. "Regardless, John needs an escort back to England. It's a wonder he made it this far without being stopped. Many of the men are in a mood to attack first and ask questions later."

John hung his head. "Like I did."

It was by now mid-afternoon, and there was faint hope that John could reach Cilcain before the burials. Even if he left this instant, the sun would be setting by the time he reached the chapel. Still, if John's interest in Adeline had been more than that of a friend, he deserved the chance to see her face one more time before they put her into the ground.

Gareth made an appeasing gesture with one hand. "With my lord's permission, I can take you to her—to Cole too, if you like. At the very least, you can speak to witnesses other than Gwen and me who saw them both." He glanced at Hywel, who nodded his assent.

"I would be grateful," John said.

Then Gareth moved to Gwen's side and lowered his voice. "Can you stay here this time?"

"There's as much danger for me here as in Cilcain," Gwen said, "maybe more if the nobleman we're searching for is among King Owain's retinue."

"I didn't say I wanted you to stay here to keep you out of danger, *cariad*." Gareth's voice was low and steady.

Gwen's eyes widened as she took in what Gareth was saying. He was suggesting that she take up the role she'd played for Hywel before she married Gareth—to act as a spy in King Owain's court and to report what she discovered.

Gwen nodded. "I haven't had a chance to see to King Owain, and this will give me a perfect excuse to stay by his side and to meet everyone who currently surrounds him. If our murderer is here, I will do my best to find him."

"Safely." Gareth gazed down at her, a warning look in his eyes. "Please do not take any risks, even necessary ones!"

Gwen would have much rather either stayed with Gareth or returned to her daughter, whose absence was becoming as constant an ache in her heart as Gareth's had been earlier. But she appreciated Gareth's trust in her and that he wasn't barring her from the investigation just because danger was all around them. They were in the middle of a war. Danger was a way of life.

She put a palm flat on his chest. "I will do my best."

"You'd better."

Prince Rhun approached, having caught the end of their conversation. "I'm hoping you've just told Gwen to stay with my father."

"I have," Gareth said, "and she will."

"Those medicines are still in my bag. I'll get them." Gwen moved towards the rickety stable in which the horses sheltered, deciding she'd had enough of standing in the drizzling rain. John stayed where he was, still eyed suspiciously by Cynan, Madoc, and Godfrid. However, Rhun, Hywel, and Gareth walked with Gwen and halted beneath the overhanging roof.

One of the stable boys had removed Gwen's saddlebag, brushed down her horse, and given him a blanket. He was warm and dry now—warmer and dryer than Gwen herself. Her bag rested on a shelf near the horse's head, and she went to open it.

Gareth's horse was tied next to Gwen's. He lifted the saddle from its rest near Gwen's bag and settled it onto Braith's back. Rhun waited while he tightened the belt and then said, "You have less to fear regarding discovery this time. With the army moving forward, we are no longer worried about alerting Ranulf to our presence in Cilcain. Let his spies tell him we have moved. He will know it for certain soon enough."

Hywel bumped Rhun's shoulder with his fist. "While Gwen sees to Father, we should put in an appearance at the camp to make sure everything is progressing smoothly. The men will march soon."

Rhun's eyes brightened for a moment, in anticipation of movement, but then his face fell. "I should stay—"

"No you shouldn't." With the box of medicines tucked under her arm, Gwen approached the princes. "I can talk to him about staying behind without you. He's either going to listen to me or he isn't. Whether or not you are looking sternly at him over my shoulder won't make a difference."

Rhun gave way with relief, and he and Hywel moved to where their horses were tethered, giving Gwen and Gareth some privacy so they could say their goodbyes. Gareth put his arm around Gwen, and she kissed his cheek. "Be careful," she said.

"You too, *cariad*." A smile flashed across his face. "King Owain's temper being what it is, it is you who have the more dangerous task."

14

Gareth

Gareth was neither pleased to be parted from Gwen nor excited to return to Lord Morgan's fort and the tedious job of questioning every one of the inhabitants of Cilcain as to whether or not they'd seen Adeline, Cole, or strange goings-on before midnight the evening Adeline and Cole died. John, at least, seemed to have taken hold of himself and his emotions.

"She was your betrothed?" Gareth said, at last asking what he—and everyone else who'd watched John's reaction to the news of Adeline's death—had assumed.

"No," John said.

"No?" Gareth glanced at him, truly surprised.

John didn't look at him, instead continuing to stare straight ahead. The track was ten feet wide for the first leg of the journey, allowing them to ride side-by-side, but both men's hoods were up against the drizzle so Gareth couldn't see John's face. They were riding to Cilcain on the same path he and Gwen had come down a few hours earlier. Gareth would have taken the main road to Cilcain, but he wanted show Cole's burial site to John and give himself another chance to look at it to see if he'd missed anything the first time.

"I've known her since childhood is all," John finally said. "She's my sister's closest confidant, and they were each to be married come spring—to brothers."

Gareth felt a tug of relief. He had felt uncomfortable prying into the man's personal life, but if Adeline had been intended as his future wife, that would have given John a very different stake in her death than if she'd been merely an acquaintance or friend of his family.

Gareth's next comment, therefore, was somewhat more matter-of-fact. "One might conclude that Adeline was looking forward to her marriage with something less than anticipation."

John barked a laugh. "You could say that. My sister's future husband is a good man, but Adeline was set to marry his older brother, with whom he works closely in their business as cartwrights. He is well respected within the community and comfortably well-off, which is why Adeline's father accepted his offer for her hand, but he has a temper, and Adeline wouldn't have chosen him for herself. I understood from my sister that Adeline had always had her eye on someone else."

"You?" Gareth said.

Another laugh. "Not I. It was one of the sheriff's men-at-arms she wanted."

"Somehow I don't see taking up with a known criminal as the best way to attract the attention of one of the sheriff's men," Gareth said.

"You wouldn't think so." John's laughter subsided, and he was back to sighing. "It was never easy to tell that girl anything."

"Who was her father?" Gareth said.

"A weaver in Shrewsbury—and a good one," John said, "but his wife died at Adeline's birth, and he didn't remarry. Adeline has always run a bit wild, though with the upcoming marriage, we hoped she'd settle down."

"Did you investigate Adeline's disappearance specifically?"

"Her father asked the sheriff to look into it, and we made some inquiries, but she had been seen with other men over the weeks before her disappearance, from sons of merchants to the aforementioned man-at-arms at Shrewsbury Castle. None could give an account to us of her last day or could be distinguished as the last person to see her alive."

John turned his head to look at Gareth. "As it turns out, she was simply biding her time until she could run away."

Gareth nodded, only half-listening, because he was really thinking about the possibility that the weaver's wife had given her husband a daughter fathered by another man, namely Meilyr, Gwen's father. If the weaver knew of the deception, it was good of him to raise the girl as his own.

Only Meilyr could tell them the truth now, and that was a conversation Gareth was not looking forward to having with his father-in-law. It would be up to Gwen whether or not they had it at all, because now that Adeline was dead, perhaps the identity of her real father didn't matter. The same could be said of Cole in regards to Gareth's family. But if Cole had been a long lost brother, Gareth felt strangely unaffected by the loss.

"What about you, my lord?" John said.

"What about me?" Gareth said.

"How did you come to be involved in these deaths? Surely your skills are wasted on two English miscreants from Shrewsbury?"

"I wouldn't say that, even if a miscreant was all Cole was," Gareth said. "Every unlawful death deserves the best effort of the man sent to investigate it. Why would you think investigating their deaths beneath me anyway?"

"You consort with kings."

Thankfully, their arrival at Cole's grave gave Gareth an excuse not to respond to that statement. He didn't really know how to anyway, or what to make of John's comment. To his mind, all he was doing was his job.

Except to Hywel and Gwen, he never talked about his role in the investigations he undertook. Solving murder was at times interesting, but mostly Gareth endeavored not to relive the moments of tension and terror he'd felt during past investigations. He certainly didn't pretty up the details over a shared carafe of wine or a cup of mead, even when those details were true.

It was quite dark under the trees, even though sunset wasn't yet upon them, so after Gareth tethered Braith to an overhanging branch, he removed his fire starter from his pack and made a makeshift torch out of a stick and a wad of oiled cloth he kept for such a purpose. Then, lit torch aloft, he walked with John to the hole, which Morgan hadn't seen fit to refill when he'd left.

"This is it?"

Gareth canted his head. "Not much of an end."

"We all end up in a hole in the ground eventually, I suppose." John's head came up, and he looked around the little clearing. "Did you find any clues as to the identity of the killer?"

"A few boot prints. Nothing else." Gareth circled the clearing. "Wait a moment."

He moved to the place where Gwen had spotted the blood and then beyond it. The whole area had been covered in snow when they'd been here earlier, and it had been impossible to properly survey the ground. It was only Gwen's keen eyes that had allowed her to find the blood in the first place.

Now, the torch light glinted off something in the grass about five feet from the bloody leaves. Bending, Gareth retrieved a small silver coin. And then he found a second one a foot away from the first.

John had followed him and, at the sight of what Gareth held in his hand, bent forward with his nose practically to the ground looking for more coins. "There's one! And another!"

Gareth stabbed the end of the torch into the ground, and soon both men were on their knees in the wet, searching more with their hands than with their eyes until they'd collected eleven silver coins and two gold pieces. It was a small fortune.

Gareth sat back on his heels, peering into the trees and trying to picture a scene where the coins would have been thrown across the grass. Then he spied a small leather purse that had caught on the end of a branch in a bush a few feet away, looking very much like a long brown leaf. He stood to retrieve it and brought it back to where John waited with the coins he'd found.

"What happened here, Sir Gareth?" John's mouth was slightly agape and maybe even watering at the sight of so much coinage.

"Why don't you take a guess?" Gareth said.

His eyes narrowing in thought, John stepped backwards a few paces to give himself a wider view of the whole area. He looked to the grave, and then to the blood, and then to the pile of coins and the bag. He walked towards the river and bent to gather a handful of pebbles.

Then he moved back to Gareth. "May I?"

Gareth gave him the bag but kept the coins.

John poured about half the stones into the purse while leaving the rest loose in his palm. "Hit my hand with yours so the stones scatter towards the trees."

Impressed and amused at the same time, Gareth swung his arm, backhanding John's hand such that the stones and the bag flew into the air in a trajectory that had them landing not quite as far—but not too far off—from where they'd found the coins. It seemed Gareth hadn't hit John's hand quite as hard as the man who'd scattered the coins. If that man had been Cole, and he'd refused payment for the murder of Adeline or because he didn't think the money he was being given was enough, he'd died angry.

Gareth clutched the coins in his fist, each one burning a hole in his flesh. They represented blood money, quite literally, and even worse, they had been last touched by the man who'd murdered Cole. Gareth didn't want to claim Cole as a long lost brother, repelled as he was by what Cole had done, but he was equally repulsed by standing where his killer had last stood and handling the coins Cole had refused.

Gareth stooped to collect the bag, which had fallen near to the original bush but hadn't caught in it, and slipped the coins inside it.

Ever since they'd found them, John had been eyeing the coins with a certain sort of eagerness, but when Gareth slipped the bag into his own purse to keep it safe, he sighed and nodded. "You must give them to your lord and let him decide what to do with the money." Then his brow furrowed. "It is a very rich man who leaves coins strewn amidst the grass."

"You're right on one hand," Gareth said, "but on the other, if the owner of the coins was also the killer, he had more urgent tasks to complete. In the dark and the cold, he'd be hard pressed to find the coins again after burying Cole."

They mounted their horses again and rode the last distance to Lord Morgan's fort, chased by the black clouds that seemed to have settled over their heads, even though the drizzle had temporarily abated.

Gareth raised his hand to the gatekeeper. "I have returned, bringing with me the undersheriff of Shrewsbury."

"Welcome back, my lord." The gate swung open to admit them.

Gareth had greeted the gatekeeper as if he and John hadn't been visible to watchers from the top of the palisade ever since they'd left the river road. It was a courtesy on the gatekeeper's part not to imply they'd been watched the whole way, and on Gareth's to pretend he didn't know. But because of it, Einion, having been forewarned of their arrival, immediately hurried down the steps to the hall to greet them.

Gareth pushed back his hood and leaned down towards the steward without dismounting. "Is the body of the dead man we found already in the ground?"

"The funeral service for both the man and the women was to start at sunset at the chapel in Cilcain. Father Alun thought it fitting to bury the pair together. Lord Morgan left the fort not long ago in order to attend the service."

Gareth checked the sky. Travel almost always took longer than he wanted it to, but even with the stop at Cole's death site, he and John had made better time than Gareth had hoped, and they still had a half-hour until dusk.

"Thank you." He turned his horse's head, prepared to ride to the chapel immediately.

"Wait!" Einion said.

Gareth looked back.

"Lord Morgan instructed me to ask you, were you to return, if the rumor of King Owain's coming advance is true."

"It is. By tomorrow evening, you'll be overrun," Gareth said. "You should prepare."

Einion's face fell as he internally calculated his stores and wondered how depleted they might become before this war was over. He had people to look after. He couldn't afford to feed King Owain or his court for very long, but he also had no choice but to provide whatever hospitality the king required.

Gareth didn't try to assuage the steward's fears because he didn't know himself where King Owain would choose to lay his head, if he came east at all.

"Come, John," Gareth said to the undersheriff.

The pair rode back the way they'd come, down the road from Morgan's stronghold. Rather than heading back into the mountains, however, they took the ford across the river that would lead them to Cilcain.

Once on the main road, Gareth spurred Braith. With the continued cloud cover and mist, it would be hard to tell the moment that the sun actually set, but sunset had to be soon. If John was going to be given the chance to see Adeline's face, it had to be now, before dirt covered her body for the second time. Father Alun would be less than willing to accommodate a request to dig her up again just for John's peace of mind.

Still, racing to a funeral was unseemly, no matter the reason, so as they reached the village and then the crossroads at the village green, they slowed as a courtesy to the few who'd remained in the street.

The village tavern lay to the west on the main road, and as he passed riding north, Gareth noted the empty tables and benches, though a wisp of smoke curled from the hole in the roof of the accompanying hut. Gareth hoped people might gather at the tavern after the service, especially if the rain didn't start up again. He intended to be one of them if they did. There wouldn't be a better time than now to hear all that Cilcain had to say.

The villagers had turned out in force to attend the service, even if most were doing so more for a chance to gossip and to remark on the spectacle of it than out of any sense of loss at the death of two strangers. The Welsh honored their dead. It was what separated them from barbarians.

Gareth urged Braith past the last few mourners straggling towards the church and dismounted in front of the entrance to the graveyard, in the same spot he'd left Braith the evening before. A lifetime ago.

A branch overhung the wall, and he looped the horse's reins around it. John dismounted too, with somewhat less enthusiasm than he'd shown up until now—not surprising, given that the funeral was for a friend.

Gareth hesitated for a moment in the archway to the grounds, his eyes scanning the congregants, who were spread out among the graves to the west of the church. Adeline's and Cole's burial site was about as far from Lord Morgan's grandfather's, to the northeast of the chapel, as it was possible to be and still have them both in the same graveyard.

Lord Morgan had placed himself at the front of the crowd, and his head was bowed. Several of his men stood near him. Gareth thought he recognized the shape of Bran as well, made more likely by the presence of his sheepdog tied to the leg of the bench upon which Father Alun had sat last night in front of the chapel entrance.

The service had already begun, but as he raised his hands to give the blessing, Father Alun caught Gareth's eye, and Gareth bent his head in greeting.

Fortunately for John, this funeral was typical for Wales, and the bodies weren't yet in the ground. They lay in their temporary coffins, which after today would be stored away against the day they were needed to carry another dead parishioner to his funeral. It was only after the crowds had dispersed that the gravediggers would remove the bodies to bury them in just their shrouds. At that point, John would be free to look upon the faces of Adeline and Cole.

Gareth was relieved to have made it in time, though probably not as relieved as John. Until the undersheriff confirmed for himself who the victims were, Gareth didn't want to say definitively that he knew their identities.

"I hate funerals," John said to Gareth in an undertone from his position just to Gareth's right.

Others had said those words to Gareth in the past, including his own wife and Prince Hywel, and he always felt like saying in reply, "who *likes* them?" Gareth would be far more concerned about John if he'd told him he was looking forward to it. But Gareth, as always, refrained from any response at all. He understood that some people disliked the necessities surrounding death more than others, and their level of animosity was often directly related to the number of loved ones who'd died and whose funerals they'd attended. So Gareth could be forgiving.

Gareth's own parents had died when he was young. As he stood and waited for Father Alun to finish, the dripping of water onto the back of his neck from the overhanging trees had him recalling that day.

It had been much the same time of year as now, and Gareth could almost see in his mind's eye, even twenty-five years later, the boy he'd been, standing before the open graves of his mother and father. He could almost feel the rain falling on his bared head, the pressure of his uncle's hand on his shoulder, and the fog of his own stunned grief. At five years old, he'd barely understood anything of what was happening, other than the obvious fact that his parents were never coming back.

Most recently, Gareth had attended the burials of the men who'd fallen in battle against the Earl of Chester's forces. And for that reason, Gareth could say, equally with John, that he hated funerals too.

15

Gareth

This funeral was soon over, however, and since they hadn't had the chance to tell Father Alun the names of the dead before the service, it had a particularly perfunctory air. The crowd dispersed quickly. Nobody cared to stand around in the wet grass and the dark to watch the interment of two people they hadn't known. The main focus of the mourners was to get to their mead so they could discuss the funeral in detail and speculate on the identity of the dead and their killers. The former point, at least, could be made clear to everyone as soon as John had a chance to look at the victims' faces.

Gareth and John waited until the last of the mourners had turned away before stepping forward from where they'd watched the funeral. Gareth moved first to the smaller of the two coffins, which had to be Adeline's, and put out a hand to the gravediggers, indicating that they should hold. They'd been about to lift her body out of the box to put her into the grave.

"Sir Gareth." Father Alun had been overseeing the work, and he gave Gareth a nod of his head in greeting, as well as a small smile.

"You chose a nice spot for them," Gareth said.

"They may have died violently and unshriven, but that doesn't mean they can't rest in peace," Father Alun said.

Gareth canted his head. "Excuse the interruption, but I'd like to present to you John Fletcher of Shrewsbury, who arrived today at King Owain's headquarters on a similar quest to your own."

"More men have been murdered?" Father Alun said, aghast.

Gareth gave a tsk of dismay. "I phrased that badly. I should have said that he came to King Owain looking for these two. He has been searching for them for some time." He gestured John closer, adding, "He thinks he can identify them for us."

Father Alun's face collapsed into an expression of pure relief. "That I had to bury them unnamed has been a weight on my heart since Lord Morgan told me that you'd returned to Prince Hywel."

"Is that what he said? That we'd abandoned the investigation?" Gareth looked around for Lord Morgan, but he'd left with the other mourners. Gareth hadn't made himself known to him, and since the only light came from several torches surrounding the gravesite and two lanterns on the step of the church, Morgan could perhaps be forgiven for not noticing Gareth's arrival. "He was the one who practically ordered us to go."

As soon as he spoke, Gareth wished he could take back his words. Father Alun might be gentle, but he'd proven last night that his mind worked as well as anyone's. Gareth had implied that Lord Morgan had lied, which was a mistake.

Father Alun frowned. "Maybe I simply inferred it."

"I'm sure it was something like that," Gareth said, backtracking. "As it is, I've returned and am ready to continue the investigation."

Father Alun gave a slight bob of his head. "Thank you, Sir Gareth."

Gareth held up one hand. "Don't thank me yet." He turned to look at John, who was crouched over Adeline's coffin. He hadn't yet moved aside the part of the shroud that covered her face.

"Are you ready for this?" Gareth was beginning to think that John himself may have lied—in this case either about his relationship with Adeline or his experience with death and murder.

John looked in Gareth's direction and waved a hand dismissively. "I've seen bodies before, of course."

"Of course," Gareth said, "but it is a very different thing to examine closely someone who has been murdered, particularly if you knew her in life. Anyone would be feeling queasy about now."

A swift breeze came from the west, thankfully blowing away any foul smell that might be developing in the corpses. They were reaching the end of the grace period when a body *had* to be put into the ground. Instead of commenting on it, Gareth moved to crouch beside John, deciding to remove from John's hands the burden of unwinding the cloth from Adeline's face. Gareth also wanted to make sure that the death wound on her neck wasn't revealed. Undersheriff or not, used to death or not, John didn't need to see it.

A few swift movements and it was done. Gareth's stepped back and left John to it. The undersheriff looked into Adeline's face for a count of ten, pausing long enough that Gareth suddenly feared they'd been mistaken about her identity. But then John nodded. "That's Adeline." He carefully rearranged the cloth so it covered her face again.

"God bless her soul." Father Alun stepped to the side of the coffin, opposite Gareth, and made the sign of the cross above her body.

"Will you look upon Cole as well?" Gareth said.

One of the gravediggers had already exposed his face—without fuss, Gareth was glad to see. He hadn't questioned either of them yet, but he reminded himself to do so. Since they'd been involved in the uncovering of Adeline's body, they might have a different perspective on the circumstances of it than Father Alun.

As an answer to Gareth, John straightened to a standing position and walked the few feet to where Cole lay in his coffin. John didn't crouch beside the body this time but just gave another curt nod, and Father Alun signaled that the gravediggers could complete their work.

Gareth remained concerned about John's wellbeing, and when John looked over at him next, his expression had turned even more severe, the worry lines around his eyes deepening.

"What's wrong?" Gareth gestured with one hand. "Beyond the obvious, I mean."

"When you unwrapped the cloth from Adeline's face, you tried to hide the wound at her throat, but I saw it anyway."

"I was trying to spare you grief," Gareth said.

John gave a mocking laugh. "Instead, I almost missed seeing it, which would have been regrettable."

"Why?"

"The wound is identical to that of a man murdered in Shrewsbury not two weeks ago. You were right in thinking that my experience with murder is minimal. In fact, the murder of which I speak was the first I'd seen. The victim's throat was cut with the same slashing blow that killed Adeline."

"Cole killed Adeline," Gareth said, "or so we believe."

John bit his lip. "Before this moment, nobody had thought to place responsibility for the death of the man in Shrewsbury on Cole's head. He was a thief, not a murderer."

"And now you may have to," Gareth said. "It will relieve your sheriff to learn that he doesn't still have a murderer running loose in Shrewsbury. Who died?"

"A Welshman traveling as emissary from King Owain Gwynedd to King Stephen of England. He was on his way home when he passed through Shrewsbury and met with my sheriff."

Gareth felt his jaw drop. "What? You didn't think to mention this earlier?"

John had the grace to look sheepish.

"By the saints, man! You were at King Owain's court not four hours ago!"

"I-I-I thought you already knew," John said, shrinking back against a gravestone. "Nobody mentioned King Owain's emissary, so I didn't either."

"By God's teeth, why did you not say something anyway? At least you could have apologized for not keeping him safe!"

"I didn't know how to tell Prince Rhun—"

"Did you think the princes would hold this death against you?" Gareth said, still incredulous, though his initial anger was waning at the stark fear in John's face. Gareth believed without a doubt that John was telling the truth.

John gave a jerky nod.

"It never occurred to you that they might want to question you as to the circumstances of his death? That I might have some insight, given my experience with death and your lack of it?"

"I didn't want to confuse the issue," John said. "I was seeking Cole; I wasn't on a quest to inform King Owain of the death. The sheriff had already done that."

Gareth thought of the letters Gwen had carried from Aber. One had been from King Stephen, but she'd brought others as well. Taran may not have opened a sealed missive from the Sheriff of Shrewsbury. Even with King Owain ill, Rhun might not have read any of the letters yet either.

When Gareth didn't answer immediately, John added, "You know the man of whom I speak?"

"Of course I know him!" Gareth ran a hand through his hair and found himself pacing among the graves. "He has played the role of emissary for King Owain many times over the years in which I've been associated with the court of Gwynedd. Llywelyn was the man's name, was it not, if we are speaking of the same person?"

John nodded. "Yes. We knew him by that name too."

"King Owain knew he was missing, you see, because Llywelyn's servant returned to Aber without him."

Gareth didn't question why Llywelyn had passed through Shrewsbury on his way home: it was one of the few cities in the whole of western England that still held for King Stephen. Gloucester, the seat of Earl Robert, Empress Maud's brother and right hand, was located twenty miles to the south. From there, the earl's power stretched far into the Welsh borderlands and adjacent counties.

Two years ago Gareth had saved the life of Maud's son, Henry, and relations between King Owain and the Empress remained cordial. Robert himself, however, had been ill on and off this past year. King Owain intended to maintain good relations with both sides against the day one of them finally achieved victory over the other.

"What were the circumstances of his death?" Gareth said.

John gave a helpless shrug. "He'd dined with the sheriff in the evening, but because he was staying at the monastery instead of the castle, he bid goodbye to the sheriff as the hour neared midnight and departed. The weather was fine that day, one of the few sunny days we had this autumn, and he told the guards he wanted to walk unescorted. His servant wasn't with him.

"One of the city boys found him dead beside the Severn River the next morning. Unlike here, the killer had made no attempt to bury the body—and we found no clues or evidence as to who had killed him or why."

"Why should have been obvious," Gareth said. "He was an emissary from King Owain to Stephen."

John grunted an acknowledgement of what that meant: Llywelyn had been on his way home from his meeting with King Stephen. Whoever killed him didn't want word of an agreement he'd reached on King Owain's behalf to reach Gwynedd.

Gareth could well believe, given Llywelyn's intelligence and long experience, that he'd realized he might be a target, and that was why he'd sent his servant to bring the letter home in his stead. Gareth could even believe that Llywelyn had stayed in Shrewsbury, dining with the sheriff and walking home without an attendant, to mislead his attacker, or even to draw him out. Unfortunately, he hadn't survived the encounter.

It might be, however, that the killer didn't know the letter had arrived safely at Aber—and then been delivered into Hywel's own hand by Gwen.

"When did Cole come into this?" Gareth said.

"He didn't. Cole was caught on the road to London, standing over a man he'd struck down for his gold," John said.

"But the man didn't have a slit throat?" Gareth said.

"No," John said. "In fact, he lived, though he retained no memory of the chain of events that had led up to the robbery. Cole claimed to have come upon the merchant lying in the road and tried to help him. He was arrested on the spot, but the arresting officer was young and inexperienced, and Cole caught him unawares and escaped before he could be brought to the castle."

Gareth finally understood what was going on, and why John had such mixed emotions about all of this. "You."

John bent his head. "Me."

"You were lucky Cole didn't slice your throat," Gareth said. "There was nothing to stop him."

"I wasn't worth it," John said. "It may even be that he was telling the truth. He could have happened upon the merchant lying in the road moments before I reached the same spot. Bad luck for him."

"The fact that Cole ran suggests guilt, however." Gareth tapped a finger to his lips as he thought. "A month ago, Cole is captured robbing a merchant but escapes. Two weeks ago, he murders Llywelyn. He moved up the ladder of crime rather quickly."

"Unless he'd murdered before somewhere else," John said, "and only came to Shrewsbury when it wasn't safe for him in that other place."

Cole's initial arrest and Llywelyn's death had come after Gareth had lost his belongings in the river. Suddenly, Gareth felt like he was a hair's-breadth away from a real discovery, as if he needed only one more piece of the puzzle and all would be made clear. But while he was so close to understanding he could taste it, he didn't have that piece yet.

By the time of Cole's arrest and Llywelyn's death, the villain behind this plot had already collected Gareth's gear from the river. Had he known of Cole's existence and in a single lightning strike of inspiration seen a chance to implement his evil plan?

"Any idea what Cole might have been doing since then? Did you learn of any more murdered men on your way north?"

"No," John said.

"Or how Adeline and Cole were connected, beyond their resemblance to Gwen and me?"

John's mouth turned down. "No. It does seem that it is in their appearance that your answers must lie. It seems unlikely that Cole himself would have had reason to murder Llywelyn, for example, or to impersonate you, unless he was working for someone else. You truly have never seen him before?"

"No."

John plucked at his lower lip, much calmer now that he knew Gareth wasn't going to strangle him. "I imagine that wouldn't be something you'd forget."

Gareth sighed. "Now that we know Cole and Adeline were from Shrewsbury, and it is in Shrewsbury that Llywelyn died, it may be that I must travel there to discover the truth."

"I'm sorry for your difficulties," John said. "I can't express to you how much we'd hoped she'd merely run off with another man."

"She did run off with another man," Gareth said, as gently as he could. "Cole."

"Do you think so?" John said.

Gareth felt himself taken aback that John might question such an obvious point. "Who else?"

"Perhaps the one she ran off with was the man who killed Cole," John said. "Didn't you suggest that he bore a sword and had the skill to use it? I find it much more likely that Adeline would leave Shrewsbury with him rather than with a brigand such as Cole, even if he was charming, a fact to which I cannot attest one way or another. She'd had her eye on a man-at-arms. How easy would it have been to transfer her affections to another man who bore a sword?"

Like a nobleman. Gareth thought the words but didn't say them. John needn't be privy to all that Gareth knew. The undersheriff had grasped the essence of the investigation quickly, but once again, Gareth was irritated with himself for how little actual investigative work he'd accomplished so far. It was in the footwork that murderers were caught—speaking to witnesses, canvassing neighbors—not in speculation and supposition, even if that speculation was based on observation.

He couldn't catch the murderer by guessing his name. He needed proof enough to convict the man before the king. The coins in his purse and the length of rope in his pack weren't enough to do it. He needed witnesses who could identify him.

Unfortunately, he didn't know of anyone who'd been to Shrewsbury in the last month, or even the last six months. He supposed that some of the visitors to the festival at Aberystwyth at the end of the summer could have come from there, but he hadn't met any personally.

"Where do we go from here?" John said.

Gareth studied the young man. "I am more grateful than I can say that you undertook this journey, but you need to be on your way." He stuck out his arm to the young undersheriff.

"What are you talking about?" John shook Gareth's arm on instinct, but his expression was one of dismay.

"Cole and Adeline are dead. Your work is done." Gareth released John's arm, bowed to Father Alun, who lifted a hand in acknowledgement, and urged John towards his horse.

John dug in his heels. "Are you not concerned about bringing their killer to justice?"

"I am very concerned about that," Gareth said, "but you have a duty to your sheriff that should not wait."

"We don't know who killed Cole!"

"Such was not your charge," Gareth said. "You were to track down Cole and return him to custody in Shrewsbury. Your sheriff gave no consideration to an outcome in which you found him dead by another's hand. Surely you must see that your only choice is to return to England ahead of this war, which you should have no part in. Besides, the murder occurred in Welsh lands. As my princes so vehemently pointed out, your lord has no writ here."

John opened his mouth to protest again but then broke off at the faint sound of drums in the distance.

Gareth could tell from the rhythm and tenor that the music was being played by men from Gwynedd, which meant King

Owain's army was coming today as promised. Last Gareth had heard, the plan had been to cross the River Alyn to the east of Cilcain and set up camp on the highest point just west of the village of Gwern-y-waun. With the army approaching Cilcain, they had only a mile and a half to go.

"The princes are coming," Gareth said, unnecessarily, since the drumming was growing louder. The army had taken the same road from their camp as Gwen and Gareth had with Father Alun, which meant they'd come into Cilcain from the west, instead of by way of Lord Morgan's fort.

"Will you come with me to Shrewsbury, then?" John said. "It appears that it is in my city that many of your answers may lie."

Gareth looked east, his heart sinking at the thought of entering England. He'd heard good things about Shrewsbury's sheriff, but he was English and so not to be trusted. Gareth was sharply reminded of his cordial relations with the castellan at Chester, only to have it come out later that he was a spy and a villain. If he rode with John, it would be John who spoke for him in enemy territory, not the other way around.

And even if Gareth went today, the trail was very cold. He'd followed cold trails before, but they were more difficult than warm ones.

The sound of drumming grew louder, making Gareth's decision for him. "Please tell your lord that before long I may come to Shrewsbury."

He held the bridle of John's horse, essentially giving John no choice but to mount. Gareth wanted him on his way before he was overtaken by King Owain's men. The young man didn't seem to realize the true danger he could be in, caught traveling alone between the two opposing armies.

"I wish you were coming now. I feel like I'm abandoning Adeline."

"I will learn more if I can and send you word of whatever I find," Gareth said. "For now, my duties lie here just as yours lie elsewhere."

"Yes, my lord." John finally gave way. He bent forward and stuck out his hand to Gareth once again. "Good luck."

Gareth grasped John's forearm. If his only means of finding out more about the deaths of Adeline and Cole lay in Shrewsbury, Gareth would follow the trail there eventually, but until then, the drums had reminded him that his duty was here.

With one last parting look, John turned his horse's head and rode away.

16

Gwen

Gwen was folding the king's freshly laundered sheets when Rhun returned. "May I borrow Gareth's helmet? I'd like to bring it to the smith to have a copy made. Mine fell in the river, back when Gareth's and my belongings were lost. We never recovered it."

Cloth half-folded, Gwen swung around to look at the prince. "I would think so."

While Gareth's helmet sported a red plume so that his men could distinguish him on the battlefield in a sea of similarly dressed men, the armorer had crafted distinct designs on the helmets of Prince Rhun and Prince Hywel as well. A golden crown marked King Owain's, not that he would be wearing any helmet, crowned or not, in the upcoming battle. He would be lucky even to be able to stand by then.

"I'm surprised Gareth didn't take it with him," Rhun said.

"My lord, you must know he hates wearing it and does so only when he goes into battle," Gwen said. "I thought you all felt that way?"

"Oh no." Rhun gave her a quick smile. "I look forward to wearing an upside-down pot on my head which prevents me from seeing anything beyond what is directly in front of me. I love in particular wearing a device which allows the sweat to run into my eyes and blind me, but which I can't then remove to address the problem."

Gwen smiled too. "If it protects your head from an errant blow, wearing a helmet is worth it."

"So I have concluded. To make a new one, I need a proper armorer with a proper forge, but we don't have one here. Until I return to Aber and can get fitted, I must make do with what I have. Since Gareth isn't here, and didn't take his with him, borrowing from him seemed like the next best thing. So, thank you."

Rhun put his heels together and gave Gwen a bow. Coming from him, it had to be genuine. If it had been Hywel doing the asking, the bow would have most definitely been mocking. Gwen found it endearing that Rhun, a prince of Wales, felt awkward about asking for a favor. Angharad, his betrothed, was a very lucky woman.

Then Rhun's eyes strayed to the doorway of the adjacent room, in which King Owain lay ill. "How is my father?"

"His manservant tells me that the bouts of vomiting were so frequent last night that they followed one on top of the other. Sleep is what he needs now, and hopefully his stomach will be calmer when he wakes," Gwen said.

"Will Father be able to come to Gwern-y-waun?"

"I really can't say," Gwen said. "I know you need him there, but sleeping outside in a tent won't be good for him. Here, at least, he has a fire to warm him."

"I appreciate you taking care of him." Then Rhun hesitated.

"What is it?"

"You haven't seen Lord Goronwy anywhere, have you?"

Gwen's raised her brows at the question. "No." Lord Goronwy was Queen Cristina's father. He was also King Owain's cousin and long-time companion, which was one reason Owain had married her. The marriage had healed a rift in the royal family of Gwynedd caused many years ago by King Owain's father. "I thought his men were advancing on Mold from the south."

"They are," Rhun said. "He sent word that they are moving now, as we are. But he was supposed to come here to confer one more time before joining his men."

Gwen held up both hands. "I have no answer for you."

Rhun tapped the side of his thigh with the flat of his hand and looked towards the fire. In an undertone, he said, "What are you up to, uncle?"

For once, he wasn't talking about Cadwaladr. Gwen cleared her throat. "Do you have reason to believe Lord Goronwy is up to something?"

"He has made himself scarce recently," Rhun said. "Up until last week, he was in and out of my father's headquarters nearly every day. But I haven't seen him in nearly a week. He just sends messages." Then he looked directly at her again. "Gwen, you should be very careful."

"Are you saying I should be careful of Lord Goronwy?" Gwen said. "He has always been kind to me, though I admit that Queen Cristina has been something of a different story of late."

"I didn't mean him, necessarily, but with my father ill, the other lords are circling like vultures."

"Then it is you, my lord, who should watch his back." Gwen put a hand on Rhun's arm before he could protest or think too hard about what would happen if his father died. "No matter the source of this illness, your father will recover, my lord. Do not fear." Gwen couldn't truly promise that, but King Owain was a strong man. She had sat beside him over the course of two hours, spoon feeding him broth, some of which he kept down for a time before vomiting again. That he could keep it down at all was a hopeful sign.

Rhun scoffed at himself. "Don't mind me. I don't have the *sight*, but we do have a killer on the loose—a man who murdered two people who look like you and Gareth. With the coming assault on Mold Castle, all will be in chaos, and you and Gareth, as always, will be in the thick of it. Just ... be careful, as I said."

"I will." Gwen swallowed hard. "You be careful too."

Suddenly Rhun's face broke into a wide grin, reminding her very much of Prince Hywel. "I always am."

Gwen spent an unrestful night beside King Owain's bed, spooning broth into him and being spelled every few hours by the king's manservant, Tudur. A man in his sixties, he was far sprier than King Owain himself, though the king was twenty years younger. Rail thin, Tudur had a full head of a white hair, which he had a tendency to run his hands through so it stuck up on end. Gwen supposed that keeping up with King Owain had kept him fit. Certainly King Owain trusted him, and Tudur knew more about what went on in the king's household than anyone but Taran.

Having finally managed to get a few solid hours of sleep before dawn, Gwen woke to find King Owain looming over her. "Where is the army?" he said, without preamble. "How could they leave without me!"

Tudur hurried into the room, a clean basin in his hand. "My lord! What are you doing on your feet?"

King Owain waved a hand. "I am perfectly well, Tudur."

"You and I both know that is not true, sire," Tudur said. "And your sons moved the army forward because the lords and captains determined it was time to do so. The advance continues, and the assault on Mold will happen as you yourself planned. Now, get back in bed."

King Owain glared at his manservant and then turned to Gwen. "Bossy isn't he? He's worse than you." But he did move away from her at a shambling walk towards his room.

Gwen shot Tudur a relieved look. She had never heard anyone speak to King Owain that way, not even Cristina, who was generally honey-sweet with him, except when she was angry.

"I am feeling much better," King Owain said, once he was settled under the covers, and immediately proved his words untrue by leaning over the side of the bed and vomiting into the basin Tudur had put there a few moments before.

"It is the motion that upsets his belly," Tudur said to Gwen, as an aside. "This is the first time he's vomited in hours." He looked at her from under bushy eyebrows. "That's your doing, you know. You sat beside him and fed him, and it allowed him to turn a corner."

"I will keep at it," Gwen said.

Tudur helped King Owain out of his soiled clothes, and for the next four hours, Gwen sat beside the king, feeding him a spoonful of broth a dozen times an hour, waking him to do so because he would fall asleep between feedings.

At one point, however, he came more awake and seemed to focus on her more fully for the first time since he'd tried to stand. "Why are you here, Gwen? What of the dead woman? Did she really look like you?"

"Somewhat," Gwen said.

"Did you find her murderer?"

"In a manner of speaking," Gwen said.

"Tell me," King Owain said.

Gwen was opening her mouth to obey, but at that moment the king put out a hand and sunk down further into the covers. "Never mind. I just need to lie here and settle myself. I want you to send Tudur in to me while you find food for yourself."

Gwen didn't argue. "Yes, sire." Before leaving, she put a hand to the king's forehead. It was remarkably cool, especially compared to how he'd been burning up before.

Truthfully, it was a moment for which Gwen had been waiting. She wanted to stretch and eat, perhaps walk around the monastery grounds to get the smell of the sick room out of her nostrils. She had also made no progress towards her charge of spying on the men in King Owain's court. She hadn't even seen anyone with especially big feet. When Gareth had suggested she stay with King Owain, neither of them had realized how sick the king really was, and how little she'd be able to leave his bedside.

As she walked from the king's quarters to the kitchen, the corridors of the monastery bustled with minor lords, their servants, and guardsmen. All of them were waiting for King Owain to get well and were no doubt chafing at being left behind. Everyone wanted to be with the army.

Upon entering the passageway that led to the kitchen, Gwen almost ran into Cynan, King Owain's next oldest son after Hywel. She was heading towards the kitchen, and he was coming from it. They both pulled up short.

"What are you doing away from the king's side?" Cynan said in a demanding voice.

Gwen hardly knew the man, and his vehemence made her take a step back. "Tudur is with him. King Owain suggested I take a moment for myself since I've been sitting with him since dawn and haven't eaten today. It's already noon."

Cynan took a step towards her, his anger vanishing like mist and his face pale but hopeful. "You mean ... he spoke to you?"

"Yes." Gwen looked at Cynan warily. "Why wouldn't he?"

"We'd heard—I mean, the men had understood him to be at death's door, and that he would not recover from this illness."

Gwen tried to nod and shake her head at the same time, anxious to dispel his fear for his father. Cynan might not have spent very much time at the king's court at Aber Castle and be newly anointed as the captain of the king's *teulu,* but that didn't mean the king hadn't always been the hub around which the spokes of his world revolved.

"He's very ill," Gwen said. "He has been very ill, but he's on the mend now. His fever has fallen, and he is keeping down broth for the most part. Who told you otherwise?"

Cynan's face darkened. "One of the other captains. Lord Goronwy's, I think."

Gwen licked her lips. "I don't know what to make of that. But no, the king will live. He was even able to stand, though Tudur shooed him back to bed right away. Motion is bad for his composure. I—" Gwen broke off as Cynan's attention was caught by something behind her.

He brushed passed her, hurrying down the passageway to the doorway that led into the cloister. He went through it, turning to the left and disappearing. Curious as to what could have made him so concerned, Gwen darted after him. As she reached the doorway between the passage and the cloister, she saw him disappearing into the courtyard of the monastery. Continuing to follow, Gwen reached the courtyard and found it in disarray.

King Owain, under no obligation to do what anyone wanted him to do, hadn't listened to Tudur's wisdom or hers. With an alarmed protest, Gwen dashed forward to where he was pulling himself into the saddle. "Please no, my lord!"

Cynan stood at his father's stirrup too, looking up at him. "Is this wise, my lord? It was only a moment ago that I learned from Gwen that you were recovering. You shouldn't risk your health just when you are finally on the mend."

"Wise? Perhaps not." King Owain looked around at the men in the courtyard. Many were smiling and bore relieved expressions on their faces. "Necessary, yes."

Cynan bowed his head. "I give way." He strode to where one of the men-at-arms was standing holding the bridle of his horse and mounted.

Then King Owain actually smiled down at Gwen from his seat on his horse. "Don't worry so much, my dear. I have been King of Gwynedd for ten years. Trust me to know what I am doing."

17

Gwen

"This is mad, Tudur," Gwen said in an undertone as she waited for her own horse to be brought from the stable.

"I know," Tudur said. "He wouldn't listen to reason, so we must be the reasonable ones instead. We will ride with him and wait beside him when he needs to rest. At least the rain has held off today."

Gwen was still shaking her head as one of the stable boys boosted her onto her horse. The *teulu* formed up around the king, along with the half-dozen noblemen who'd come to fight this battle with him, and an equal number of servants and workers who accompanied the king wherever he went. The noblemen had their own retinues as well, their own tents, and their own carts. She knew some of them from Aber, but many were from eastern or southern Gwynedd, and she'd seen them only in passing in the times they'd come to pay their respects to the king.

The more she examined the faces of each confidant to the king, made small talk with them, and rode among them, the more the hair on the back of her neck stood straight up. One of these men could easily be the killer. But which one? And why had both Cynan and Prince Rhun mentioned Lord Goronwy? Was his absence significant, given that his longtime companion, son-in-law, and king was so ill?

Gwen thought that riding even the few miles to Lord Morgan's fort was a very bad idea, but the king was right in a way—if rumor had it that he was dying, what better way to combat that rumor than to appear in the courtyard, cloaked and booted for war?

For Gwen's part, if it meant sleeping on a pallet with Gareth another night instead of alone at the monastery, she could hardly be sorry. She *had* suggested that the king send a fast rider to the fort to warn Einion that he was coming; King Owain had agreed it would be unwise to descend upon the local lord with a hundred men to feed and house with no more notice than the time it took for them to ride up the road to the gatehouse.

"I want to visit Cilcain's chapel too," King Owain said, "even if it isn't on the way."

Gwen had a vision of Father Alun making welcome the royal company, which would proceed to run roughshod over the villagers, causing Gareth no end of grief. But again, she acquiesced and promised to bring him there before turning south to Lord Morgan's fort. Privately, she didn't think he would make it that far and, unfortunately, she was right.

Shortly after riding through the pass south of Moel Arthur, Cynan made a stab with his hand for his father and shouted, "He's going over!"

Everyone pulled up as the king fell more than dismounted from his horse. He landed on his knees beside the road and brought up what little he'd eaten and all the water he'd recently drunk. Then he lay on his side in the grass, shaking and shivering, unable to rise to continue the journey even in the back of one of the carts.

Gwen and Tudur were beside him instantly, working to get a blanket underneath him. Gwen covered him with two more. Then she hovered over him, wrapping her arms around his bulky shoulders in hopes of warming him. The snow had long since melted, so he wasn't lying in it, but the grass beside the road was wet and the ground water-logged. The damp would soon seep through everything.

"I'm sorry, Gwen," King Owain said, his teeth chattering. "I shouldn't have come."

The truth of his statement was so obvious it needed no reply, so Gwen said, "My lord, may I suggest that you send everyone who isn't absolutely needed for your guard on ahead to the princes' camp? They can tell Prince Hywel and Prince Rhun what has happened. Perhaps they can return with help."

King Owain gave a jerky nod. "Better that my nobles don't see me in my weakened condition for longer than necessary, eh, Gwen? You would have made someone a fine queen. Politics is in your blood."

He waved a hand at Cynan, who'd been standing close enough to be attentive but far enough away such that he remained out of range of King Owain's sickness.

Gwen had meant only that they were holding up the whole caravan, and the nobles would soon be anxious and irritated at the delay. It was still the right choice, however, as was clear once Gwen explained her suggestion to Cynan. His expression lightened.

"Madoc can take them." And then he gave a swift grin. "It will serve him right to have to speak to people and lead them for once. Being the younger brother, he doesn't often have to."

There was no bite in his tone—just mischievousness and love. Rhun and Hywel had a similar relationship, except Hywel was more outgoing than Madoc, and Rhun was the heir to the throne instead of third in line like Cynan.

Soon the only people left in attendance were a reduced guard of fifteen, Tudur, Cynan, and Gwen. They'd been left a cart and a driver too, for when the king found the ability to rise, they would need it.

The bed of the cart had been full of cooking supplies, but it had been a matter of a few moments work to disperse them among the other carts. King Owain's men set to work building a fire, and soon it blazed up, bathing everyone in its heat. Meanwhile, they moved the king to a dryer spot under the spreading branches of an old oak tree and covered him with more blankets that Cynan had collected before the carts departed.

The new spot they'd chosen was damp, but that was the extent to which the weather was a problem. If need be, they could erect the king's tent around him right beside the road. After a brief consultation, they deferred doing so for now. While a tent would protect him from rain or snow, he couldn't lie as close to the fire if he was inside it.

"We have less than a mile to go to the village," Gwen reassured the king. "We will get there, if not this hour then in the next one."

"If I don't live to see them again, tell my boys that I love them," King Owain said.

Gwen felt at the king's forehead. His fever had returned. Until this moment, he'd managed to sustain a gap of almost six hours between bouts of vomiting, which was probably why he'd decided he was well enough to ride. According to Tudur, the previous day, King Owain hadn't kept anything down for longer than the time it took Tudur to empty the chamber pot and return.

"You're not going to die," she said flatly. "Two steps forward, one step back, my lord. You're recovering. You've just done too much today."

And her words proved true, because now that he was lying down again, he was no longer vomiting. If she could keep him warm, and if she could eventually get him settled in a bed so he didn't have to move, she could start over with the regime of broth and put him back on the road to health.

King Owain looked somewhat mollified. "You really believe that, don't you?"

"I do." What she didn't say was that he would still be believing it too if he hadn't refused to listen to her and Tudur.

"If I lie on my left side and don't move at all, I can contain myself."

"Then don't move," Gwen said. "I'd like to eventually get you into that cart bed, and then you can sleep there all night if you have to."

"The driver can park me in the stable." King Owain actually managed a slight laugh. "If it was good enough for our Lord and Savior, it can be good enough for me."

Gwen remained beside the king as the sun slowly lowered behind the hills to the west. She didn't have any broth, but she warmed mead in a pot they'd been left and fed him that. It was sweet and soothing—and something with which to fill his stomach, which was all she cared about.

The king slept for a time; when he awoke, he seemed better until he tried to rise, at which point he vomited yet again. As he shuddered and shook in his blankets, curled up around his belly, the king gripped Gwen's hand. That it was a strong grip gave her hope that what she'd told him was true: he wasn't dying. But then he tugged her closer so she had to put her ear right next to his head.

"I never should have allowed your father to leave Aber."

"Sire, please—"

The king squeezed her hand again. "My temper has been my downfall all my life. It was the same for my father, though some might say it was the fire in him that gave him the drive to overcome every obstacle to regain his throne. But it also sent my brother to his death. I pray that my stubbornness never sends my sons to theirs."

Gwen didn't know how to answer that except to say, "You are not your father."

"We'll see." The king's eyes closed. For a moment she thought he had returned to sleep and that his outburst had been a form of sleep-walking, but then he said, "I never should have married Cristina either."

Gwen made no reply to that, because there was none to make, and she glanced around quickly to make sure she was the only one within earshot. Then the king's hand loosened in hers, and he really did sleep. A coldness ran all through her that wasn't due to the breeze that had risen now that the sun was going down.

King Owain shouldn't have married Cristina. Everyone at Aber had known it long before the wedding. If Cristina knew the king had regrets about their marriage, she would be anxious and enraged, never a good combination in their queen. Her jealousy of King Owain's other women and her protectiveness of her sons were already troublesome.

The last time Gwen had seen Cristina and the king together, a shouting match had erupted between them in the queen's quarters, ending in the king storming from the room. He'd left a few hours later for the front lines of this war and had not returned to Aber.

As the king slept on, Gwen calculated and recalculated the time it would take to get to the camp and hoped that Rhun or Hywel would come at any moment. Gareth had said that it lay only a mile and a half beyond Cilcain, but perhaps her sense of time and distance was distorted by her anxiety for the king.

Cynan, for his part, maintained a constant vigil on the road. He paced back and forth along it, leaving them occasionally to scout the road at either end beyond the limits of what they could see from where the king lay. Afraid of Ranulf's men coming upon them unawares, Cynan sent other men in all directions.

At one point he came back to her and said under his breath. "I almost regret sending Madoc with the others instead of going myself. I hate waiting, and I would have returned with help by now."

Privately, Gwen thought Madoc would have stayed behind and done all the same things, but without the nervous energy Cynan displayed.

But then at last, before another half-hour had passed, Rhun rode around the corner to the east, accompanied by Godfrid and his men. Cynan ran forward to catch the bridle of Rhun's horse as he reined in, and Rhun dismounted and loped towards his father, with Cynan beside him, detailing all the while what had happened. Rhun fell to his knees beside Gwen. At the sound of his eldest son's voice, King Owain lifted his hand weakly in greeting, a vague smile on his lips, though his eyes remained closed.

Rhun took King Owain's hand, even as he said to Gwen, "You were supposed to keep him at the monastery."

Gwen gave a gasp of protest, but before she could actually speak, Rhun made a dismissive motion with his hand.

"Ignore me. I was a fool to think anyone could stop my father from doing what he chose, when he chose. He is pig-headed."

King Owain opened his eyes. “Don’t blame Gwen or Cynan, son. I’m a stubborn old fool.”

“You are not,” Cynan said staunchly. “Put it down to how healthy you’ve been for so long. You have no patience for illness.”

“Now that’s the truth there, my boy,” the king said, and he even managed a wink at his younger son.

Leaving King Owain to Cynan and Rhun, Gwen rose to her feet and went to where Godfrid waited with his company.

“This wasn’t what we needed today,” he said when she reached him.

“Has something else happened?” Gwen said.

“The king’s spies near Mold say we are too late. The castle is refortified,” Godfrid said. “Both he and Ranulf moved at the same time, but Ranulf beat us to it.”

“Will we keep on?” Gwen said.

Godfrid grunted. “What can we do? For now, we’re committed to the assault, but none of your nobles have the stomach for a long siege, which, of course, is what Ranulf is counting on.”

“We’ve had victories elsewhere,” Gwen said.

“You have, but not this week, and now with this—” Godfrid gestured to where the king lay. “Some will be questioning Gwynedd’s leadership. You need a victory here, or you will be forced to retreat with your tail between your legs.”

“Have you said as much to Hywel?” Gwen said.

“I have.”

Gwen didn't like the image Godfrid had drawn, and none of the men would like it either. King Owain led the coalition of nobles who formed the Welsh side of this conflict. Those in Gwynedd owed him loyalty as a matter of course, but those from Powys or from regions to the south followed him because his leadership led to victories, which meant land, money, and power.

In King Owain's absence, the responsibility for delivering those victories fell to Rhun and Hywel, as his elder sons. That King Owain hadn't actually fought in a battle in years and this arrangement was no different from normal (except for the king's illness) was irrelevant.

In short order, Rhun accomplished what Gwen and Cynan could not, which was to ride roughshod over the immediacy of his father's illness and order the men to lift the king bodily into the cart. The king vomited twice in the process, but once he was settled in the cart bed, braced against Cynan so he wouldn't rock too much, his stomach calmed down again. Gwen waved Tudur onto the seat next to the driver, and she took a spot in the back next to the king.

The cart set off, and after a half-mile, the king fell asleep to the rocking motion.

Cynan's face remained tight with concern. "His condition is such that he could fall asleep and never wake!" He spoke in loud whisper so Gwen could hear him over the clopping of the horses' hooves and the rumble of the cart wheels on the road.

"I will tell you what I told Rhun: he is very ill, but he isn't at death's door. I do hope, though, that he will sleep even after we reach Morgan's fort. I told him I'd leave him in the back of the cart rather than disturb him."

That got a smile from Cynan, though it disappeared instantly. He twisted in his seat, trying not to disturb his father's rest but anxious about how much farther they had to go. It was fully dark now, and Gwen couldn't see anything but the shadows of trees that lined the road and the faint outline of fields beyond. The only light available was thrown out by the torches carried by Godfrid's men.

Like Cynan, she sat leaning against the side of the cart. She had her feet tucked under her cloak and a blanket wrapped around her shoulders and tried not to crack her teeth at the jostling of the cart on the rough road. She'd take a horse any hour over this.

When they reached the village of Cilcain, however, Rhun didn't turn south to Morgan's fort. Instead, he led them right through the crossroads. Gwen tried to hail him unobtrusively, not wanting to question his leadership or his sense of direction in front of the other men, but Godfrid pulled up beside the cart and shushed her.

"Trust him, Gwen. He knows what he's doing."

She subsided, and before another hour had passed, they arrived at the new encampment, King Owain still asleep.

The camp for the kings and princes sat on a hill above the plain and was reached by a road that switched back and forth across the face of the hill, much like the road to Lord Morgan's fort. The slopes were well forested, since the hillside was no good for farming. It did seem as if the top had once housed a settlement, since it consisted of a cleared space, a hundred and fifty yards by two hundred. The larger camp for the spearmen and archers was located to the southeast (and downwind) of the hill.

Gareth appeared beside the cart the moment it came to a halt, and Rhun was all business again, insisting on overseeing the transfer of his father from the cart bed to his tent, which had already been set up.

"I am happy to see you, *cariad*, but not the king in this condition." Gareth held out his hand to help Gwen out of the cart. Once her feet hit the ground, she staggered a bit, her legs and back stiff from the ride. Gareth embraced her, and Gwen felt tears pricking at the corners of her eyes again. She fought them back. She was *so* tired and worn out.

And cold too. A dozen fires blazed from within stone rings, raising the temperature of the surrounding area. The rain had continued to hold off, but now that the sun had set, the air was genuinely cold again. Gwen hoped it wouldn't snow by morning, and she shivered at the thought.

Gareth tightened his hold on her, his fingers clenching the wool at the back of her cloak. "The princes weren't pleased to hear that their father had left the monastery and fallen ill beside the road."

"I can't say I was either!" Gwen looked up into her husband's face. "The king sent me away from the sick room to get some air, and by the time I discovered what he planned, he'd already mounted his horse. He's seen the error of his ways, obviously."

"It is hard for a king to admit he is wrong," Gareth said. "I'm sorry to run off on you, but I can't be here to assist you or the princes. I have business in the village."

"In Cilcain?" Gwen said.

"Not Cilcain, though I spent all day questioning the villagers there," Gareth said. "To no avail, mind you. I don't know which of us had the more tedious job."

Gwen gave him a commiserating smile.

Gareth scoffed at himself. "It would be unfair to think my day was worse than yours, I admit. But no, this time I'm headed to the village of Gwern-y-waun, and my task isn't related to the investigation, though if the chance appears to speak to someone about Adeline and Cole, I will."

"How can what you're about to do not be related to our investigation?" Gwen said.

Gareth smiled. "We are at war, *cariad*. I am tasked with subduing the village, not that it should amount to more than a brief show of force followed by friendly mingling over cups of mead. Or at least I hope that's all it amounts to. Madoc and I will be off in a moment—and Godfrid too if he wants to come."

"If nothing else, those two will keep you well entertained." Gwen gave her husband another hug.

He laughed. "Two more different princes could not be found, except they both are intelligent in their own way. It has been helpful to hear their thoughts on the investigation, even if what they've concluded hasn't brought us any closer to finding our killer."

"Have we given up on the idea that Cole was murdered by a different man than the one who created the deception as a whole?"

"Not necessarily." Gareth stretched his back, trying to warm his muscles. "If such a man exists, either he killed Cole for murdering Adeline, or he killed Cole because he thought he was me. I don't much like the idea of such a man running around free, but he isn't my chief concern right now."

Gwen nodded. "It's the man behind the deception you're most worried about."

"My only comfort is that he may not yet know we are on to him," Gareth said. "Only a few of the king's men are aware of our travels during the last few days, and whatever we have done is surely overshadowed by the coming siege. If he doesn't know we're aware that a plot against the king is afoot, we still have a chance to sneak up on him unawares."

Gwen shivered again, and not from the cold this time. "You may have had a brother you didn't know about, Gareth."

"If Cole was my brother, I don't care to claim him." Gareth looked down at her, his face full of concern. "Stay near the king or the princes while I'm gone, will you?"

"I won't wander off. I promise," Gwen said, "and you keep your eyes open too."

"Always."

And then she had to watch Gareth walk away again. Bereft, she didn't even know which tent was his, though that wouldn't be hard to find out. Because this camp was just being established, the activity leaned closer to chaotic than organized. Men were still digging the latrine pits and setting up tents. Her stomach growled as the smell of stewing mutton reached her.

Most wars were conducted in summer, due to the better weather, but going to war after the harvest, as they were now, made sense too. Food was momentarily plentiful because King Owain had received tithes of grain and animals from his people. While eating up his supplies so early in the winter might not bode well for next spring, it did mean that he could feed his army.

"Gwen."

She was started out of her reverie by Prince Rhun, back again, but this time accompanied by Hywel.

"Is the king—"

"He is resting and no worse than before," Rhun said.

"I will go to him now," Gwen said.

Rhun stayed her with a hand to her arm. "Can we talk again about poison?"

Gwen made a rueful face. "We can talk about it. Men fall ill with the flux during wartime. I assumed—" She broke off at the dark look Hywel sent her, but then said, "We assume things every day, my lord. If I feared poison every time a man became ill or murder every time a man died, I'd end up hiding on my pallet with the blankets pulled over my head and never come out again."

Hywel softened his stance slightly. "I despise the word and the concept."

"Is fear of poison why you brought the king here instead of to Lord Morgan's fort, which would have been more comfortable for him?" Gwen said to Prince Rhun.

"That is exactly why," Hywel said.

Rhun put a dispelling hand on his brother's arm before focusing again on Gwen. "If it were poison, what could it be?"

Gwen considered King Owain's symptoms, which included nausea, vomiting and diarrhea, of course, but also a fever, and some incoherence. Gwen had attributed the last symptom to a combination of exhaustion, fever, and dehydration. Taken together, King Owain's illness appeared to be a severe presentation of the flux, except—

"Wait here." Gwen hurried back to her horse, and opened her saddle bag, though not without fumbling with the ties that kept it closed because her fingers were cold. She pulled out her box of herbal remedies, set it on the ground to get it out of the way, and then returned to the bag to find her book of poisons, illnesses, and cures.

Hywel had come with her, and he peered over her shoulder at the book. "What is that?"

Gwen glanced at him before returning her eyes to the pages. "Back in Aberystwyth, during the time I was first with Gareth, I encountered a lawyer whose task was to defend a thief. He had a little book like this one, smaller than the palm of my hand. The laws of Wales had been recorded in it, along with all his notes and addendums.

"It was only when we were in Aberystwyth last summer that I remembered it. After we returned to Gwynedd, I asked Taran to make me a book, except with the pages still blank, to more permanently record what I learned from the investigations

Gareth and I undertake. Gareth keeps scraps of paper in his bag to sketch images of suspects and victims, why not a little book for me?" In fact, she'd spent much of the lonely autumn filling in the pages with everything she knew about murder.

"And you wrote about poisons in there?" Rhun said.

"I did." She put her finger on a passage. "I don't think the king has been given one of the deadly three: monkshood, hemlock, or belladonna, because the symptoms are wrong, but he could have taken foxglove or even peony. Given in lower doses, these both cause nausea and vomiting." Gwen picked at her bottom lip with the nail of her pinky finger. "Not mandrake either."

"Why not?" Hywel said.

Gwen looked over at him. "Some of these herbs are so poisonous there's hardly a safe dose that will only cause the kind of vomiting he's experiencing. Mandrake will put a person into permanent sleep." Gwen closed the book, shaking her head. "I don't know. I'd have to work backwards from what he ate and when it happened to be able to tell you more, but we aren't even at the monastery now."

Rhun gave an uncharacteristic growl that rumbled low in his chest. "For all that I can't condone my father's decision to ride with his men, I am not sorry he's here. We're safer—and stronger—when we're together."

18

Gareth

The look on Gwen's face as he left her behind had told Gareth all he needed to know about how her day had been. The king was very ill—maybe not as far gone as Gareth had been led to believe by the rumors swirling around the camp, but ill nonetheless. Either his illness had made a dramatic improvement, or the men he'd spoken to had exaggerated the danger. Perhaps both. Sometimes supposing the worst was preferable to being surprised by it later.

As he'd told Gwen, Gareth had spent the whole day in Cilcain going from house to house and questioning the inhabitants of the village as to what they'd seen the night Cole and Adeline had died. What he'd discovered was a bucket full of nothing. Nobody had seen them. Nobody knew anything about riders passing through the village in the night. It had been a relief to leave the unanswered questions behind him and return to his regular duties as Prince Hywel's captain.

To that end, Gareth had gathered up a mixed group of men to ride to Gwern-y-waun, located just down the hill to the northeast of the princes' camp. Godfrid and his men rode among them. Though nobody was paying the Danes in gold, effectively they were mercenaries. They had fewer definitive tasks to accomplish, which was one reason Rhun had taken them with him when he'd gone to fetch his father.

The men of Rhun's own *teulu*, while a strong fighting force of themselves, were also the leaders of other men, and those in the general army looked to the knights and men-at-arms who served the princes and the king for guidance. The common men didn't entirely trust, and thus would be reluctant to take orders from, a Dane. Too many Welshmen had died on Danish swords, some not that long ago, for most Welshmen to relish fighting alongside them.

That said, the men-at-arms who served the princes mingled well with the men of Dublin, speaking in a mix of Welsh and Danish without regard for proper grammar or pronunciation. Gareth enjoyed listening to the banter, which even without Madoc would have meant for an entertaining evening. With Madoc, as was evident within moments of setting out, the result could be downright dangerous. He may have kept nearly silent in the presence of his elder brothers, but something about the Norsemen had him far more talkative than usual. Currently, they were trying to teach him Danish profanity, to general hilarity all around.

The men needed their fun, because tomorrow—or the next day—they would go to war.

Infected by the mood of his men, Godfrid reached out from where he was riding beside Gareth and punched him on the upper arm. "I want to know all about the progress of this investigation."

Gareth rubbed at his arm, thankful for the mail that protected it, because otherwise the punch would have stung. "I intend to tell you everything I know over a large draught of mead just as soon as I can run one to earth."

"That should go down well," Godfrid said, complacently.

Hywel was convinced that spies for Ranulf were hidden in plain sight in the countryside, which was why he had asked Gareth to lead this overt show of force. No village headman would ever think to counter a company of thirty mounted men-at-arms and knights, especially when their numbers might be comparable to the number of men in the whole village. Armed men were daunting. Drunken men even more so.

Gareth's men weren't drunk, but they were giving a good impression of it, which was all to the good. It gave the villagers the chance to prepare to greet them, as well as fair warning so they had time to spirit away their daughters to some place safe. Likely, Prince Godfrid had already thought of that, which was why he had encouraged his men's play.

In short order, they reached the village green where, to no one's surprise, the village headman met them with what looked like every man in the village backing him up.

Thirty soldiers. Thirty village men. Just as Gareth had expected.

Several of Gareth's men carried torches, and combining these with the dozen in the hands of various villagers meant that everyone could see everyone else clearly, even if the light blinded their eyes to movement beyond the green.

Gareth dismounted and tossed his reins to one of his men. He could have remained mounted and spoken to the headman from on high, but that wasn't how he wanted to be perceived. If it had been up to him instead of a direct order from Prince Hywel, he would have ridden down from the camp with five men, brought a jug of mead as a sign of goodwill, and drunk it right here on the green with them.

Still, now that he was here, he could forgive Hywel for ordering the larger force. He hadn't done so because it was the better plan, but because he was angry and fearful about his father's health, the plot against Gareth and Gwen, about which they still knew far too little, and the coming assault on Mold.

So Gareth stuck out his arm to the headman with aplomb and goodwill. "We have descended on you in force, but you have no need to fear us. My lord has pledged not to strip your homes or your lands of food or possessions. Or your women. The main body of the army is camped a half-mile to the south of you here, and orders have been given for the men to keep to it tonight."

The headman had initially greeted Gareth's proffered arm with suspicion, but at his words, real relief swept across his face. "Thank you, my lord. I am Sion ap Robat, and I welcome you and your men to our village."

"We were hoping to be welcomed to your inn as well," Gareth said.

Sion bowed. "My home is your home, my lord." He straightened and gestured to the east. "Please come with me."

He set off towards the inn. Gareth waved the rest of the soldiers off their horses and then fell into step beside him. "I'm surprised your village can maintain an inn."

Taverns such as the one at Cilcain were common, since (as in the great hall at Lord Morgan's fort or at Aber), men and women liked to gather together at the end of the day at a place where they could drink and talk. With winter coming, nights were growing longer, and a man could sleep only so much. To have the village together in one place most evenings saved on candles and firewood. It was friendlier too.

But an inn was something else entirely, requiring the resources to build a structure on the scale of a manor house and the commerce to justify it.

"Ach, I know what you're thinking. With Mold Castle or Lord Morgan's stronghold so close, why would anyone stop here instead of there? Here's the real truth." Sion leaned in close to whisper conspiratorially. "We have the best mead and the best cook in all of Gwynedd. People come for miles to sample our fare. Just the other day, a fine lord from west of the Conwy by his accent stopped for the night with his companions."

Gareth's step faltered for an instant. He covered up the hesitation with an extra-long stride and said, "When was this?"

"Hmmm. Three or four nights ago?" Sion said, his brow furrowing. "I'd have to look in my ledger."

"What was the lord's name?"

"He called himself Gareth ap Rhys."

Gareth almost choked on his own saliva. *What had he been expecting? The man to name himself?* He cleared his throat. “Had this Gareth ever stopped here before?”

“No, my lord.” Sion’s expression was one of studied neutrality.

“This lord did not comport himself well?”

“I would never speak ill of a customer. We don’t get many men as high as he.”

“*And a good thing too*, are the words you aren’t saying.”

Sion shrugged. “Still, we’re full up five nights out of six.”

Gareth looked at the headman with new respect, even as his stomach tied itself in knots yet again. “You own the inn.”

“My father built it with his own hands,” Sion said. “Most people don’t understand that a better life can cost nothing more than time and effort.”

Gareth almost laughed at the sudden smoothing of Sion’s elocution. The last words he’d said had been a quote from someone else. “Is that what your father used to say?”

“Every day, God rest his soul,” Sion said.

“Would I have known your father?” Gareth said.

“He was a man-at-arms in the Earl of Chester’s retinue.” Sion drew in a breath before holding out a supplicating hand to Gareth. “My loyalties lie with King Owain, of course.”

“Of course,” Gareth said, but he felt the chill that had fallen between them at the innkeeper’s words. He tried to dispel it, if only because Sion was so voluble a talker and a wealth of information. Gareth wanted to know more about the man who'd given Sion his name. "So, your father retired to run an inn."

Some of the tension that was showing in Sion's manner eased. "He did. Have you ever been to the inn before tonight, my lord?"

"No, but I'm looking forward to it."

"And we are happy to welcome you." With an extravagant bow, he gestured Gareth's men inside.

Gareth was used to the dampening effect his presence had on the joviality of a tavern, so he held back at first and allowed everyone else to enter ahead of him. Madoc stepped to one side as well. At Madoc's own request, Gareth hadn't introduced him to the headman as a prince of Wales. He was very glad that he hadn't given Sion his own name either.

"Did I overhear Sion say that a lord stayed here a few days ago?"

"You did," Gareth said. "He called himself *Gareth ap Rhys.*"

"Holy hell," Madoc said. "What did the man look like? Was it this Cole?"

"I would imagine not, since Sion didn't blink an eye at my appearance," Gareth said.

"Christ, man. Why didn't you press him further?" Madoc said.

"I didn't want to show too much interest in his visitor in case my queries made him clam up too soon," Gareth said. "I thought I'd take it slowly. The night is young."

"What if I were to speak to him?" Madoc said.

Gareth nodded as he studied the young prince. Ten years younger than Gareth, Madoc had the surety of a much older man. That's what came from being one of a dozen sons of the King of Gwynedd.

"I would be grateful," Gareth said. "It goes without saying that we're trying to be discreet."

"Indeed." Madoc put a hand on Gareth's shoulder. "Leave it to me."

The inn consisted of a large main room, almost the size of Morgan's hall, with an adjacent smaller, more private chamber. The sleeping rooms were above, accessed by a stairway that ran against a side wall. Great beams supported the roof, and a large fire burned in a stone fireplace, which was built against the wall opposite the stairs. An overhanging smoke canopy vented out the back wall and prevented the room from being filled with smoke. Gareth was pleased to see that it was doing a reasonable job—better than the vent in the tavern at Aber, which had been designed poorly and tended to draft inwards instead of out.

Thirty of the village men had met Gareth's force on the green, but a few—mostly elderly—had stayed behind at the inn near the fire. Gareth headed towards them, not because he was cold in his thick cloak and leather gloves, but because he had learned over the years that the aged tended to look upon authority with more favor than the young. He didn't order a drink but instead settled back into the corner to watch the crowd for a while. His stomach growled. He had missed dinner and wished he wasn't on duty because he would like to take the opportunity to taste the fare here.

It was probably just as well he didn't, however. Sion might think he was obligated to serve Gareth for free.

That Sion's father had been a man-at-arms in the company of the Earl of Chester explained a great deal, mostly about how he'd acquired the money to build an inn in the first place. Whether or not he, in fact, had constructed the inn himself by hand, the land had to have been given to him by an overlord. In Saxon England, a village was carved out of the land belonging to the lord, and the homes were paid for by him too.

Bigger market towns like Shrewsbury had petitioned the English crown for independence from local lords. Merchants there owned their own land and houses. In Wales, more often than not, towns grew up next to a castle, or as in the case of Gwern-y-Waun, next to a mine and quarry. It was the productiveness of the lead mine, along with the beauty of the limestone found here—a source of building material for his castles—

that was one of the reasons King Owain had been so eager to press forward and take Mold Castle. The people here tithed to the Lord of Mold, which today happened to be the Earl of Chester.

Tomorrow ... well, they'd see about that.

19

Gareth

"You don't have a drink in your hand, laddie."

Gareth blinked and straightened, focusing on the man speaking to him, one of the elderly gentlemen at the nearest table. His face was deeply lined and his hair snow white. Gareth had been neglectful both of his manner and of his duty.

He smiled. "I don't, do I? If I were to acquire one, may I get another for you as well?"

"Four." The man nodded, looking very pleased with himself.

Gareth stood up, laughter on his lips. He had expected no less, since the man had three companions as aged as himself and knew a soft target when he saw one. Gareth edged his way through the crowded benches and tables to the serving area located against the wall opposite the fire. The old men would be more likely to answer Gareth's questions once they had another drink in front of them.

"Five." Gareth held up one hand, fingers spread wide, in case the bartender couldn't hear him over the hubbub.

An elbow dug into his ribs, accompanied by a grating voice. "If it isn't the incorruptible Gareth ap Rhys. Not so much on your high horse anymore, are you?"

The man next to Gareth was seated on a stool, drinking with a companion, and from the smell of him, which was wafting unpleasantly up to Gareth's nostrils, he was extremely drunk.

"How is that?" Gareth said, his cheerful mood dissipating in the face of yet another man confusing him for Cole.

"I knew you were just like the rest of us."

Gareth's eyes narrowed as he gazed down at the top of the man's head, sure he knew him from somewhere but unable to place him. Gareth bent forward, his elbows on the bar, trying to act nonchalant, though his heart was pounding loudly in his ears.

To hear his full name again, though in a completely different context from how Sion had used it, almost had him confused about who he was supposed to be. Sion's *Gareth ap Rhys* had been a lord from west of the Conwy River. Now he was either Lord Morgan's traitor or a brigand such as John Fletcher would have recognized.

The man glanced up at him, drained his drink, and gave a belch. The bartender had already placed two drinks in front of Gareth, and Gareth instantly swapped out the man's empty cup for a full one. He was glad it wasn't Sion tending the drinks and hoped Madoc was questioning him in a corner somewhere.

"Do I know you?" Gareth said.

The man grinned, showing yellow teeth, the same color as the mead he was drinking. "Served Prince Cadwaladr once upon a time, didn't you? Left because you didn't want to follow his orders if they sullied your hands. They're well and truly sullied now, aren't they?"

And with this last phrase, Gareth recognized the man by the way he talked. Looking many years older than when Gareth had last spoken to him, Morien had been a man-at-arms in Prince Cadwaladr's retinue at Aberystwyth when Gareth had belonged to the garrison. Now, instead of becoming angry at Morien's smirking face and ongoing insults, Gareth braced his right side against the bar and affected a curious look. "I wouldn't say so. Why do you?"

"Because we know the truth, don't we?" Morien said.

"Do we?"

"What are you going on about, Morien?" the man beside him said. Then he looked at Gareth. "Don't mind him. He's in his cups and doesn't know what he's saying."

"I'd like to hear it anyway." Gareth couldn't recall the newcomer's name. He wore a full beard that obscured his mouth and chin, but Gareth thought he remembered seeing him at Aber Castle a few years ago. As a younger man he'd had less gray in his hair and been unable to grow the beard he wore now.

Gareth didn't care about the man's origins. He wanted to get to the bottom of Morien's snide remarks before the man collapsed into drunkenness or his friend succeeded in silencing him. Gareth clapped Morien on the shoulder. "When was this?"

"What do you mean, *when*?" Morien sneered into his cup. "You rode next to the prince as fine as you please, didn't you? You and your lady wife."

"We're talking about Prince Hywel, right?" Gareth said, and then was annoyed with himself for picking up on Morien's habit of ending every sentence in a question.

Morien gave him a sour look. "You know I don't mean him."

"You're going to have to say what you mean," Gareth said.

"Cadwaladr." Morien took a long drink.

Gareth felt as if someone had poured a bucket of cold water over his head, and it was even now running down his back. He and Gwen had sworn that they wouldn't say Cadwaladr's name unless all evidence pointed to him, and here was testimony falling into his lap from the lips of a drunken man-at-arms.

Morien's friend made a disgusted sound at the back of his throat, reached across Morien to put a hand on his right shoulder, and tried to turn him away from Gareth. "Of course he meant Prince Hywel."

"Get off me!" Morien shoved his friend away. "Putting on airs with the Earl of Chester himself, weren't you?"

The rage that had been building in Gareth since he'd learned that Cole had been pretending to be him threatened to overwhelm him again, but he ruthlessly shoved it back down. "You saw me with Ranulf, the Earl of Chester, in the company of Prince Cadwaladr?"

Morien's friend growled. "Close your lips, Morien."

To Gareth's great relief, Morien ignored his friend, though his face had sunk into a sullen mask. "No."

Gareth crashed to earth. Was this not what he thought it was? He studied Morien through a half-dozen heartbeats and then said, "What exactly do you think I've done if you never saw me yourself?"

"I saw you," Morien said. "We all did, and we heard about what you'd done."

"From whom?"

Morien hesitated, seeming to realize for the first time that something might be amiss, either with him or with Gareth. "From one who was there."

"This is at Chester Castle?" Gareth said, taking a guess.

"No." Morien frowned again at Gareth, his puzzlement at Gareth's ignorance finally breaking through his mead-saturated brain.

Gareth bent closer to Morien, enduring his foul breath. "Go on."

"It was at Mold. Why are you asking all these questions when you were there yourself?" Morien said.

The man beyond Morien became more agitated than ever. Holding Morien's upper arm in a tight grip, he whispered something Gareth didn't catch into Morien's ear.

Morien jerked away so his elbow connected with his friend's chin. "I know who it was." He pointed at Gareth. "Gareth ap Rhys!"

His friend was shaking his head in little jerks, his eyes a bit wider than they should be. Sweat beaded on his forehead. The room was warm, but it wasn't that warm, and again he tugged on Morien's arm.

Morien took a long drink from his cup and slammed it down on the bar in front of him. "Another!"

Finally, the friend spoke loudly enough for Gareth to hear. "It was someone else, Morien!"

The man's urgency finally penetrated the drink in Morien's head. He gaped at his friend. "Of course it was him. You saw him too!"

His friend shook his head, and his eyes flicked from Morien's face to Gareth's and back again, trying to get Morien to *look*.

"It's too late to take back what's been said. You are surrounded by my men. Tell me what he's talking about." Gareth paused. "Pawl." He'd finally remembered the man's name. "Why did Cadwaladr meet with Ranulf?"

"How would I know?" Morien burped hugely and wiped the back of his hand across his mouth.

Gareth kept his eyes on Pawl's face, since it was he to whom Gareth had directed the question.

"It wasn't you, was it?" Pawl said.

"Whatever you think I've done, or have been told I've done, it's a lie. Again I must ask, why was I supposed to have met with the Earl of Chester at Cadwaladr's side?"

Pawl shot a glance around the tavern as if he might find a way out before he had to answer.

"You have nowhere to run. Your only choice is to tell me what you know."

Pawl licked his lips nervously. "As proof."

"Proof of what?"

"That Cadwaladr had support for his plan."

It was relief to have the truth laid out before him. Gareth hadn't even had to work that hard for it. The initial racing of Gareth's heart slowed, and his brain started to function again. He had most of the answers now. If he'd known that all he needed was one conversation with a drunken man-at-arms in Cadwaladr's retinue, he would have cornered one days ago. The truth was, he avoided interaction with Cadwaladr's men and for years had walked the other way if any approached.

In part, he hadn't wanted to be reminded of his ignominious departure from Cadwaladr's service, but he also hadn't wanted to thumb his nose in the faces of men who'd stayed. Nothing was more abhorrent than a self-righteous man.

"And what was that plan?"

Pawl shook his head. "I wasn't privy to that."

"But you know something," Gareth said. "What did Cadwaladr hope to get from Ranulf?"

"Men. Money."

Now they were really getting somewhere. "What are you two doing here in Gwern-y-waun?" Gareth said.

Blinking sleepily, Morien burped again. He seemed to have already forgotten what he'd told Gareth.

Pawl gave him a sour look and said, "Prince Cadwaladr's camp lies to the north of the village. We were given leave to enter the inn once our duties were done, same as you. There should be more of us soon."

That wasn't quite the same reason Gareth had brought his men to the village, but Pawl didn't need to know that. It did mean that Gareth had very little time before many more men would descend upon them. Gareth wanted to avoid a confrontation between King Owain's men and Prince Cadwaladr's on the village green. They might all be Welsh and ostensibly allies in this war, but they did not get along as a rule. On top of which, the last thing Gareth wanted was for word to get back to Cadwaladr that he was here—and that he'd been seen with Morien and Pawl.

"You two are part of the prince's *teulu*, aren't you?" Gareth said.

Morien laid down his head on the bar. "An honor."

When Gareth had known them before, they hadn't yet risen so high. He met Pawl's eyes above Morien's head. "How many of you in the prince's *teulu* believe my loyalties lie with Prince Cadwaladr?"

Pawl's brows came together. "What are you talking about? Nobody thinks your loyalties lie with Cadwaladr."

Gareth felt like his head was full of stuffing. "Then why would I ride to Mold at Cadwaladr's side?"

"To represent Prince Hywel and Prince Rhun to Ranulf, of course," Pawl said.

Gareth's mouth tasted of ash, and he only just managed to keep the shock from showing on his face, wiping it clean of all expression in an instant. *Cadwaladr had used Cole to convince Ranulf that the princes had allied themselves with Cadwaladr against their father*. And his whole *teulu* believed it.

And why wouldn't they? Welsh brothers and uncles had been at each other's throats since the beginning of time.

It was hard for that many to keep a secret, however, though the fact that Cadwaladr was allowing his men to leave their camp indicated how little he was worried about the rumor getting out. And again, for good reason. None of the king's men would ever believe that Hywel or Rhun would side with Cadwaladr. Even were Morien to walk right up to them and mock them with it, they would dismiss the idea out of hand. It was only because of the dead imposters that Gareth was taking him seriously.

Gareth craned his neck to look above the heads of the crowd gathered in the tavern. Sighting Madoc talking to Godfrid, Gareth signaled to him with one hand above his head.

While both princes made their way towards him, Gareth turned back to Pawl, "What orders has Cadwaladr given you specifically?"

"To obey our captain, as always."

"To what end?"

"As Morien told you, we don't know," Pawl said. "He hasn't said."

And as unlikely as it might seem, Gareth believed him. Whatever Cadwaladr's plot, it surely made no sense to tell the details of it to anyone but his closest confidants until right before they were asked to act. Gareth felt a little better. Whatever treachery Cadwaladr had planned remained in abeyance, at least for tonight.

Morien gave a huge burp. "Run back to your king and leave us be."

Gareth's brows drew together, and Pawl's face paled as he realized the mistake Morien had just made. He'd said, *your king*.

Pawl and Morien knew something more, even if they didn't know how it was meant to play out. It was time to go. Gareth jerked his head to Madoc. "These two need to come with us. Quietly if possible."

"Who are they?" Godfrid said.

"Cadwaladr's men. There are more on the way."

Godfrid snapped his fingers at two of his men, who closed in on Morien and encouraged him to move towards the door. He took a few unsteady steps, and then they grasped his upper arms because he needed assistance to walk. Before Pawl could leave, however, Gareth caught his arm in a tight grip and asked the question that always burned in his gut whenever he encountered one of Cadwaladr's men. "Why do you still serve him?"

"I'm paid to do so." Pawl drained the rest of his drink and then dabbed at his mouth with his sleeve. "What are you going to do with us?"

"It isn't what *I'm* going to do with you that you have to worry about." Gareth tugged him towards the door, following Morien, who'd already disappeared through it.

Pawl gave no trouble, allowing himself to be dragged outside. The moon had risen and shone weakly down at them through the scattered clouds. It had grown colder while they'd been inside the inn too, and Gareth could see the fog of his breath in the air.

And with that, Pawl slugged at Gareth's face with his free hand, jerked away, and made his bid for freedom. As Gareth reeled from the blow, Pawl raced away, his boots pounding heavily on the road and his shape appearing as hardly more than a black shadow in the night.

Gareth took off after him. As he hadn't drunk anything and was thinner and younger than Pawl, he gained on him quickly. After fifty yards, Gareth caught up to within a few feet. With an indrawn breath, he launched himself at Pawl, wrapping his arms around the man's hips and bringing him to the ground.

Pawl fell with a squeal and a thud. Scrabbling and jerking, he tried to get away, but Gareth held onto him tightly. Within a few moments, six others arrived to subdue Pawl more fully, two of them jerking him upright and away from Gareth. Evan was among the newcomers, and Gareth grasped his proffered hand in order to rise to his feet. He brushed the dirt from the road off his legs and arms, while Evan swiped at the back of his cloak.

"You're pretty spry for an old man," Evan said.

Gareth smirked. "You're older than I am."

"Which is why it was good that you reacted first," Evan said. "Better you than me."

"That was well done." Godfrid strolled up, Madoc in his wake. Neither had deigned to be among the men who'd run either.

Gareth's men tied Pawl's hands behind his back, which Gareth should have done in the first place. Before they could take Pawl away, however, Gareth stepped close, his face inches away from Cadwaladr's man. Because Gareth was the taller of the two, Pawl had to look up at him. "You have served Cadwaladr for too long. Your only hope of survival is to tell us everything you know."

Pawl swallowed hard, real fear in his eyes for the first time. Gareth jerked his chin to Evan, who led him away. Morien had already been coaxed onto a horse, too drunk to walk.

Madoc stepped beside Gareth. "I spoke with the headman."

Gareth had forgotten all about his request. "You wouldn't be telling me of it if you didn't have something important to say, my lord. I can see it in your face."

"Sion described to me the lord who passed through Gwern-y-waun four nights ago," Madoc said. "Big, burly, blond going gray."

A frisson of satisfaction coursed down Gareth's spine.

"He was accompanied by several men-at-arms and a married couple," Madoc went on. "The headman specifically mentioned that the married man, who went by the name Dai, not Gareth, bore a striking resemblance to you. When you dismounted on the green, his first thought was that you were the same man. As soon as you spoke to him, however, he knew he was mistaken."

"What a relief," Gareth said, mocking. "One wonders why the Earl of Chester didn't realize it too."

"The Earl of Chester?" Madoc said. "What does he have to do with this?"

"Everything," Gareth said. "With your permission, my lord, I will explain it all once we're back at the camp. It would be better to tell everyone at the same time."

It was only as Gareth mounted Braith, having ensured that his prisoners were secured, that he realized he'd never brought the old gentlemen their drinks.

20

Gwen

"Psst! Gwen!"

Gwen looked up to see her husband silhouetted in the doorway of King Owain's tent.

Gwen glanced first at the king, who was huddled before his brazier on a stool, wrapped in a blanket and sipping broth in a cup he was holding without assistance, which in and of itself was a huge triumph. He remained weak and shivery, but the fever had broken, and he claimed to be hungry. She rose to her feet and went to the doorway.

"I need you to come with me," Gareth said.

"I can't leave—"

"We're just here." Gareth indicated the fire circle closest to the king's tent, all of ten yards away. "You'll be able to respond immediately if he calls out to you."

"Go on, Gwen." Tudur ducked under Gareth's arm and entered the tent. "I can care for him a while."

"Did you sleep?" she said.

"Enough."

Gwen didn't believe Tudur, but she let Gareth lead her to the fire circle, where the companions waited for her. She pulled up short to see Cynan and Madoc among the listeners too. Before yesterday when they'd talked in the monastery warming room, they had never been part of the circle of confidants she'd known Hywel and Rhun to have, but it seemed they were in the thick of it now.

She liked them fine, as far as liking a pair of Welsh princes was something one even did, but she didn't know yet about trusting them. Hywel and Rhun clearly did, however, and that apparently was going to have to be good enough for her.

King Owain's tent was set back from any others but Rhun's and Hywel's, so they were far enough from the other soldiers in the camp that they couldn't be overheard. She glanced towards Hywel's tent, shadowed underneath some nearby trees. They could have met in there, except the walls gave the illusion of privacy without actually providing it. Gwen agreed that this was better.

Gareth held Gwen's hand to steady her as she stepped over the fallen log currently being used as a bench seat, and then he sat down beside her. The air was colder than before the sun had gone down—colder than in King Owain's tent where a brazier burned next to his bed. Happy for the warmth, she put her hands out to the fire. Her gloves were back in the king's tent.

It was Hywel who spoke first. "Gareth has new information that effectively brings his investigation into the deaths of the false Gareth and Gwen to a conclusion. While I might want more solid evidence than we have, I can't wait on it. We must act. I have called you here because what Gareth has discovered is so volatile that whatever we do from here on out must take place with one mind, one goal."

The prince then nodded at Gareth, who launched into a narration of his conversation with Pawl and Morien. As he talked, Gwen felt herself shivering, and no amount of heat from the fire was going to warm her. *Cadwaladr.* Gwen hated even to hear his name.

Gareth concluded with the information that Morien and Pawl were being held inside Hywel's tent, which explained further why they hadn't met in there. The knee of her husband's breeches also had a tear, which hadn't been there when she'd seen him earlier, indicating there had to be even more to this story than he'd told them. She could feel the looks being shot at them by the soldiers sitting at nearby fire pits. A number of them had been present when Gareth had gone to the village. They knew something was happening. They just didn't know what.

Gwen had no idea what Hywel and Rhun were going to tell them. How does one say to one's men that Prince Cadwaladr had betrayed them all again with the very man against whom they were supposed to be fighting?

Rhun tipped back his head and expelled an audible breath. "*That's* why Cadwaladr wanted Cole and Adeline with him—as proof that Hywel and I supported Cadwaladr?"

Hywel glanced at Gwen and Gareth. They had feared from the very beginning the role someone had wanted Cole to play. But this was so audacious a plan that it wasn't any wonder Rhun could barely believe it.

"Yes, my lord," Gareth said. "If Ranulf could be convinced that the two of you had switched sides and supported Cadwaladr against your father, then not only would Ranulf be more likely to throw in his lot with Cadwaladr, but the odds of his plan actually working would go way up. Cadwaladr's problem was that he needed me to convince his own men too. They needed reassurances that they could betray the king and get away with it. But that was a secret too great to keep."

"You are incorruptible," Hywel said, "which is why Ranulf took your presence as testimony that working with Cadwaladr might gain him Gwynedd." He glanced around at the others. "That's what our uncle wants, isn't it? Our father's throne."

Cynan grunted his assent. "Ranulf tried to work with Cadwaladr before. The plot failed because it was uncovered—by you, Gareth, I might add. Only a powerful incentive could have encouraged him to work with Cadwaladr again, and I can see how the sight of Cole acting as you might have been just what Ranulf needed."

"And then Cadwaladr killed Cole." Gareth drew out a bag and spilled the coins stored inside into his hand so everyone could see them. The gold and silver glinted in the firelight. "Or had him killed."

"Judas required thirty pieces of silver to betray Christ," Gwen said.

"There's eleven here," Gareth said. "Given that they were discarded on the ground, it seems Cole believed himself underpaid."

"How did Cadwaladr even know about Adeline's and Cole's existence?" Madoc said.

Hywel clutched his knees with his hands, staring into the fire. "Unless my uncle confesses, we may never know, and though I don't like guessing, in this case I will: his wife's family has lands in Shropshire. He's been to Shrewsbury many times. He could have seen the woman six months ago ... a year ... two years, and then a chance meeting with Cole, who was already something of a brigand, put the idea of impersonating Gareth into his head."

"He did look very much like Gareth," Gwen said.

"When Gareth's belongings fell into the river, the plot was born," Hywel concluded.

Rhun made a chopping motion with his hand. "It doesn't matter how, only that he did it. It's an easy forty miles to Shrewsbury from here. A few days' journey, a few pieces of silver as down payment, and he has his false Gareth and Gwen."

"Don't forget the death of Llywelyn. Cole could have killed him on Cadwaladr's orders," Gwen said, and then at the men's surprised looks, she added, "What? He killed him for someone, didn't he? Cadwaladr wouldn't want King Stephen's message to reach King Owain. It makes sense if it was he."

"Or perhaps it was for Ranulf, who would have objected equally to an alliance between King Stephen and Gwynedd," Hywel said.

Rhun stood abruptly. "We must take it as a given that everything we've planned for the upcoming campaign has reached Ranulf's ears through our uncle. Ranulf knows we're coming. He knows when. He knows how many men we have. Everything."

Hywel looked sharply at his brother. "Where is that letter from King Stephen?"

Rhun gaped at Hywel through several heartbeats and then said, "It's addressed to Father. I didn't open it."

"Maybe we should," Hywel said.

"I'll get it." Rhun disappeared inside his tent, which was to the left of King Owain's, and returned immediately. Once back at the fire, he sat with the missive on his lap for a moment, and then with a swift slice of his belt knife, broke the seal. As he unfolded it, complete silence fell on the companions.

Rhun read, his eyes flicking quickly across the page. "It says he is prepared to launch a joint attack on Chester and asks father to send a representative to meet with him to discuss the action as soon as it's convenient." He handed the letter to Hywel. "We already knew from Father Alun that Ranulf is facing an assault by the king's forces on his eastern flank."

"King Stephen may have given up waiting for a response," Gwen said. "He's never been a patient man."

"An alliance among his enemies is exactly what Ranulf would have wanted to avoid if he's working with Cadwaladr," Gareth said. "King Owain's sons would have wanted that letter to disappear too, were you really working with your uncle and Ranulf."

"I will send a man to Stephen immediately with our acceptance of the alliance. Mold should have been as good as ours, but with Cadwaladr feeding information to Ranulf, we have to wonder what traps he may have laid for us." Rhun gazed around at the others. "Our uncle has gone too far this time. I see now that there is nothing he won't do and no desire he won't put ahead of his family."

For her part, Gwen had come to that conclusion a long time ago, though it was a relief to hear someone else say it. She hated Cadwaladr, and hated herself for hating him because it ate her up inside. If it wasn't only she who felt this way—or how Gareth, Hywel, and she felt—it made it easier to let the emotion go.

"I admit the lengths to which he has gone are astounding." Godfrid stretched his legs out towards the fire and crossed his ankles. He was the only one among them who appeared relaxed.

Cynan was shaking his head. "I know what my uncle has done in the past, but even knowing that the plot is real, it seems far too elaborate and complicated to ever work."

That was too much for Gwen. "You don't know him like I do. Cadwaladr would never simply murder a woman and bury her in the woods. He would think it clever to hide the body in someone else's grave. He wouldn't simply conspire with the Earl of Chester. It's totally in character for Cadwaladr to create copies of Gareth and me in order to convince Ranulf that Rhun and Hywel had betrayed their own father."

Gareth nodded. "Elaborate plans and overthinking are *exactly* like him."

Rhun laughed mockingly. "Without the discovery of the bodies, Gareth might have dismissed the words of Morien and Pawl as drunken ramblings."

"We have to end this, Rhun." Hywel had finished reading the letter from King Stephen. "Our uncle can't be allowed to go free this time."

"We have to kill him, you mean," Rhun said.

Gwen swallowed down a gasp, less that the words had been spoken out loud, but that it had been Rhun to say them. Cynan and Madoc didn't look shocked at all, however, and Godfrid merely stroked his beard in a contemplative way.

"We can't just do it, though," Hywel said, "not without at least speaking to Father."

"We can't talk to him about this tonight, though," Rhun said. He and Hywel kept their eyes focused on each other. "He isn't well enough to hear it. They're still brothers."

"If Father is too ill to see justice done, that it must be we who do it," Cynan said.

We. All of the men in the group relaxed a little. *Yes. We're in this together,* the younger princes were saying. *We're brothers too.*

Hywel turned to the others, having concluded whatever silent communication he'd been having with Rhun. "We have to bring Cadwaladr in. He can't be allowed to roam free."

"We don't have real proof yet," Gwen said, remembering all those times King Owain refused to believe the worst of his brother, even when it was true.

"We have the word of two of his men, and the innkeeper in the village should recognize him," Hywel said. "It's true that if confronted, Cadwaladr could come up with any number of lies that would explain what he was doing in Shrewsbury recently or why he met with Ranulf. He might not even have killed either Adeline or Cole himself, further confusing the issue."

Rhun took in a breath. "We have enough proof for me. More importantly, we have leverage we can use against Ranulf that could bring us Mold Castle without a fight."

"We do?" Cynan said.

Rhun looked at his younger brother. "We have the letter from Stephen. We have proof in Gareth's own person that Hywel and I have not betrayed our father. Ranulf thinks that we have allied with Cadwaladr and are about to rise up to overthrow Father before Mold falls. We have not, of course. Cadwaladr lied to him. If we told Ranulf that we have uncovered Cadwaladr's plot and that the men he has given Cadwaladr are walking into a bloody fight, he might see better of this alliance."

"He will cut his losses," Hywel said. "Ranulf, like Cadwaladr, is only concerned about himself and his power. Losing a company of men will not aid him in that regard."

Godfrid lifted a hand. "Perhaps I can help—"

Just then, Tudur came out of the king's tent and approached the fire. He bowed to four Welsh princes and said, "Your father requests your presence."

The brothers looked at each other with consternation, but then as one they rose to their feet. Hywel still had the letter from

King Stephen in his hand. Godfrid, Gwen, and Gareth stayed seated, but Tudur gestured to them as well. "He wants all of you to come."

"He knows something's going on," Gareth said to Gwen and Godfrid in an undertone.

"He always knows," Hywel said grimly, having overheard. "I've been trying to lie to him and failing my entire life." They all followed Rhun toward King Owain's tent.

Godfrid put his hand on Hywel's shoulder. "Better if I don't come with you."

Hywel stopped in the doorway, half in and half out of the tent. "You said you had an idea?"

Godfrid made a dismissive motion with his head. "I will tell you later. It might no longer be appropriate, depending on what your father says."

Thus, only the four princes, Gareth, and Gwen filed into King Owain's tent. It was more of a pavilion, at least thirty feet on a side with a grass floor. A hole in the roof allowed the smoke from the fire burning in the brazier, a portable iron grate, to escape the tent. King Owain's bed had been placed right next to the fire, along with the stool upon which he'd been sitting when Gwen had been in here earlier.

As soon as she entered, Gwen went straight to the king to feel his forehead. She allowed herself a small sigh of relief at how cool he felt. Whether or not he'd been poisoned, he was on the mend.

King Owain reached up to remove her hand from his head, though he squeezed it once before letting go. "Help me to sit up."

"Father—" Rhun started forward.

King Owain actually waved his son closer instead of refusing his help. "I am much better, but I need this pillow behind my back." Between Rhun and Gwen, they maneuvered King Owain into a more upright position, propped against several pillows. "I want to hear what has you all so concerned. Gwen tried to tell me about the investigation yesterday, but I was incapable of hearing it."

There was a moment's pause as the companions looked at one another, nobody wanting to be the one to speak first. Then Hywel took in a breath, taking it upon himself to begin. He raised his hand to show his father the letter from King Stephen—

—but then without warning, King Owain leaned over the side of the bed and vomited up the broth he'd so confidently drunk. A chamber pot had been placed in that spot for just such an occasion. Gwen moved it closer, holding it in both hands, her head bent towards the king.

Tudur hastened to take the basin from her, his brow wrinkling in concern. "Really, Gwen, he's been so much better."

"I know," Gwen said. "This is the first time he's vomited since we reached the camp."

The king sighed and flopped back against his pillows, sweat on his forehead and his face ashen. Gwen allowed Tudur to take her place and backed away, motioning with her hands to shoo the others out the door. They went, but Rhun hesitated, and then stepped to his father's side to put a hand on his shoulder. "We'll talk later, Father. It isn't important for you to hear this now. Rest."

King Owain flapped a hand weakly in his son's direction but didn't speak. He turned on his side to curl up around his belly, a position in which he'd lain almost exclusively for the last two days.

"I'll get more broth," Gwen said, resigning herself to another night of spooning liquid into the king's mouth.

Once outside again, Rhun set off determinedly after his brothers in the direction of the fire where the Danes had established themselves on the north side of the camp, adjacent to the kitchen area, which Gwen suspected wasn't a coincidence. Gwen followed, since she was going that way anyway.

Gareth, Hywel, and the others reached Godfrid first, and by the time Rhun and Gwen arrived, his face had turned grave. "You had no chance to tell the king anything?"

"Nothing," Rhun said. "He didn't even hold King Stephen's letter. We need to hear your idea."

"Hmmm." Godfrid looked towards the campfire where his men were clustered. Most weren't actually sitting, and their stances implied tense anticipation. "The more I consider it, the worse my idea becomes, but it might be the only option available to us."

"Tell us," Hywel said.

Godfrid shrugged. "I had a thought that some of us might take a little trip."

21

Gareth

"What kind of trip?" Gareth said. They were all still standing, which was good for Gareth since he was too agitated to sit.

Godfrid canted his head, indicating that they should move farther away from the campfire and his men. While he claimed to trust every one of them, he'd misplaced his trust before—as they all had at one time or another—and been betrayed. With Cadwaladr involved, it could easily happen again.

"Before I go into detail," Godfrid said, "you have to be absolutely sure that you believe Cadwaladr has conspired with Ranulf. The plan is risky, so it has to be worth the cost if it goes astray."

"We're sure, Godfrid," Rhun said. "Let's hear it."

"It's simple, really," Godfrid said. "I will take Gareth and Gwen with me and my men straight into the lion's den."

Gwen had tight hold of Gareth's hand, but she didn't speak or ask what Godfrid meant. Everyone in the little circle knew what he meant.

"You want them to walk into Mold Castle and speak to Ranulf of Chester?"

Gareth could hear the laughter in Hywel's voice at the audacity of Godfrid's suggestion.

Godfrid spread his hands wide. "Who else and where else? That's where the scouts say he is, don't they?" He looked at Rhun.

"They do," Rhun said, "and where Pawl and Morien say the false Gareth dined with him."

"And if he isn't there?" Cynan said.

"We'll ride all the way to Chester if need be," Godfrid said. "There's an agreement between him and Cadwaladr, and Ranulf thinks the princes are betraying their father. He might find the news that they aren't worth hearing. As Rhun said, if Ranulf has given Cadwaladr support in the form of men, money, and weapons, he could lose them all."

"You're suggesting that we give him another option," Hywel said.

"He won't switch sides," Gareth said.

"No, but he might be interested in a truce," Godfrid said. "He might see the benefit of giving up Mold Castle in exchange for a cease fire. He thought Cadwaladr was going to stop the siege before it started. He may not have refortified the castle at all, because he was counting on your father's fall and Cadwaladr's withdrawal of your forces."

"He should recognize Gareth and Gwen from the time they saved Prince Henry," Rhun said.

"In his arrogance, Ranulf barely looked at you at the time," Hywel said, "so I can see how he could have been deceived years later. He may have thought when he saw Cole and Adeline that they were you, but as soon as he sees both of you together in the flesh he will know the truth."

"It is different this time, isn't it?" Madoc said softly. Everyone looked at him. As usual, he hadn't said two words up until now. He gave a small smile, as if in acknowledgement of that fact, before continuing, "We're in the middle of a war. Men are dying." He gestured to King Owain's tent. "Father could be dying. The stakes this time are much, much higher. Does Cadwaladr know it?"

"He has to," Rhun said.

Madoc canted his head. "I don't know that he does. He has lived so long with deception, he might not be able to see how far down the road to perdition he's come. I don't think he can see his own sin anymore. He has fallen so far into evil that he has lost the ability to recognize when he's committed a crime that can never be forgiven. If he ever had that ability. If he was caught."

"Which makes it all the more important that we act," Hywel said.

His back straightening with resolve, Gareth said, "I will go to Ranulf."

Godfrid shook his head. "Gareth, I know you want to protect Gwen, but you both have to come with me. Cadwaladr used you both, and it may be that Ranulf will have to see you together to realize he's been deceived. If it's any consolation, I think if you allow Gwen to come, it will be safer for all of us. When a woman rides among men, the party is no longer one of war."

Gareth ground his teeth but didn't deny Godfrid's words.

"Knowing that Cadwaladr lied to him and involved him in his schemes under false pretenses might not be enough to stop what is already in motion," Cynan warned.

"It might not be," Rhun said, "so we have to act on this end too. At first light, Gareth and Gwen will go to Ranulf, with the letter from Stephen, and negotiate for peace on our behalf. If Ranulf reconsiders his support for Cadwaladr, as I think he must, then we need you to ride hell bent for home to stop the siege before it starts."

Hywel nodded. "Meanwhile, we must continue to move our men forward, to put pressure on Mold. If we don't hear from you, we'll know Ranulf chose to fight and that the war is still on. The sooner you return, the fewer lives will be lost."

"And what will you do about Cadwaladr?" Gareth said.

"I will stop him," Rhun said.

Because he was the son of the deposed King of Dublin, the one aspect of this scheme that nobody questioned was Godfrid's role. He could get them to Mold Castle. Anyone who saw him would assume that he had come to Wales for the reason he *had* come to Wales—to seek allies for the overthrow of Ottar, his father's rival. That he had gone to Gwynedd and the court of King Owain first need never be mentioned. Ranulf would admit a company led by him into Mold.

Gareth, in particular, would have to be well hooded and cloaked so that nobody would recognize him until he was through the defenses around the castle. It would have been better to ride under the cover of darkness for that reason, but for Godfrid's mission to appear true, he had to arrive in broad daylight.

Once decided, there was very little they had to do in preparation. Mold Castle lay all of two miles from their current camp, on a little mound north of the village of Mold. The castle had been built on practically the only high ground for the whole of those two miles.

Meanwhile, they could sleep.

Maybe.

Because Gwen had to ride in the morning, Tudur had relieved her of her vigil at King Owain's bedside. Gwen rolled over, out of Gareth's arms, but he could tell from the way she was breathing that she wasn't asleep. After another count of twenty, he said, "What are you thinking about?"

"Tangwen," Gwen said immediately.

Gareth turned onto his side and tucked his arm around Gwen again. "Are you worrying about her? You've been here only a few days."

"That's a few days longer than I've ever left her before." Gwen raised one shoulder. "I tell myself she's fine, and I know she's fine. She has her grandfather and the entire castle wrapped around her little finger. I know that. But I'm her mother. I worry."

"If this goes well, you could be back in Aber by the end of the month," Gareth said. "You haven't been gone even a week yet."

"I know," Gwen said. "Truthfully, worrying about Tangwen is better than worrying about tomorrow."

Gareth relaxed, pillowing his head in his arm. "I am not worried."

Gwen rolled half onto her back, craning her neck so she could look into his face. "Truly?"

"Truly. Ranulf isn't going to harm either of us, and he will welcome Godfrid with open arms."

"How can you be sure?" Gwen said.

"He has no reason to harm us," Gareth said. "We are his enemy in this battle, but we will be riding under a banner of peace. *And* we will be bringing news he doesn't want to hear but needs to know."

"It is a great responsibility Rhun and Hywel are giving us," Gwen said.

"Ranulf can't be ignorant of the fact that he's in bed with a treacherous snake, but he might believe that the alliance he's forged is a true one," Gareth said.

"Using us as surety of it," Gwen said sourly.

"Even so," Gareth said.

Gwen sighed. "At times like these, when I'm worried or scared, I tell myself that no matter what happens, by tomorrow night it will be over."

Gareth pulled the blanket higher onto Gwen's shoulder as she turned onto her side again. He'd told her the truth. He wasn't worried—except for that niggling fear in the back of his mind that it would all be over tomorrow because they'd both be dead.

The morning came, as mornings tended to, no matter how terrible the future that came with it. The companions rose in the pre-dawn light in preparation for their journey. They wanted to reach Mold as quickly as possible, and with only two miles to go, it wouldn't take them long.

Godfrid had quested among the spare gear his men had brought and come up with armor and clothing that made Gareth look Danish instead of Welsh. Gareth couldn't grow his beard back overnight, but he had a few days' growth on his face, which would have to do. When he was completely dressed, down to the axe in his belt (in addition to his sword and belt knife), Godfrid appeared in front of him with a big grin on his face and a helmet under his arms. To Gareth's horror, it sported ram's horns on either side of the main casement.

"*What* is *that*?" he said, though he had a bad feeling he knew.

"The English will see only the helmet and not the man wearing it. One of my men made it one day to see what it would be like to wear," Godfrid said. "He loves what he looks like in it, though we mock him for it."

With great reluctance, Gareth allowed Godfrid to put the helmet on his head and adjust the straps. He wiggled his head, feeling the awkward weight of the horns. "Don't tell me he's actually worn this into battle. Godfrid, it's terribly unwieldy!"

Godfrid laughed, and then Gwen did too when he turned to her. She held up both hands to keep him away. "Any Welsh woman would run screaming from you if you arrived on our beach wearing that!"

Gareth growled and reached for her. She squealed as he grabbed her arm and pulled her to him. Then he kissed her, despite Godfrid's presence. When he released her, Godfrid gave Gareth a deep bow. "I apologize to your ancestors for the behavior of mine, my friend." His bow was mocking, but his words were not.

"Your ancestors and mine are drinking mead together in heaven right now, so all is forgiven." Gareth clapped his big friend on the shoulder. "Let's do this."

Godfrid hadn't attempted to turn Gwen into a soldier because the whole point was for her to be arrayed as a lady. To that end, she wore the better of the two dresses she'd brought, covered by an all-encompassing cloak. Gareth was happy to see her belt knife at her waist. Even though all his instincts screamed against it, he was taking her into enemy territory, and she needed to be able to protect herself.

A cold fog shrouded the hill, not unusual for a winter morning in Wales, and they waded through it to where the horses waited. Hywel was standing next to Gwen's horse, and he held out his clasped hands to Gwen in order to boost her up. Then the prince turned to Gareth, grinning to see him wearing the absurd helmet. "You always have all the fun."

"Your definition of fun and mine are clearly not the same, my lord."

"Oh yes, they are," Hywel said. "You live for this sort of thing."

Gareth shook his head. "Once. Not anymore." Because, of course, Hywel was right that exploits like this had once been a way of life for him. Hywel had sought them out, Gareth at his side. Sometimes Hywel's escapades had been a bit more fraught with peril than had been to Gareth's taste, but he'd gone along with them.

They were both older now, however, with wives and children, and Gareth's willingness to risk everything, even for great reward, had been tempered by a strong dose of caution. In his current state, he found it easier to remember that adventure was usually accompanied by fear, hunger, and the unexpected in equal measure, in none of which Gareth had any interest anymore.

"Please don't begin the assault on Mold before we get back," Gwen said from her perch on her horse. "I'd hate to be stuck there until your eventual victory."

Hywel waved a hand. "Madoc and Cynan will be moving out with the bulk of our men within an hour of your departure. They'll be right behind you, regardless of how your meeting with Ranulf goes. If you don't return by nightfall, we'll know that you are in need of rescue, which will mean the siege will be as much for your benefit as ours."

"I suppose that's some comfort." Gareth's horse shifted, and he leaned forward to pat Braith's neck.

"I looked in on your father this morning," Gwen said. "He was awake and talking, but you haven't told him what we're doing, have you?"

"No," Hywel said.

Gareth gathered the reins. "Are you sure that's wise?"

"All will be made clear soon enough, one way or another," Hywel said. "We are committed. My brother himself leads the company that rides to Cadwaladr's camp. They've already gone. Soon Cadwaladr won't be able to do us harm ever again, and we will tell my father everything we know when you return."

"What do you think Cadwaladr's plan was?" Gwen said. "The siege is supposed to begin tonight. At what point did he intend to betray the king?"

"Rhun and I have discussed it. Given my father's illness and inability to travel, we think it would have been late this afternoon. All the captains were to have met here before sunset, in order to finalize any last details. Our army would have been—and still should be—in place around Mold by then, ready for the last push forward after dark."

Gareth nodded. "You would have let him and his men into the camp, and then he would have turned on you. He wouldn't have had enough men himself, but if his *teulu* had been augmented by a company of Ranulf's men as Morien said ..." Gareth's voice trailed off at the horror of it. If he hadn't gone to the inn, they would have been too late to uncover Cadwaladr's plans. It had been a very near thing.

"Does Cadwaladr know about Morien and Pawl?" Gwen said.

"I don't know," Hywel said. "Anyone looking for them should assume they're under a bush sleeping off a drunken stupor, but regardless, in another hour it won't matter."

Gareth let out a sharp breath. "Cadwaladr may not submit without a fight."

"That's why Rhun left before first light. He will surround the camp quietly, taking out the sentries if necessary, and go straight to my uncle. With my brother's blade to Cadwaladr's throat, his men will surrender."

"Does Rhun have enough men with him for that?" Gwen said.

"He is riding with more than just his own *teulu*." Hywel nodded to Gareth. "Evan is with him, along with many of my father's men and mine."

"You don't want to kill him without laying all this before your father first," Gwen said.

"I hear you, Gwen," Hywel said, "but we will do what we must. Leave Cadwaladr to Rhun and me. Your task is to make Ranulf aware of the truth, negotiate for Mold if you can, and return as quickly as possible. With Cadwaladr in chains, Mold is ours, whether by force or by treaty."

"What about his men?" Gwen said. "His *teulu* are genuinely loyal to him."

"Not to mention the fact that you need his spearmen and archers to take Mold," Gareth said.

Hywel grimaced. "Rhun and I will assess his men, just as we did three years ago at Aberffraw."

Then Gwen leaned down to Hywel, surprising Gareth by saying, "My lord, have you spoken with Lord Goronwy recently?"

Curiosity entered Hywel's face. "No. Why?"

"It's a niggling thing, but his men seem to have been the source of a rumor that your father was dying." She shrugged. "Now that we're sure Cadwaladr is a traitor, I'm not so worried about Goronwy, but I would advise you to keep an eye on him."

"You never said anything about him to me, Gwen," Gareth said.

"With all that's happened, I forgot about him until now," Gwen said.

"His captain does have very large feet," Gareth said.

"So do dozens of men I've seen in the past few days—including Llelo!" Gwen said. "His are like boats."

Hywel was no longer listening. His eyes had strayed to the north, not in the direction of Goronwy's camp, but towards Cadwaladr's. His look was one of determination.

And in that moment, Gareth knew what his lord's look meant. Hywel meant to see that his uncle died, if not by hanging, then in battle, regardless of what Gareth and Gwen negotiated with Ranulf. As he looked down at the top of the prince's head, Gareth eased out a breath, nodding silently to himself. *Yes. It would be a better end.*

Hywel had killed in secret before to protect his sister. Gareth had covered up that crime for him, and he would cover up this one too. He would even help Hywel if need be.

Godfrid and his men had been mustering near their tents, and now they picked their way through the rest of the Welsh camp to where Gwen and Gareth waited at the entrance. Godfrid reached down to Hywel and the two princes clasped forearms.

"Good luck," Hywel said.

"You too." Godfrid held Hywel's arm for a moment longer than necessary. Perhaps Godfrid also knew what was going on in Hywel's mind and was telling him, one prince to another, to do what he must.

Then Hywel turned to Gareth. "If our scouts are wrong and Ranulf is not at Mold, you must seek him out wherever he may be, all the way to Gloucester if necessary. We must know the whole truth of what my uncle has done, once and for all."

"Yes, my lord." Gareth nodded to Hywel again, and they were off.

They rode two abreast on the narrow track, Gwen and Gareth directly behind Godfrid and his captain, Alfred. The remaining eighteen men stretched out behind them as they navigated down the road towards the village. Gareth couldn't help glancing to the north as they rode, looking for signs of movement from Cadwaladr's camp and wishing he'd been among those sent to arrest him instead of riding away from the fight.

Then the trails of smoke from the cooking fires were behind them. Today's journey took them east and slightly south towards Mold. As they reached the valley floor, a rare winter sun rose up in the east and burned through the fog. The light shone on the riders' faces, which meant the watchmen on the castle walls would be able to see Godfrid's company long before Gareth could make the watchmen out.

The two miles flew by, and in less than a half-hour, they were within striking distance of Mold. The English had been busy building a system of earthworks around the castle, which would make the Welsh assault all the more difficult. Looking up at the towers, Gareth could almost feel the eyes of Ranulf's archers on him. Their arrows would be put to the strings of their bows, ready to fire if the captain commanded it. Ranulf was one Norman lord who paid Welshmen to fight against their own people.

Gareth could never understand it himself, even if he knew why men did it: money, land, revenge. These were all the same reasons Cadwaladr fought against his brother. Long ago, Gareth had recognized the danger inherent in one Welshman fighting another while the Norman rulers of England looked on and laughed—and took advantage of their rivalries to carve out a bigger piece of Wales for themselves. It always amazed Gareth when a fellow Welshman took Norman gold and told himself that Norman lies were truth.

Cadwaladr didn't even have to go that far. He simply believed the lies he told himself.

Godfrid rode without his helmet, and his blond hair reflected the sunlight as much as the steel of his armor. Without any sign of fear, he led his company up to the gatehouse and halted before the gate. The castle was built in wood. The keep perched on a motte above them and was surrounded by a wooden palisade.

Directly behind the gatehouse lay the bailey, which itself was surrounded by a second wooden palisade. As Gareth had told Gwen, King Owain could burn the whole thing to the ground, and thus render it impotent, but then it wouldn't still be standing for him to refortify. He wanted to rule the surrounding lands from within it.

Godfrid called up to the gatekeeper, who poked his head over the top of the wall. "I am Prince Godfrid of Dublin. I seek an audience with Earl Ranulf of Chester." Godfrid had used the muscles in his belly to support his voice, and his challenge resounded against the thick wooden door in front of him.

The gatekeeper leaned over the top of the palisade. "Save your ire. He isn't here."

Gareth had feared this, though he hadn't done more than mention it to Hywel in passing. That Pawl, as well as Hywel's scouts, had reported that Ranulf was at Mold said nothing about whether or not he'd remained here. The earl might think himself too important a man to risk being burned out or captured, if by chance Cadwaladr failed to overthrow King Owain.

"I must speak with him urgently," Godfrid said.

The gatekeeper gazed down at the company, an insolent expression on his face. "He is at Chester,"

"We will seek him there." Godfrid swung his horse around.

So well trained were Godfrid's men that they turned their horses smoothly in place. Gareth and Gwen spun with them, and within three breaths, they were following the Danish prince away from the castle at a gallop. No arrows rained down among them.

The encounter had been very brief, and with so few in number, the Danes posed little threat. It would only be later that the garrison captain might wonder if Godfrid was working with King Owain and had come to Mold for the sole purpose of asking if Ranulf was there.

As the company thundered away, Godfrid flicked a hand and spoke in Danish. Two of his men peeled away from the company and raced off, back to Hywel's camp. Gareth urged Braith a little faster so as to come abreast of Godfrid.

"That was nicely done," he said.

Godfrid bared his teeth. "You think so? I would feel better about all of this if Ranulf had been there and at least one thing Pawl told us had already proved true."

"You think this is a ruse to draw you and your men—and Gwen and me—away from the camp?" Gareth said.

"You were the one who said that Cadwaladr loved elaborate plans, my friend," Godfrid said.

22

Gwen

No horse could gallop all the way to Chester. It would have been unwise to do so even if one could. They were in enemy territory, and the city had to be approached with caution.

Thus, it was past noon by the time the company reached a point where the city was laid out before them. Large by Welsh standards—or even Norman ones—Chester wasn't Mold. That castle was a simple motte and bailey construction. Chester's city walls and castle had been built in stone, and a curtain wall fronted by a ditch circled the entire city, enclosing the dwellings of at least two thousand people. Four gates in the cardinal directions allowed admittance into the town, and they'd have to ride through one of them before they reached the castle and Ranulf.

Thus, after consultation with Godfrid, they changed their strategy. Gareth removed his outrageous ram's horn helmet and returned it to its owner, who lovingly stowed it in his pack. It was Gareth's face that would gain them admission here. He was known from a previous investigation, and no gatekeeper worth his salt would allow a Danish company—even under the banner of peace—

into the town during a time of war on the merits of Prince Godfrid's word alone.

The company had ridden east from Mold, but it was to the south gate they rode now. The gatehouse, with its two massive towers, was fronted by a narrow bridge that crossed the River Dee as it passed around the city to the west and south. When they reached it, the bridge was nearly deserted, which surprised Gwen until she realized that the guards had cleared the bridge in anticipation of the company's arrival. As at Mold, they would have been seen from the battlements long before they made their way down to the Dee.

Gareth reined in before the gate, which was blocked by a portcullis, and called in English to the gatekeeper: "I am Gareth ap Rhys, in the company of Godfrid, Prince of Dublin. We ask admittance to speak to the Earl of Chester."

The gatekeeper stared through the iron bars at them. Gwen's English was limited, but since she'd understood Gareth, she hoped the Saxon guard had too. He looked from Gareth to Godfrid, who'd come to a halt beside him.

The Saxon raised a hand. "Wait here." He disappeared into the city behind him.

Gwen gripped her horse's reins reflexively and then forced herself to relax.

A half-dozen other guards peered through the gatehouse tunnel at the visitors, while many more crowded on top of the red stone wall above them. Nobody spoke, either among the company or on the wall.

Gareth and the Danes wore swords, but none were armed with bows. If it came to a fight, the company had intended to rely on the speed of their horses to escape rather than standing and fighting. The silence was broken only by the slap of water against the base of the supporting walls of the bridge as it flowed by and shouts and calls beyond the gate where the normal business of Chester was ongoing.

After possibly a quarter of an hour, quick footfalls echoed underneath the gatehouse, and a man stopped, half in the shadows under the archway so the angle of the sun shone on the lower half of his body. He could see their faces, but Gwen couldn't see his at all.

After a quick assessment, he waved to the guard. "Raise the portcullis."

The guard began to ratchet it up, and the newcomer stepped into the light. Sporting a thick brown beard tinged with red, he was a man built along the lines of Godfrid's Danes, wearing martial gear with the Earl of Chester's colors on his surcoat.

"Sir Gareth."

Gareth dismounted. "Dafydd."

Dafydd came forward, confident and sure, but then he faltered in midstride. "Sir ... Gareth?" He stared.

Gareth gave a low laugh and spoke in Welsh. "I gather I am not the Sir Gareth you last saw, Dafydd?"

Gwen understood then that this was the half-Saxon, half-Welsh guard who'd assisted Gareth with an investigation in Chester before their marriage.

"No." Dafydd rubbed at his bearded chin, still staring at Gareth with something like awe. "You are not, and I should have known when I saw that other man, even in passing and from a distance, that he could not be you. You would not have betrayed your king under any circumstances. We all should have known better."

Gwen let out an audible breath, but she was far enough back in the company that neither Dafydd nor Gareth heard her. Relief coursed through her. If even Gareth's supposed enemies realized their error when they saw him, then perhaps, if rumor of his treason had spread far and wide, it wouldn't be as hard to convince his friends that Cadwaladr's betrayal had been none of Gareth's doing.

"He looked very much like me," Gareth said, "and it has been several years since that day we met."

Dafydd stuck out his hand in greeting. "Why are you here?" He pointed with his chin towards Godfrid and his men. "And in such august company."

Gareth gripped Dafydd's arm. "As you can imagine, we have something important to discuss with Earl Ranulf, if he is here."

"It may be that he has something to discuss with you too." Dafydd stepped back.

With an accord reached between Dafydd and Gareth, Godfrid dismounted and waved the rest of his company off their horses.

Gareth came to Gwen's side to help her dismount, squeezing her waist briefly as he did so. "We're going to be all right."

"I am pleased to welcome you to my city," Dafydd said.

"Good man." Godfrid clapped Dafydd on the shoulder as he passed him.

Gwen had seen men driven into the ground by that sign of affection from Godfrid, but Dafydd took it well, not even rocking back on his heels.

Leading the horses, the company walked with Dafydd from the gateway. Once in the city proper, Gwen's head turned this way and that. She'd never been to Chester before, and the city lived up to Gareth's description. There were so many people and houses in it, Gwen didn't know what to look at first.

Unfortunately, she couldn't look long, as Dafydd led them down the street to the northwest corner of the city, which Chester Castle guarded. Its walls formed part of the city walls, and although the castle itself wasn't large, it sat on a low hill that overlooked the city to the east and the landscape to the west.

Obviously trusted, Dafydd took them right through the castle gate without more than a word to the guard there. The portcullis protecting the bailey was already up and, once inside, Dafydd turned again to the company. "If just a few of you could come with me?"

Godfrid spoke to his men, who nodded, though Gwen herself couldn't understand his words. And so it was that only Godfrid, Gwen, Gareth, and Godfrid's captain, Alfred, followed

Dafydd towards the keep. Gwen glanced back once, pleased to see that several of Godfrid's men were drifting towards the gatehouse and that the portcullis remained up. The rest spread out throughout the courtyard in pairs. Anyone who wanted to take them on was going to lose men doing it. Still, very little activity was occurring in the bailey, which Gwen thought odd until she asked Dafydd about it.

"We are in the midst of a war, my lady. Most of the soldiers have gone."

Gareth had Gwen's arm, and he squeezed her elbow significantly. The war and where those men had gone to was, of course, why they were here.

They reached the keep. A wooden stairway led up to a higher floor where the great hall lay. Dafydd directed them up it and then through a narrow door, which would be a last defense against attack if the main gateway was breached.

A handful of men were gathered around a table in front of the dais, Earl Ranulf among them. Most looked up as Gareth and Gwen entered the hall, and even from thirty feet away, Gwen could see the sneer that crossed the faces of several of them at the sight of Gareth walking beside Dafydd.

But then Gareth tugged Gwen forward, and as they approached the table, the men's expressions faltered, just as Dafydd's had. Gwen felt a sense of grim satisfaction at their reactions.

One of the men said, "My lord," speaking to Ranulf, who—typical of the man—had continued to study the map spread out flat on the table in front of him rather than paying attention to the newcomers.

"What is it—?" He looked up and caught sight of Gareth and Gwen.

His control was better than that of his men. Except for a slight hardening around the eyes and mouth, nothing in his face changed. Ranulf stepped away from the table and, with his eyes fixed on Gareth's, said, "Clear the room. Now."

The earl kept his face impassive, but his men interpreted his anger correctly and moved with alacrity, passing Gareth and Gwen on the way to the front door, which was the only exit from the hall. Several stared at them on the way, though others kept their eyes averted, as if they didn't want to see what was plainly before them.

The hall in which they were standing was a smaller version of the one in which Gwen had last met Ranulf, that danger-filled week after her marriage to Gareth at Newcastle-under-Lyme, when she and Gareth had traveled to England with Prince Hywel. Instead of rich tapestries, weapons—mostly spears and axes—adorned these walls. A fire blazed in the fireplace built to one side.

No matter his surroundings, however, once met, nobody could forget this volatile Earl of Chester.

"So," Ranulf said, speaking in French. "I was deceived."

"You can't be surprised about that, given that it was Cadwaladr you were working with," Gwen said, surprising *herself* at speaking first and so bluntly.

Ranulf stared at her for a moment, perhaps really seeing her for the first time. When he didn't speak, she feared he was about to lose his carefully contained temper, but then he threw back his head and laughed. And he laughed. Tears sprang from the corners of his eyes, and he wiped at them.

Finally, shaking his head, he moved towards the end of the table at which he'd been working. A carafe with several cups stood on a tray. He lifted the carafe, still smirking. "May I offer you mulled wine?"

"Thank you," Gareth said, speaking for all of them. Then he gestured to Godfrid, who'd been waiting patiently throughout Ranulf's display. "May I present to you Godfrid, Prince of Dublin."

Ranulf put down the carafe, having poured only one cup. "Oh my. This is a delegation, isn't it?" He put his heels together and gave Godfrid a slight bow. "Ranulf, Earl of Chester."

Godfrid came forward and bowed in mimicry of Ranulf. "My father sends his greetings."

"So." Ranulf handed the cup to Gwen, and then poured more wine, distributing the other cups to Gareth, Godfrid, and Alfred, and keeping the last for himself. "Why have you come?"

"We come in peace, in hopes of bringing this war to a conclusion that does not involve the bloodshed King Owain's brother has planned," Gareth said.

Ranulf tsked through his teeth. He took a swallow of wine, observing his guests over the rim of his cup, and then he lowered it. "How much do you know?"

Gareth considered the earl for the same amount of time he'd kept them waiting, and then he said, "The bodies of two people, bearing close resemblance to Gwen and me, were found in shallow graves two days ago."

Ranulf gave a bark of laughter. "Ah. And after you learned of it, you did what you do, and the trail led you here. Good." Ranulf gestured with his cup to Gareth and Gwen. "We can dispense with evasion then. I met your dead imposter five days ago."

Cold relief swept through Gwen. It was exactly as they suspected, and exactly what they hadn't wanted to hear. "You should have known that you couldn't trust him."

Ranulf's eyebrows went up. "Straight to the point as always, my dear. And, of course, you are right."

"What was the bargain, exactly?" Gareth said.

"Cadwaladr wanted what he has always wanted: the throne of Gwynedd," Ranulf said. "In exchange, he would see to it that the siege of Mold never came about, and I would keep my lands in eastern Gwynedd."

"While he ruled in the west?" Gwen said.

Ranulf gave a curt nod.

"What about Hywel and Rhun?" Gareth asked. "Cadwaladr claimed that they'd allied with him, correct?"

"They would each have their lands, and in exchange, I would assist them in overthrowing their father, who'd become an irrational despot."

"I hope our presence here confirms for you that nothing Cadwaladr told you or promised is true," Gareth said. "You face an army of King Stephen's men on your eastern border. In the west, a strong King Owain, well-supported by his barons and his sons, threatens Mold, and I have a letter here from King Stephen offering an alliance between Gwynedd and England against you. The tide has turned, my lord. Continuing this charade with Cadwaladr will only result in more loss and death."

"I see." Ranulf looked at Godfrid. "Dublin stands with Owain as well?"

"It does, though I came without knowledge of this war. I am here on behalf of my father," Godfrid said, "who seeks alliances to overthrow the tyrant Ottar."

Ranulf's eyes narrowed briefly, though not in suspicion, Gwen didn't think. More in acknowledgement of his change in circumstance. He faced Gareth again. "What is your offer?"

Gareth stood very straight. "You withdraw your men whom you've sent to support Cadwaladr. We will give them free passage back to Chester. You surrender Mold to us now, and we will cease all hostilities. You will then be free to concentrate your forces on King Stephen's army."

Ranulf gave him a wide smile. "What of this promised alliance between Gwynedd and Stephen?"

"I first must ask if you had anything to do with the death of the king's emissary," Gareth said.

Ranulf looked genuinely puzzled. "Who would that be?"

"A man by the name of Llywelyn," Gareth said.

"I am sorry he is dead, but I had no hand in it," Ranulf said. "He died recently?"

"In Shrewsbury."

"Oh." Ranulf gave a slight smirk. "I am not welcome there, so it had nothing to do with me."

"Or your men?" Gwen said.

Ranulf turned his gaze on her. "I will ignore the insult to my honor if Gareth answers my earlier question."

Gareth's head bobbed. "King Owain might send a few men to support the king's cause. It would be a small matter to you, given the cessation of the fighting in the west."

Ranulf turned away and began to pace back and forth in front of the fire. "You should know that my men have already left for Cadwaladr's camp. I might agree to this—" he threw out a hand in Gareth's direction, "—but it may be too late to change what's coming."

"And what was that supposed to be?" Gwen said.

"Not a bloodbath, if that's what you're thinking," Ranulf said. "With the princes allied against their father, King Owain would have been taken without a fight and his men subdued, since they would have been surrounded by not only the forces of Rhun, Hywel, and Cadwaladr, but mine as well."

"And what was to become of the king?" Gareth said.

"Prison," Ranulf said. "Exile. I gave Cadwaladr leave to do with his brother as he pleased."

23

Cadwaladr

"Prince Rhun is coming!"

His face contorted in sudden anger, Cadwaladr swung around to look at his captain, a man named Geraint. "Have I not warned you against using my nephew's title?"

Cadwaladr felt satisfaction as Geraint cowered before him. "Yes, my lord."

"When?"

The man's expression went blank. "When what?"

Cadwaladr growled. He was surrounded by incompetents. "When will Rhun be here?"

Geraint's expression cleared. "Within the hour. Less. His men were mustering when our man learned they were riding here and not to Mold, though he is not clear on the reason for it. He didn't stay to find out, thinking that it was more important to tell us of it."

"How many men does Rhun have?"

"Nearer to one hundred men than fifty," Geraint said. "More than just his own *teulu* rides with him."

"He knows all, then. Or enough." A grimace crossed Cadwaladr's face. *To have come* so *close.* "This never would have happened if you hadn't left the body of the girl in the graveyard."

Geraint's face fell. "I told you already, it was Cole's idea. He botched the girl's death. I thought—"

Cadwaladr didn't want to hear Geraint's excuses again. "And I have told you many times that your job *isn't* to think! It is to obey. If you'd just left her back in the woods like I told you to—"

"It would have been fine if not for that meddling priest. The ground was hard, my lord, and we were afraid someone would come—"

Cadwaladr made a chopping motion with his hand. "What's done is done."

Geraint's expression turned mulish. "You were the one who murdered Cole."

"And I brought a shovel, didn't I?" Cadwaladr strode to the door of the tent and looked out.

"You didn't bury Llywelyn."

"That was Cole also, as you well know." Cadwaladr gazed at his men, counting them and calculating the odds of surviving an outright battle with Rhun's force. He might be able to slip away himself, but then he would be on the wrong side of the border with no support.

He shook his head. "We don't have the numbers to make a stand, and we don't have time to get word to Ranulf of the change in plans."

"The prince—" Geraint froze at Cadwaladr's glare, cleared his throat, and adjusted what he'd been about to say, "Rhun may merely be coming to confer, my lord."

"Not with those numbers," Cadwaladr said.

"Your foresight in placing a spy in your brother's camp has paid off, my lord," Geraint said ingratiatingly.

"Bah!" Cadwaladr said. "He should have reported back sooner, given me more time to respond. Get out!" He pointed through the open tent flap. "Get the men up and riding. I want this camp cleared within a quarter hour. We leave no man behind for Rhun to question."

"Yes, my lord!"

Cadwaladr caught Geraint's elbow before he could depart. "Ensure that we bring every weapon and enough supplies to last us several days. I don't know how long it will take us to reach England."

Geraint swallowed hard. "It will be done."

Cadwaladr still didn't let him go. "We also need to make sure Ranulf's livery is safely stowed. We will need it once we cross the border if we don't want to draw attention to ourselves."

"Of course, my lord. It will be done."

Cadwaladr nodded, and Geraint exited the tent. A moment later, Cadwaladr could hear him shouting at the men to roust them.

Cadwaladr smoothed his beard, glad he'd had the foresight to grow it. Having a beard would make it easier to pass as a Norman. Before him lay the dilemma of what path to take out of here. He couldn't ride east, because an entire army of his brother's men stood between him and safety. He couldn't take the road directly south for the same reason. If he did that, he'd meet Rhun riding towards him.

But he could go west and then south, traveling behind the Clwyd range. And then, when he was a safe distance from his brother's camp, he could strike out due east for Chester.

He would run today, but not forever.

* * * * *

Cadwaladr glanced at the sky. The sun was about to set. All day, he'd hoped to stay far enough ahead of Rhun's force to reach England and safety before sunset. But it was too far, and he'd had to take too circuitous a route, not daring to ride too close to Mold and his brother's army.

If it hadn't meant killing the horses, Cadwaladr would have ridden on to Chester, but even his beast had been staggering for the last mile. If Cadwaladr had pushed him for one more, the beast wouldn't have been able to continue the rest of the way.

And then, when the scouts Cadwaladr had sent ahead reported that they'd made contact with Ranulf's men, the promise of augmenting his *teulu* had him pulling off the road in anticipation of their arrival. One of the reasons he'd brought his men this way in the first place was because he'd arranged to meet Ranulf's men on the road to Chester, not far from here, back when the plan had been to surprise Owain in his camp.

That wasn't going to happen now, though when he'd heard that Ranulf's men were coming he'd thought about instituting the original plan again. Cadwaladr ground his teeth in frustration at the need to run. So much had gone into what he'd perceived as a brilliant plan, only to have it foiled. He didn't yet know how or why, but if it was in his power, he would discover the truth.

"It's Gareth who rides against us, my lord."

Cadwaladr swung around to look at Geraint. It was always he who brought him news, good or bad. Cadwaladr had long since dispensed with any other close confidants and regretted his inability to find allies among his father's men, though he'd been working on Cristina's father, Goronwy, of late. He had no true friends, and he knew it—but then, a man in his position couldn't afford any.

"What? How so? You have seen him?"

"His force has stopped to cross the ford not a half-mile from here. I can show you."

This could be the very opportunity he'd been waiting for. If it really *was* Gareth at the root of his undoing, he would take payment for all that he had suffered. It would be one last bit of retribution to make up for having to flee before his brother's wrath.

Cadwaladr's men had settled themselves within a stand of trees to the south of the road. Leaving the bulk of them where they rested, Cadwaladr, puffing slightly and cursing the slight paunch that had grown around his middle since he'd turned forty, followed Geraint through the trees and up a rise that overlooked the ford of the River Terrig. By his calculation, they were now directly south of Mold. He might have already crossed the border into England, but it did him no good. If the full extent of his plot had really been discovered, then Rhun—or Gareth if this was indeed he—would pursue him to the ends of the earth.

"There!" Geraint pointed west, to where the river broadened enough to allow a crossing.

Rhun's men had bunched up, some resting, some already across the river. If Cadwaladr had thought about it—and had had more men at his disposal—he would have set up an ambush right there, but it was too late for that now.

But maybe it wasn't too late in principle.

"I don't see him." Cadwaladr swept his gaze across the mass of men.

"He's in the back, my lord. He watches from the rise to the north."

And there he was. Cadwaladr couldn't see his face, of course, not from this distance, but the bit of sun peeking through the clouds shone off his red-plumed helmet, making his identity unmistakable. Gareth's second, that pie-faced Evan, was there too. He'd pulled off his helmet, revealing his shock of blond hair, not dissimilar to Cadwaladr's own color when he was younger. A column of rage blazed up inside Cadwaladr that it had been Gareth who'd been charged with bringing him before his brother. He'd had to leave his camp with his face half-shaven. The ignominy of it stuck in his craw.

Cadwaladr swung around. "We're going to kill him."

"My lord—" Geraint looked shocked.

"With Ranulf's men, we outnumber them." Cadwaladr shooed all the scouts off the hill. "Go! We'll set up an ambush on either side of the road. I know just the place!"

Gareth. He'd hated him for ten years, ever since the whelp had stood in front of him, legs spread and hands behind his back, and refused a direct order.

And not only had he refused it, he'd told Cadwaladr why.

No man could do that and get away with it. For ten years, Cadwaladr had had to put up with Gareth's self-righteous meddling.

No more.

24

Gareth

They rode from Chester as if the hounds of Arawn themselves were at their heels. Ranulf sent Dafydd with them, as emissary to his men, were they to meet them on the way. The company that Ranulf had given to Cadwaladr had left Chester by the western road, which was why Godfrid's company had missed passing them on their way into Chester.

Ahead of them, the sun was sinking below the Clwyd Mountains. They'd come halfway from Chester, ten miles, but with perhaps another hour at least until they'd reach Hywel and Rhun. The knowledge that Ranulf had not only listened to him but agreed to a treaty burned like a warm fire in Gareth's belly. If Ranulf stayed true to his word, the princes only needed to give him two days to clear out of Mold, and then it would be theirs.

Victory, true victory, and an end to this war before Christmas.

"What is that noise?" Godfrid, who'd been riding beside Gareth at the head of the company, put out a hand and slowed.

Gareth hadn't heard the first shout, but as the thunder of hooves from the company's horses lessened, the words came clearly through the air—a dozen voices intermingled with his own name unmistakable as it was shouted to the skies: “Kill him! Kill Gareth! Kill the traitor!”

Gareth pulled on Braith’s reins, and she danced around so he could see the faces of Godfrid, Gwen, and the other men. Everyone was looking around, straining to see where the enemy force was coming from. But nothing stirred the air except a slight breeze and a few birds, swooping from one tree to another.

“What’s going on?” Dafydd urged his horse closer.

“I don’t know,” Gareth said.

“I don’t care,” Godfrid said. “I only know I heard your name.”

“It can’t be directed at me,” Gareth said. “We aren’t under attack. The shouts are coming from up ahead.”

“Someone is under attack,” Godfrid said. “Let’s find out who it is.”

They spurred their horses, thundering up a rise and then down the other side. They’d reached a valley through which the road ran in a straight line until the ford of the Terrig River. Fields, ditches, and stands of trees lined the road on either side—and right below them, a hundred yards ahead, a pitched battle was taking place.

It didn’t seem possible for so many men to be fighting in such a small space. The fighters nearest to Gareth wore surcoats indicating their allegiance to the Earl of Chester, and these were set against an equal number of men showing the crest of Gwynedd.

Gwen, riding beside Gareth, opened her mouth in horror. "Do you see? It's Rhun!"

Gareth looked again, and there in the middle of the fight was the prince—distinguishable from his men by Gareth's own helmet.

Godfrid didn't wait to confer but raised his sword above his head. "Forward!"

Gareth flung out a hand to Gwen. "Get off the road!"

Gwen obeyed, and as Gareth urged Braith into a gallop, out of the corner of his eye, he saw her horse leap a stone wall and canter into a neighboring field to the south of the road.

"Ride!" Gareth said, as if Godfrid's men needed any more urging.

With nothing more than a jerk of his head, Godfrid organized his men into two tight columns. They had only twenty men, but they were mounted and their sword arms were rested. They would drive right into the back of Ranulf's men. Side by side, Gareth and Godfrid directed their horses straight down the center of the road.

Forty yards. Twenty yards.

And then they were upon them. A large Englishman with a broad back lifted his axe above his head to strike the final blow to a Welshman on the ground at his feet. Gareth swept the edge of his sword across the back of the man's neck, one of the few places he wasn't protected by armor.

The man dropped to the ground, and Gareth didn't stay to watch him die, already moving on to the next fighter. Braith danced among the downed men, picking her way with a sureness that far exceeded Gareth's capacity to guide her—were he even paying attention to anything but the Englishmen he intended to kill.

Then Alfred, Godfrid's captain, gave a ululating cry that sent shivers down Gareth's spine, and with an accompanying roar, the rest of the Danes surged into the fight. Gareth hadn't thought they'd been particularly silent in their approach, and to his mind, hours had already passed between sighting the battle and launching the attack. But it had been fewer than a hundred heartbeats, even if Gareth's heart was beating out of his chest at twice its normal pace.

A hundred English soldiers versus twenty Danish cavalry might not be considered a fair fight to anyone but the Danish, but their arrival gave life to the Welsh defenders. They fought with renewed vigor in defense of their prince, and there were more of them still alive than Gareth had thought at first. He even saw one man rise, hale and whole, from within a pile of fallen men to rejoin the fight.

Gareth continued to urge Braith with his knees, pressing towards the far side of the battle. His arm rose and fell, hacking at one man after another, completely devoid of finesse. A detachment filled him, and it was as if time slowed down. He could see the outlines of the fight with complete clarity.

There was Gwen, flitting into a stand of trees at the base of a hill.

There was Godfrid, his expression a rictus of hate, bringing his sword smashing down on the head of an Englishman who'd lost his helmet.

There, finally, was Prince Rhun, hard pressed, fighting two Englishmen at once, but standing back to back with Gruffydd, his captain, and Gareth's friend, Evan.

And at the sight of the prince, time resumed its normal speed. Gareth urged Braith through the press of men, slashing at one after another, almost heedless of whom he might be hurting in his haste. Prince Rhun had dispensed with one of his opponents, but the effort had left him unbalanced, and he went down on one knee to steady himself.

As the prince surged upward to face the second man, that soldier raised his sword, aiming to finish him off. Gareth switched his sword to his left hand in anticipation of blocking the blow, but Braith was struggling to reach the attacker, stymied by the many obstacles on the ground.

So Gareth did what he could.

Loosening his feet from his stirrups, he launched himself off Braith, over the heads of two soldiers between him and Rhun's attacker. He caught the English soldier around the neck and shoulders, falling into him and riding him to the ground. They hit the earth with a sickening crunch. Gareth lay gasping for a moment, trying to regain the breath that had been crushed out of him. The man beneath him moaned.

Gareth lifted up, easing onto his knees, and looked down at the fallen man. His right arm was bent at a terrible angle, and one of the bones in his forearm was sticking through the skin.

Gareth would have been nauseated by the sight if he allowed himself to think about it. Instead, he looked around for the prince. Neither he nor Gruffydd were anywhere in evidence, having moved back into the midst of the battle. So Gareth grasped Evan's hand and levered himself to his feet. Their eyes met for a moment in shared acknowledgement of what they faced, and then they returned to the fray too, standing back to back, ready to take on all comers to this part of the road.

At the start of the battle, Gareth had put hope away, even as the desire for it rose in his chest. The English soldiers had thought themselves the stronger when they'd attacked Rhun's company. In turn, the arrival of Godfrid's men had sent them into a frenzy. It wasn't Prince Rhun's habit to put those who surrendered to the sword, but these men fought as if they believed that would be their fate.

Another man came at Gareth at the same moment Evan grunted with exertion behind him. A ditch protected Gareth's right side, as if a third defender were standing there, and Gareth had already used the slippery soil to distract one soldier he'd faced. This man, however, had an intensity to him that was hard to counter. Their swords clashed again as each tried to gain the advantage.

Gareth had initially focused on the man's sword, but he knew that it was often a man's eyes that foretold where the next blow would come. He looked into them, and then looked for a heartbeat longer than he should have because he knew the man—and he wasn't Saxon, for all that he was wearing Earl Ranulf's colors.

The man—his name was Aeron—had played a role in Gareth's past, just as Morien had. He served in Cadwaladr's company, and even though Gareth had known that Cadwaladr had conspired with Ranulf, he still couldn't quite believe that Cadwaladr's men were fighting in the livery of the Earl of Chester.

Gareth's surprise was almost his undoing, because he brought up his sword to counter Aeron's a heartbeat too late. Aeron's sword slid along his blade, allowing Aeron to get close, and it was only at the last instant that Gareth saw the knife in Aeron's other hand.

Gareth twisted away, heedless of the uneven ground, and instead of driving his knife into Gareth's gut, Aeron managed only to slide the blade along Gareth's right ribcage. Gareth rolled, his head tucked to his chin and his left shoulder taking the brunt of the fall, and came up five paces away from Aeron, breathing hard but alive.

And then Evan swung around and skewered Aeron right through his mail.

It was enough.

The Welsh defenders had taken heavy casualties, but the attackers hadn't been able to finish the job before Godfrid's company arrived, and that had been their undoing.

Gareth had killed at least four men by himself, and some of Godfrid's men had done the same, taking advantage of the element of surprise and their greater strength and wind. As Gareth surveyed the road, the bright helmets of all eighteen of Godfrid's men reflected the last rays of the setting sun. Not many were still mounted, but all were alive.

Aeron had been one of the last of the enemy to fall.

"You're bleeding." Evan pulled aside Gareth's cloak to reveal a burgeoning red stain. The narrow blade of the knife had gone right through the links of his mail, and the protective padding Gareth wore beneath it, into his skin.

Gareth looked down, puzzled. "I can't feel it."

Evan pressed a hand to the wound, trying to stop the flow of blood, though it immediately began to seep through his fingers. "You will. Where's Gwen?"

Gareth looked across the road to the other side, towards the stand of trees into which he'd seen her go. He gestured to it. "Over there."

Together they crossed over to it, reaching the stone wall that demarcated the field. Thankfully, before Gareth could panic because he didn't see her, Gwen appeared, leading her horse. "I'm here."

"Gwen." Gareth put out his hand to help her over the wall, but as he did so, a shout came from the center of the road. They all turned to look at who'd cried out. It was Gruffydd, Prince Rhun's captain. He was only a hundred feet away to the east, and Gareth could see the horror written in every line of his body.

Evan took off towards Gruffydd at a shambling run, and Gareth followed immediately after. A litany of *no, no, no* starting in his head, anticipating what he didn't yet know for sure. Evan reached Gruffydd first and gave a cry of such pain that Gareth's heart split in two. He came to a halt where Evan had fallen to his knees. A man lay on the ground face up, and while his features were obscured by his helmet, the helmet itself was unmistakable.

Evan threw himself across the body, his wailing grief rising into the air and sending shivers down the spine of every man listening. Gruffydd passed a trembling hand across his brow even as tears streamed down his cheeks. He left a smear of blood that was not his own across his forehead, and then he stared down at his hands. Gareth didn't think he was really seeing them, and it was easier to think about Gruffydd's grief than Gareth's own.

Edging Evan aside, Gareth crouched beside Rhun's body, his hands on his prince's shoulders. "My lord," Gareth said, trying wake him, even though he knew the prince would never wake again.

Gareth couldn't see an obvious wound on the front of Rhun's body, but the blood on the ground told him that he would find it if he turned him over. It was too late to save him, but the rational part of Gareth told him he had to be sure. He put two fingers to Rhun's neck. No pulse beat in it.

Gareth bowed his head as Evan's mournful cry was joined by others. Prince Rhun, beloved son and brother, the *edling* of Gwynedd, was dead.

25

Gwen

As she rode away from the battle, praying the whole time, Gwen tried to block out the sounds of fighting. It was impossible, but she directed her horse across the field, circling around to the south of the road towards a tree-covered hill where she could be safe. She focused as hard as she could on keeping her seat and staying out of sight. The woods were dark compared to the field outside, and she hoped that anyone looking in her direction would see nothing but a shadow. Not that any man in the road had a moment to look her way.

She reached a spot that gave her a good view of the battle and crouched behind a bush. She was on the edge of the woods but still close enough to see Prince Rhun, backed up as he was against Gruffydd and Evan, fending off two attackers at once.

She couldn't think about him. She couldn't think about Gareth.

She forced her eyes away, but in so doing noticed a man standing next to a tree on the edge of the woods, looking away from her. He hadn't seen her yet, but if she moved at all, he would.

And then it was he who moved, and she realized she was looking at Cadwaladr himself.

At first, she had thought it was he by his shape and the set of his shoulders, which she would have recognized from a hundred paces away. Then he stepped into the sun and she recognized him without a doubt. Gwen clenched her hands into fists so tightly she would have bled from the pressure of her nails if she hadn't been wearing gloves.

She hardly dared to breathe, and she prayed that her horse wouldn't whicker or shift. He was standing with his head down, exhausted from the ride.

As if woven into a tapestry, the three of them didn't move for thirty heartbeats, each one pounding out of Gwen's ears.

Then in the middle of the road, Godfrid rose up, bellowing in triumph with his sword high above his head.

Gwen couldn't see the expression on Cadwaladr's face, but the Dane's call seemed to decide something for him. He loped away from Gwen, heading west and skirting the hill behind her. He ended up where several unattended horses, which she hadn't noticed before, were picketed. Nobody else was there or looking at him.

Part of her wanted to race after him, to throw herself at his back, tackling him to the ground and beating on him. She wanted to rage at him for what he'd done.

But she didn't. She had neither weapons nor words to stop him. So she did what she had to, which was to stand in the shadows in silence, watching as Cadwaladr mounted a horse and rode away.

Gwen could barely speak around the lump in her throat, and what she was feeling had to be nothing compared to Prince Hywel's and King Owain's pain. Gareth had sent word of the ambush and Cadwaladr's flight to Hywel immediately. The prince had gathered the rest of his *teulu* and a half-dozen carts and ridden to the battlefield. His face had been a grim mask when he'd arrived, and he'd hardly changed expression since.

They'd made their slow way back to King Owain's encampment on the hill, the dead thrown over the backs of the horses and the wounded in carts, while the survivors walked.

As the hours had passed since Rhun's death, Gwen had forced herself to keep moving, to go through the necessary motions that accompanied the aftermath of the fight: cleaning men's wounds, offering water or food to them, bandaging the slice that Gareth had received along his ribs. Everything she did took place with a kind of numbing grief that was both emotionless and at the same time full of emotion.

It was after midnight now, and Prince Hywel remained incoherent. Having done what was needed to reach the encampment, he sat on a stool before one of the cooking fires, Gareth's helmet in his lap. He wouldn't eat or drink. He wouldn't allow anyone to take the helmet from him.

King Owain had retreated to his tent. Gwen had offered him wine and poppy juice to allow him to sleep, but he'd refused them both. "I don't want to stop thinking about him, Gwen. Let me keep my memories for now."

Godfrid, a godsend as always, had taken it upon himself to do what needed to be done. In the immediate aftermath of the battle, she'd told him about Cadwaladr's departure, and he'd sent two of his own men to track him if they could. He'd directed two more to what remained of Cadwaladr's camp, if for no other reason than to make sure the traitorous prince hadn't retreated there.

He'd asked Dafydd to return to Ranulf, to tell him of the fight on the road and the loss of many of his men. Dafydd had fought alongside Gareth and Godfrid, and though he was only one man, his contribution had been significant.

Godfrid had also sent a rider to Madoc and Cynan, to tell them of the ambush and Rhun's death. They'd sent word in return that they were pulling back the men from the forward positions they'd established and would be at the camp themselves by dawn.

More men had ridden to the village of Gwern-y-waun and then to Cilcain, to Father Alun, to ask villagers to come and succor the men who still lived.

Gwen wanted to put her arms around her husband and slide into oblivion herself, even if nobody else would take the poppy juice she offered. But Gareth sat beside his prince, head bowed and in too much pain in both body and mind to move even had he wanted to.

None of them could escape the wrenching truth: Rhun had been struck down because Cadwaladr and his men had thought he was Gareth. Almost worse, Rhun hadn't been felled by the blow of a sword or an axe in the midst of battle. It had been a thin blade that had been shoved through the links in the armor on his back, straight into his heart, that had killed him.

Godfrid appeared at Gwen's side. He hadn't had the opportunity to change his tunic, which was stained with blood. Gwen herself was coated with it, though none was her own.

"We have to talk, Gwen."

Gwen nodded reluctantly. She didn't want to talk. Four days ago, back when she and Godfrid had arrived at Hywel's camp, she'd been surprised and maybe even a little hurt to have him tell Gareth about his dying father when he'd never said a word to her about it in the days they'd ridden together from Aber.

Now, she understood completely why he hadn't. Like her fears for Gareth, and for everyone she loved, speaking to anyone about the pain inside her made it more real. Speaking of what Cadwaladr had done here would be the same. She knew Rhun was dead. She knew that King Owain's hopes for his kingdom and for this war lay in ruins around him, but she wanted to pretend otherwise for just a little longer.

Unfortunately, at this moment, Godfrid and she were the only two people still standing who knew the whole of what had happened.

"About Cadwaladr," Godfrid began.

Gwen didn't need him to finish his thought. "Your men couldn't find him."

"No," Godfrid said. "He must have gone to ground, but they don't know where. They're seamen, not foresters. I'm sorry."

Her hands shaking, unable to express what she was feeling other than grief, Gwen bent her head and the tears started to flow again. Everything had gone wrong, and there was no way to fix it. It wasn't possible to fix it.

She felt Godfrid's gentle hand on her shoulder. "You are the bravest woman I know."

Godfrid was an old friend, and like the best of old friends, he understood what was inside her without her having to articulate it. He pulled her into one of his bear hugs. "Ah, Gwen. I wish we could start the day over."

"I do too." Her voice was muffled by his tunic. "I was so scared for all of you."

"What do the sages say?" Godfrid said. "A brave man isn't one without fear, but one who acts even though he is afraid."

"Gareth has said that," Gwen said. "You and he acted. It just wasn't enough. Even the treaty with Ranulf might be in ruins now, given the loss of his men."

Godfrid released her and guided her to a stool. He crouched in front of her. "What has happened is entirely Cadwaladr's fault. If we hadn't returned when we did, Cadwaladr's men would have left no one alive.

"Gareth is suffering. Guilt consumes him." Gwen gestured helplessly towards the rows of Cadwaladr's wounded men. "I've known some of these men since I was a girl, ever since my father sang for Cadwaladr in his hall at Aberystwyth. I don't know how they will live with themselves after this."

"You feel sorry for them?"

"I don't want to. I want to hate them for following orders, but I can't even do that. Not everyone has the courage to walk away from a lord he can't respect."

"And like the coward he is," Godfrid said, "Cadwaladr has abandoned even those loyal to him."

Gwen looked up at Godfrid. "It isn't only Gareth who blames himself. King Owain is telling himself that if he'd hanged his brother years ago, or locked him up, none of this would have happened."

"Sadly, he's right," Godfrid looked away. "I have more bad news. My men have returned from Cadwaladr's camp. It is deserted. Even those servants he didn't take with him are gone."

"That's no surprise," Gwen said. "They know who and what Cadwaladr is and would have fled before Rhun arrived this morning. All of his men here wish they'd fled too. They know that once King Owain begins to recover from the shock of Rhun's death, his wrath will be unlike we've ever seen."

"My men did find these among the possessions Cadwaladr abandoned." Godfrid dropped two small purses into Gwen's lap. "Adeline's and Cole's perhaps?"

"Is there any way to tell for certain?" Gwen gazed dully at the purses. They were evidence of Cadwaladr's crimes, but she found it impossible to care.

"There will be some who doubt that Prince Cadwaladr could have been responsible for what happened here today. They will refuse to believe the testimony of honest men," Godfrid said. "They need items like these as proof. If Adeline's father were to testify that one of these was hers …" His voice trailed off as Gwen still didn't move.

But then she nodded, trying to shake off some of the gray that seemed to be covering her vision. "You're right about the testimony. Someday King Owain himself might want to see them as part of knowing the whole truth about how Rhun died. I'm glad your man found them. Please keep them against that day."

"Of course." Godfrid returned them to his pocket. "May I speak to you of what I have learned from Cadwaladr's men, one Geraint in particular?"

"Yes." Gwen made a sour face, not wanting to hear it but knowing that Godfrid needed to tell someone. "What does he say?"

"Cadwaladr's plan was to descend with his and Ranulf's men on this encampment, kill those who resisted, and capture the rest. While Ranulf's men took the king and princes back to Chester as prisoners, Cadwaladr's men would retreat back to their camp. There, they would remove their false livery, and then Cadwaladr himself was to 'discover' the ruin of his brother's camp."

"Do we believe him?"

Godfrid shrugged. "In the main, though perhaps not the details. Admitting that it was the death of the princes and the king rather than their capture that was Cadwaladr's goal does Geraint no good at all."

Gwen closed her eyes. "If Father Alun hadn't come to find us; if Gareth hadn't encountered Pawl and Morien, it might have worked. But then, because Gareth discovered the plot, Rhun spent the day chasing after him and was in the center of his men to be ambushed on the road."

Godfrid shook his head. "Geraint says, and this I do believe given what we heard shouted before the battle, that Cadwaladr wanted to see Gareth dead on that road, not Rhun. You can second-guess yourselves all you want, but both princes and Gareth did what was necessary at the time.

"Ranulf is being hard pressed on his eastern border. He did forge peace with you once he learned the truth about Cadwaladr. It does also seem, from talking to the survivors among Ranulf's men, that they had no idea what Cadwaladr had really planned. They thought Hywel and Rhun stood against their father. They thought they were providing support for a bloodless coup, not force of arms for a pitched battle."

"Who did they think they were ambushing on the road?" Gwen said.

"Gareth, same as Cadwaladr, except Cadwaladr told them a story about how Gareth had lied to everyone about his loyalties and had unexpectedly turned on Cadwaladr. Ranulf's men were happy to participate in what they thought was an easy fight."

"Did you ask Geraint who killed Cole and Adeline?" Gwen said.

"Cole killed Adeline and Llywelyn, the king's messenger, and Cadwaladr killed Cole, just as we thought," Godfrid said.

"Was Geraint there?"

"He claims not to have been. The man Cadwaladr took with him was one of his other captains who died in the fight." Godfrid tipped his head. "Geraint does have larger than normal feet."

"We could find out the truth by showing Geraint to the innkeeper in Gwern-y-waun, but it seems so pointless now." Tears choked Gwen's throat yet again.

"Only one man is at the heart of this, and we know his name."

Gwen turned in her seat and then stood at the sight of Hywel coming towards her. He and Gareth came to a halt next to Godfrid.

"Tell me what you have learned," Hywel said.

It was an order, and Gwen imagined that orders were all they were going to get from him for a while. Hywel's grip on his emotions was tenuous, but she could see his eyes in the light of the torches that flickered all around the camp. They were clear.

Because Gareth still didn't look capable of speaking, Gwen related in short sentences the details of the journey they'd undertaken to Ranulf. Hywel kept his gaze fixed on Gwen's face. She concluded with Ranulf's agreement to surrender Mold in exchange for peace.

Hywel turned to Gareth. "Tell me of this Dafydd of Chester. I understand you worked with him before?"

"Yes, my lord," Gareth said. "He knew me as soon as he saw me, and knew that Cadwaladr had deceived them all."

"Ranulf knew it too." Gwen understood what Hywel was doing. He was preparing to lay at his father's feet everything Cadwaladr had done, and he needed to have every detail clear in his mind before he did it. She could almost see the mantle of *edling* settling onto his shoulders. He was bowed by the weight of it—and his grief—but the responsibility for his father's kingdom lay with him now.

Gwen risked a hand on his forearm. "You aren't alone, Hywel."

His arm trembled under her fingers, but then he stilled. "I know, Gwen. And I am grateful." He looked at each of them. "I need to impose on your friendship, and your loyalty, and ask that you come with me now to speak to my father."

"Of course," Gwen and Gareth said together, and Gwen was glad to see her husband standing tall again.

They had all experienced death before and the settling in of grief until it became one's new reality. When her mother had died, Gwen had had hours to prepare herself, though she didn't know that the preparation had made the pain any less. It *had* allowed her to prepare to tend to her newborn brother when he needed her.

The reality of Rhun's death—and the suddenness of it—was only just sinking in. What Hywel was feeling now was anger, and Gwen understood that emotion too. He might be angry for a long time, but it was his anger that would sustain him until he returned home. Until then, it would be Gwen's job—hers and Gareth's—to moderate his decisions if they were rash and based on emotion rather than sense.

"You have no doubt, then," Hywel said, "that my uncle was responsible for what happened here?"

"I saw him leave once he realized that his men would be defeated," Gwen said.

The look in Hywel's eyes told her that it didn't matter what his father thought because he'd already made up his mind about his next course of action. Cadwaladr would be dealt with, as swiftly and decisively as Hywel could manage.

As Madoc had said, what Cadwaladr had done—regardless of whether the death of Rhun was an accident or intentional—could never be forgiven.

26

Gareth

Gareth didn't remember finding his blankets. He'd finally lain down sometime while it was still dark, after they'd spoken to King Owain, who'd listened to all that Hywel had to say—and nodded.

King Owain had told his son, in essence, that he should do what he must, adding, "Cadwaladr had to have known from the start that if his attack wasn't successful—if it was beaten back or, as turned out to be the case, defeated completely—his involvement would be discovered."

And then he'd rolled over to face away from them all and had finally taken the wine and poppy juice Gwen offered him.

Gwen lay sprawled on her back, fast asleep. He hated to wake her, but they had too much to do to sleep past the dawn. He put a hand to her shoulder, and she started up, her hand to her heart.

He leaned away to give her room. "Sorry."

"No. That's all right. I'm sorry." She shivered. "I had a hard time staying asleep, and my dreams were full of blood."

Now he really was sorry to have woken her. Giving in to impulse and what he really wanted, he scooped her into the curve of his body, and they lay back down together. "We will bury Rhun today, and then you will go home."

"And you will ride to Cadwaladr's seat in Merionnydd," Gwen said.

"If he were to dare to return to Wales, Cadwaladr cannot be allowed to think he has a refuge there," Gareth said.

"King Owain is still too ill to travel," Gwen said.

"We will leave him at Denbigh, where he can be cared for in comfort until he is well enough to ride to Aber."

"What of Mold Castle?" Gwen said.

"We will keep it, of course, if Ranulf adheres to the agreement we made with him."

"And if he doesn't?"

Gareth's hands fisted for a moment, and then he forced himself to relax. "Mold Castle will still be there in the spring."

"What will become of Cadwaladr's family?" Gwen said.

Gareth gave her shoulders a squeeze. "Are you concerned that in Hywel's grief and rage he will harm Alice and the children?"

"No, not that, never that," Gwen said. "Hywel proved himself capable of moderation in Ceredigion. I meant merely to ask if he'll bring them to Aber or send them to her family in England."

Gareth was silent. That was a question for which he didn't have an answer. He wanted to know the answer because it was a good question. Though maybe not their most pressing problem right now.

"It would be better if her children weren't raised to hate King Owain," Gwen added. "The last thing Gwynedd needs is for Cadwaladr's treachery to be passed to the next generation."

"One might ask what role Alice played in Cadwaladr's schemes," Gareth said.

"None," Gwen said.

"You're very sure."

"Alice is intelligent and practical—far more so than her husband," Gwen said. "Her concern is for her sons' inheritance. She would never have encouraged Cadwaladr in this plot because she would have known that the penalty for failure was too high. I would be more concerned about Cristina's role in Cadwaladr's plot than Alice's."

Gareth pushed up on one elbow so he could look into his wife's face. "Why do you say that?"

"Lord Goronwy's behavior was strange leading up to yesterday. I know he rode to King Owain the moment he heard the news of Rhun's death and was properly regretful and supportive," Gwen said. "I'm not saying he had a hand in Cadwaladr's scheming with Ranulf, but I wonder if he didn't know something. Neither Lord Goronwy nor Cristina would ever have colluded with Cadwaladr in a plan to overthrow King Owain, but what if Cadwaladr presented his plan as a means to clear the path for the elevation of Cristina's sons—"

"Cristina would have been fully supportive of it." Gareth's innards churned at the thought.

Cristina had already shown herself to be very vocal in her desire to have her two legitimate sons recognized as King Owain's heirs—above the claims of Rhun, Hywel, Cynan, and Madoc—and even above King Owain's other legitimate sons he'd fathered with his first wife, Gladwys.

"Can I ask—?" Gwen hesitated.

Gareth kissed her temple. "There is nothing you can't ask me." Though even as he spoke, he hoped she wasn't going to ask about the battle and his role in it. He had done what needed doing, and it was best not to say any more about it than that.

He also hoped she wasn't going to chastise herself further for not going after Cadwaladr. The treacherous prince was bigger, stronger, and missing his soul. She would only have given Cadwaladr the chance to harm her.

"Will you bring Llelo and Dai with you when you ride to Merionnydd?" she said.

Gareth gave an inward sigh of relief. This he was happy to talk about. "You can't keep them beside you, *cariad*. Cynan is their lord now, and if he is riding for Merionnydd, as I know he will in support of Hywel, then they will ride too. We were lucky yesterday that they were with Cynan instead of Rhun. Take comfort that God watched over them then, and that he will continue to do so."

Gwen put her face into Gareth's chest. "I can't bear any more death."

Gareth rubbed her back. "I know. I don't ever want to feel this way again either."

*****

Funerals were for the living, Hywel had once told him, but this funeral was for the dead, to get them into the ground as quickly as possible so everyone could get off this hill and begin the real work of rebuilding Gwynedd. Uninjured soldiers and villagers had started digging the communal grave before dawn, and every villager and herdsman within five miles who could get there had come. King Owain managed to stay on his feet for most of the ceremony, but near the end, he collapsed into Hywel's arms in his illness and his grief.

Father Alun had consecrated the newly established graveyard, in the center of what had once been the camp, for the burial of the men who'd died defending Rhun. The dead among Cadwaladr's men, along with Ranulf's fallen, had already been buried in a separate grave—also consecrated at Father Alun's insistence—beside the road to Chester.

Though King Owain's preference would have been to bring Prince Rhun home to Aber Castle and bury him there, it was too far to travel with the body, and he himself was too ill to attend to it. Hywel had insisted that Rhun would have preferred to be buried with his men, and so it had been done.

Gwen had sobbed uncontrollably in Gareth's arms earlier, but once the funeral started, she'd become still and silent. The tears refused to flow at all for Gareth, even though he would have liked the relief of them. He felt hollowed out, and while he hadn't been able to eat anything since Rhun's death, Gwen had lost her breakfast on the ground shortly after eating it. Gareth had felt her forehead, fearing she was coming down with the same sickness that had felled King Owain, but she wasn't hot. Gwen had told him it was just her emotions overwhelming her and churning her stomach.

Father Alun raised his hands into the air, speaking in Welsh and then in Latin, which comforted the listeners with the familiar ritual. Even those villagers who'd been neutral in this dispute between Earl Ranulf and King Owain, or resented the intrusion onto their lands and the disruption of their livelihood, were staunchly with Gwynedd today.

Of Cadwaladr, of course, there was no sign.

Father Alun dropped his hands, having finished the closing prayer. Silence descended upon the funeral-goers. In the past, it would have been in this moment that Hywel would have lifted his voice in song. He remained resolutely silent, however. And still, nobody moved. It was as if they were waiting for something, though Gareth didn't know what.

So it was that Gwen stepped forward, answering the call the people hadn't voiced. Since her marriage to Gareth, she rarely performed, and then only under pressure from her father. But now she moved to the foot of Rhun's grave, which lay a few yards from where the rest of the men were buried. The song she chose was an ancient one, written by a long dead Welsh poet, whose words had been passed down from one bard to the next until someone had written them down in one of the books Taran kept so carefully in his office:

Praise be to God
in the beginning and the end.
He will neither despise nor refuse
those who supplicate to him.
And to Mary, intercede
for thy great mercy's sake,
With thy Son,
Before I go into the earth to my fresh grave,
In the dark without a candle to my reckoning ...

Gwen finished the song. Gareth wished her father could have heard her, for she had done as much for King Owain and his people in that moment as all the warriors who'd so stoutly defended Rhun yesterday. As the people dispersed, Gareth walked to his wife and silently put his arms around her, while she put her cheek against his chest and held on.

Supported by Lord Goronwy, King Owain disappeared inside his tent to lie down and await the final dismantling of the camp. Gareth wanted Gwen to do the same, but the staccato of hooves coming up the road from the village had him telling her to stay where she was. He strode towards the camp's entrance. Riders had come and gone along the road in a nearly continuous stream, except during the hour for the funeral, but this sounded more like a cavalcade.

Gareth's hand went instinctively to the hilt of his sword, and he pulled it from its sheath without conscious thought. The soldiers in the camp who could still stand followed his lead, pushing through what remained of the funeral goers to form a phalanx across the entrance and protecting everyone behind them. The saliva in Gareth's mouth tasted bittersweet, and he acknowledged that he was relishing the thought of battle.

Anything to take his mind off Rhun's death.

The riders didn't come all the way to the entrance. The line of soldiers that faced them made clear the danger of any kind of move Gareth didn't like. Instead, the horsemen halted just past the last switchback. There were only six of them, and thus not the threat Gareth had at first feared, and they were dressed in the livery of the Earl of Chester. One of them held a flag of peace on a spear. Lord Morgan of Cilcain was among them.

Dafydd led them.

Gareth stepped in front of his men, his sword still in his hand, though pointed down at the ground.

Both Dafydd and Lord Morgan dismounted and approached. Dafydd held his hands palms outward. "We come in peace, Sir Gareth."

Gareth sheathed his sword. "It's hard to think of peace after yesterday."

Dafydd looked past Gareth to the hardened expressions on the faces of the Welshmen behind him. "I understand your animosity. I am not here to add to it. My lord Ranulf sends his condolences at the loss of Prince Rhun and has instructed me to confirm a temporary peace between Gwynedd and Chester."

"On the same terms as yesterday?" Gareth said.

Dafydd pressed his lips together, telling Gareth the answer was 'no' before Dafydd actually said the word. "I have brought Lord Morgan with me, in hopes that you will listen to him if not to me."

Gareth didn't speak, unable to think of any response that could convey the depth of his grief, hatred, and anger. They had been so close, though it hardly mattered now.

He felt a hand on his arm and turned to see Prince Hywel at his shoulder, buttressed by Cynan and Madoc. "I am here," Prince Hywel said. "What are Ranulf's new terms?"

Dafydd bowed. "Gwynedd will withdraw beyond the Clwyd mountains, and Chester will restrict itself to current lands. Earl Ranulf will retain Mold Castle. We stand here on neutral ground, ruled by Lord Morgan, until such a time as a more permanent peace can be established."

Lord Morgan bowed but didn't speak.

"This peace will hold for four months, until the spring," Dafydd said. "You will have time to mourn your dead."

Gareth almost wished he hadn't put away his sword. He was furious at Ranulf for taking advantage of Rhun's death to change the terms of their agreement and hated this talk of peace when he had so much anger inside him. But part of him knew that Gwynedd was weakened, the bulk of the men-at-arms and knights in King Owain's court killed or wounded in a single day. Of Prince Rhun's *teulu,* only fifteen could stand this morning.

Ranulf was under no obligation to sue for peace, and while King Owain still had enough men through those loyal to him and from his allies to pursue the assault on Mold, it had less chance of succeeding now than it had yesterday.

"Why does Ranulf offer this?" Hywel said.

"The death of Prince Rhun was never his intention," Dafydd said. "He respects the magnitude of your loss, and desires to give your king a chance to grieve in peace."

"And he would prefer not to have to surrender Mold today," Hywel said.

Dafydd canted his head. "As you say."

Hywel directed his gaze at Lord Morgan. "What say you?"

"I am here because I too grieve the loss of Prince Rhun," Morgan said. "I agreed to ride here with Ranulf's men because I played a role in all this, even if it was never my intention, and I had no knowledge of Prince Cadwaladr's activities. He murdered two people on my land."

Hywel studied Morgan through a count of ten and then turned back to the emissary. "Gwynedd accepts."

Dafydd bowed. He and Morgan backed down the hill, mounted their horses, and rode away. Hywel stood watching the road long after the small company had disappeared around the bend. Gareth stood beside him, watching too—and not with impatience. Anything that Hywel did or felt was fine by Gareth.

"Did I do the right thing?" Hywel said.

"Yes," Gareth said without hesitation.

"I am all anger, Gareth." Hywel turned to him. "Though I surprise myself at how little of that anger is directed at my uncle. I am angry that my brother is dead, but Cadwaladr doesn't merit anger. He is of as little importance—of less importance—than an ant, even as I make plans to squash him beneath my boot."

Hywel looked towards the center of the camp. Most of the tents were down, the carts loaded for travel. "We go to Merionnydd to deprive my uncle's sons of their inheritance. Will you come with me?"

He didn't have to ask, but Gareth appreciated the respect Hywel showed him by asking. "Of course, my lord."

Hywel placed a hand on Gareth's shoulder and shook him slightly. "Never doubt my trust in you, Gareth. I'm afraid—" He took in a breath. "You have taught me that honor can carry a man through any trial, but I fear what my heart tells me to do. This rage inside is the only thing keeping me on my feet."

"My lord—" Tears pricked at the corners of Gareth's eyes, just when he didn't want them to fall, and he fought them back.

"You are my conscience." Hywel's voice was as full of pain and desperation as Gareth's heart. "You and Gwen. It would be the easiest thing in the world to have lost all honor by the time we're done. Don't let that happen to me, Gareth. Even in my anger, I don't want to fall into perdition as Cadwaladr has done. I haven't traveled this far only to lose everything at the last pass. Cadwaladr has taken what my father most loved. Don't let him take what honor I have left too. All my life I have striven to be like Rhun, and it can't be because of his death that I fall short."

"You have nothing to fear, my lord." Gareth gestured to the bend in the road around which Ranulf's emissaries had disappeared. "Your first act as *edling* was to put Gwynedd's interests above your own and make peace with your enemy. Rhun would have been proud."

Hywel closed his eyes, taking in a breath and easing it out slowly.

It seemed to Gareth that some of the weight was lifted from his prince's heart, and he gripped Hywel's hand as it rested on his shoulder. "Come, my lord. We have work to do."

Author's Note

I have known since I wrote the first line of *The Good Knight* that I would eventually have to write this book. Rhun, eldest son of King Owain Gwynedd, was killed at the end of 1146. In the aftermath, Cadwaladr deserted his family and his men and fled to England to find refuge at the English court—where King Owain and Hywel couldn't reach him. Subsequently, Hywel and his brother, Cynan, marched on Merionnydd, the last of Cadwaladr's lands that King Owain had allowed him, and took them back—in much the same way that Hywel had marched on Aberystwyth three years earlier.

Up until 1146, King Owain had always forgiven his brother for his misdeeds, even to the point of overlooking murder and treason. Only a terrible act such as bringing about Rhun's death could have prompted the king to ban Cadwaladr from Wales and send Hywel and Cynan to Merionnydd. Cadwaladr—who'd spent his life carrying out brazen and terrible deeds—had finally committed a crime so heinous that he fled Wales rather than face his brother's wrath.

Though the loss of Rhun is grievous, the story of Gareth and Gwen—and Prince Hywel—continues. If you would like to be notified the moment the seventh *Gareth and Gwen Medieval Mystery* is released, you can sign up for my email list at:

www.sarahwoodbury.com

Or find me on Facebook:

https://www.facebook.com/sarahwoodburybooks

About the Author

With two historian parents, Sarah couldn't help but develop an interest in the past. She went on to get more than enough education herself (in anthropology) and began writing fiction when the stories in her head overflowed and demanded she let them out. While her ancestry is Welsh, she only visited Wales for the first time while in college. She has been in love with the country, language, and people ever since. She even convinced her husband to give all four of their children Welsh names.

She makes her home in Oregon.

www.sarahwoodbury.com

Printed in Great Britain
by Amazon